the

WARSEC

Interstellar Series

the
WARSEC
Interstellar Series

1

REGULATION

2094 – 2095

ASH GAWAIN

ASHGAWAIN.COM

Published by Ash Gawain

ISBN: 978-91-639-7449-6

Cover design, illustration & interior formatting:
Mark Thomas / Coverness.com

Disclaimer: Like all Sci-Fi, this book contains more fiction than science. Any resemblance to reality would be nothing more than the result of the random functions of the universe.

TABLE OF CONTENTS

Map of Earth: 2094

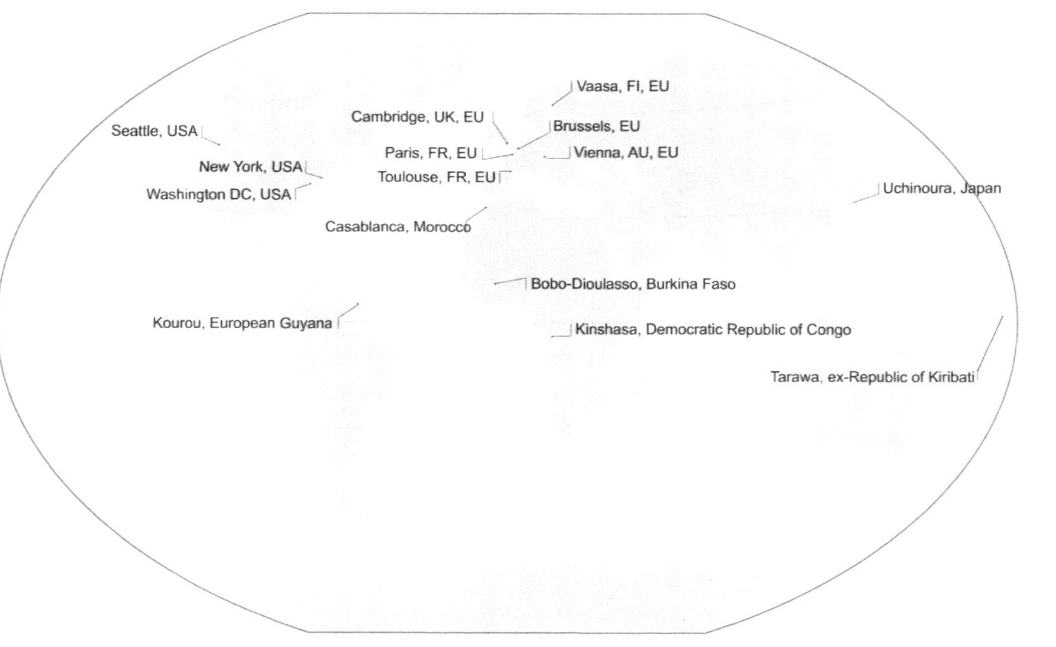

INTRODUCTION

In late summer 2094, as the world was waiting for the maiden warp-flight of the *Alcubierre*, the first spaceship ever endowed with faster-than-light capability, two opinion pieces, published in two different papers, illustrated two opposite conceptions of the conquest of space at the time.

The first Op-Ed, published in *The Wall Street Journal*, had been written by Michael Vahlroos, CEO and founder of the Vahlroos Corporation, holding company of the now booming subsidiary, V-Space. It was entitled *A Tribute to Elon Musk*:

At the origins of the conquest of space lay fierce competition. In the aftermath of World War 2, and during the subsequent Cold War, it was mostly a competition between countries and governments. Us versus the communist East. In 1957, the Soviet Union was first to put a satellite in orbit, thus demonstrating their ability to send nuclear ballistic missiles anywhere in the world. This put the pressure on us and the USA were first to land a man on the

Moon in 1969.

Competition between countries has its virtues but also a lot of inconveniences. Back in the 1960s, 4% of the nation's wealth was spent or, I would rather say, 'wasted', on NASA. And how was it financed? Through unacceptably high taxes. Wealthy people like myself had to pay up to 80% on their marginal income. No wonder Richard Nixon was elected in 1968!

The end of the Cold War in the 1990s led to another pitfall: cooperation. Cooperation removes the incentive to surpass one another. As a result, the whole space race lost its intensity. In the 2010s, the situation was so bad that US astronauts were compelled to board unsafe Russian rockets to reach the International Space Station. And what were they doing up there, in space? Making the world a better place? You bet they were not! They were wasting the tax payers' money to do uninteresting or even bogus experiments with no other purpose than to man the station.

Luckily, Elon Musk changed all this. As one of the first space entrepreneurs, he showed the world that private corporations were the right players to boldly do what no one had done before. In the 1990s, Musk had been very disappointed to see that NASA had no immediate plan to go to Mars. Later, after becoming a successful IT entrepreneur and billionaire, he founded Space X and, using his charisma, had world powers resume their ambition to reach the red planet.

Without Elon Musk's audacity and tenacity, mankind would certainly not have taken its first steps on Mars in 2053. It is only a pity he had to wait until after his 81st birthday to see it. That was due to a series of financial setbacks and unfortunate events: the burst of the artificial intelligence bubble in the early 2020s; the hostile take-over by a competitor of his car company, Tesla, which was in financial difficulties and the spectacular failure of his hyperloop prototype on the Californian coast, obliterated by the Big One earthquake in 2033. However, his tunnel boring machines, or at least adaptations of them, have eventually proven quite useful on the recent Moon Base. A pity he is not here with us to see it.

A pity also he is not here with us to see the first warping of spacetime. In a few weeks, the Russian, Chinese and Japanese space agencies will test the Alcubierre, the first spacecraft able to travel faster than light. Equipped with compact fusion reactors developed by my subsidiary V-Fusion, the Alcubierre is able to generate a negative energy field around it and resort to the Casimir Force to warp spacetime.

Should the test be successful it will open a new era for space entrepreneurs. Elon Musk has been the pioneer. We should build upon his legacy. Mining celestial bodies at an affordable cost will become a reality, enabling us to bring much needed resources back to our overpopulated earth.

Now, more than ever, private corporations are the right players to dynamize the Outer Space economy for the greater good of mankind.

Though acclaimed among entrepreneurs and venture capitalists, this first opinion piece by V-Space's CEO Michael Vahlroos had been judged by some as displaying an excessive faith in the virtues of the market economy.

It had led *The Guardian* to publish another Op-Ed, written this time by a UN diplomat, Ralf Åhman, director of the United Nations Office for Outer Space Affairs (UNOOSA). While Vahlroos's column radiated passion and enthusiasm, the diplomat's response had been drafted in an insipid manner. Not that diplomats were necessarily boring as individuals but, on the public stage, they had to act like it. It was part of their job description. His piece was entitled *An urgent need for space regulation*:

The office of which I am the director, the United Nations Office for Outer Space Affairs (UNOOSA), was created in the heat of the Cold War to assist the General Assembly's Committee on the Peaceful Uses of Outer Space (COPUOS). It has been a quite successful office. Not only has it supported the COPUOS in establishing major space treaties, from the Outer Space Treaty to the Moon Treaty, but it has always strived to keep a high standard of cooperation in outer space affairs, regardless of the geopolitical differences between the nations of this world.

And it has succeeded, not only in terms of cooperation between nations or between their respective space agencies but also in terms of cooperation between nations and private space corporations.

However, claiming that private corporations are the right players to boldly do what no one has done before is a daring statement.

When Martian soil was stepped on for the very first time on 9 March 2053, this was the result of a joint mission by the various national space agencies at that time. Though it has to be conceded that the assembly in orbit of the mission spaceship back in 2050 was mostly due to Space X's rockets.

After the cancellation of the Martian exploration program in 2057 due to lack of public funding, it was a private corporation which established the Martian colony at Elysium Planitia in 2075. The seventeen couples taking part in that experiment were meant to stay on the red planet, waiting for the colony to grow, while their lives were broadcasted on Earth in what was called The Martian Show.

Except that no further colonization waves arrived. The Martian Show Corporation had proven unable to raise additional funds. Supplies sent to the Martian colony became scarcer. The colonists building the colony exposed themselves to too high solar radiation doses until they all developed some form of cancer. They had the instinct to keep their children inside their compounds, protecting them from the sun, but most of them suffered from lack of vitamin D and bone reinforcement medicines.

Did it occur to the Martian Show Corporation to organize a rescue mission and bring the survivors back to earth? No, they filed for bankruptcy. There is now only one survivor left at the Martian colony and it is my office, the United Nations Office for Outer Space Affairs, which is coordinating her rescue. Why? Because all other players have failed to take their responsibility.

If successfully tested, the Alcubierre will soon be put to use to repatriate the last Martian colonist.

It will not take long, however, before private space corporations launch their own spaceships with warp technology. Given the current space legislation, it could have tremendous consequences for all of mankind.

I therefore believe that the time has come for the nations of this world to turn to the UN and negotiate a new treaty to regulate space activities.

Yes, private corporations have had a positive influence on the claiming of outer space by mankind. But no, their space activities should not be permitted without additional regulation.

01: THE MARTIAN COLONY (15 SEPT 2094)

Standing in her flashy green Martian suit by the crane-truck, Sanne van der Maas was contemplating the rocket she had eventually assembled, the rocket that would help her off Mars.

At her feet, her shadow was gradually stretching on the orange soil toward the sleek erected spacecraft, glittering in the sun. She cast a quick glance behind her. The sun was plummeting toward the horizon, behind the settlement made of pipes and orange bumps popping out of the ground. The Martian colony was located near the equator, at Elysium Planitia, and the night would naturally fall in no time.

She went back to into the truck's cockpit and ensured the crane was in idle mode. She grabbed her control pad out of her Martian suit's kangaroo pocket and commanded the insect-like robots to regroup at the assembly tent, where they would spend the night.

She had received the eight insect-like robots six months

earlier in a cargo shipment from Earth, together with a load of high-tech components. The plan had been to build a rocket with the resources available on Mars.

She jumped out of the crane-truck, headed for the base of the rocket and started to climb up the fuselage's ladder.

It was a very primitive rocket. The first stage was only 16 m (52 ft) high and was made of a single combustion chamber squeezed between hydrogen and oxygen tanks. Using their 3D-printing arms and the alloy produced at the colony from locally mined minerals, the robots had built it in less than two weeks, following pre-programmed procedures. The production of alloy-powder to feed their 3-D printers had been a more time-consuming business, due to the limited availability of energy at the colony.

On the fuselage ladder, Sanne had reached the second stage of the rocket, which was the space module itself.

She had had to put more manual labor into it, as the robots had only contributed to the manufacturing of the frame and secondary engines. The steering chemical thrusters and most of the spacecraft's cockpit had had to be assembled by hand using the parts received from Earth. It had been tedious and laborious and Sanne was still wondering how she had fixed it, as she opened the hatch and slid into the module.

She was now standing in the cockpit of the rocket that would allow her to escape the Martian gravity, the first necessary step of a much longer journey to Earth. She had spent two weeks inspecting the space module in the assembly tent. The module was now docked on top of the first stage and she only had to follow one last checklist to ensure the two stages had been properly connected.

Except that it took her ten minutes to complete. Over the last six months, it had seemed that her life had been all about following checklists. Eventually, she was also done with that one and the rocket was completed. She would fill the tanks after the week-end.

She extricated herself from the cockpit, shut the hatch and climbed down the ladder. Her green Martian mountain bike was waiting by the crane-truck. She grabbed it and pedaled away.

The sun had now disappeared below the horizon and Sanne could barely make out the different units of the colony in the Martian twilight. She first biked past the power station and the oxygen and hydrogen tanks of the outer colony ring. She followed a set of pipes lying on the ground leading to the colony's workshops, all equipped with 3D-printers. She rode on to the greenhouses, where she had to halt. There, she dismounted her bike and put it over her shoulder to climb over another set of pipes.

Pipes connected the various buildings of the colony for the transport of electricity, oxygen, hydrogen, water and organic waste. The Martian permafrost had made it impossible to bury the pipes. Not far from her lay an abandoned electrically powered tunnel boring machine that the colonists had tried to use to dig in their settlement. It had proven impossible, precisely because of the permafrost.

Sanne cast a weary look at the boring machine. It had been because of this failure that the Martian Show Corporation had failed to raise additional funding to pursue the colony project. The thirty-four colonists had been left on their own, with no hope of reinforcement and no plans for evacuation, their lives being broadcasted to billions of followers on Earth.

Unable to bury the colony, they had built it on the surface, exposed to deadly doses of solar radiation. In order to reduce their exposure to it, the buildings had been covered with thick alternate layers of gravel and ice, making them look like artificial dunes on the Martian ground.

Sanne had been irradiated long enough for the day, she thought, as she resumed her biking toward the living compound. She had done most of the assembly work at night, back in the tent, but that final stage had been easier to complete in daylight.

Between the buildings were large fields of solar panels. Above her head, with lights twinkling in the night, were some wind turbines built around air balloons. They floated about half a kilometer above the ground, where the Martian winds were strong enough to generate power, despite the thinner atmosphere than on Earth.

Redundancy perhaps best described the design of the Martian colony, where all installations were duplicated as backups. This was a must on such an exposed ground as Mars. If a building were to be damaged, the other buildings would provide the facilities to restore it. It had protected the settlers against accidents, but not against cancer, Sanne thought bitterly.

It was almost entirely dark when she arrived at one of the four living units. She braked just in front of the airlock, opened it, and biked into it. Inside, she dismounted her bike, shut the outer door, opened the inner door and moved into a large room equipped with a kitchen area, and furnished with a long, bare metallic table surrounded by metallic chairs. There was also a sofa section and desk corner.

Sanne got out of her flashy green spacesuit, went straight to the kitchen area and poured herself a large glass of water she drank avidly. She was a tall but skinny and very certainly malnourished eighteen-year-old girl with tired brown eyes. Her short brown hair was in a mess. Not that she cared: The Martian Show Corporation had gone bankrupt five years earlier and life in the colony had stopped being broadcasted to Earth. Sanne had herself disconnected all the cameras, and it was a relief not to be spied upon.

On the wall beside the freezer, a group picture was hanging. It had been taken twelve years earlier. On it were 33 adults and five children, including herself, the eldest of them. On the picture, her younger self had already a weary smile.

She remembered. He parents would not let her go out in daylight, lest she may take in a too high a dose of solar radiation. Throughout her youth, she had been confined in the living compound all day. It was only after the first colonists had developed some forms of cancer that she had understood the purpose of staying inside. The other children on the picture, all with their merry smiles, had had more freedom. They would go out whenever the wanted. Too bad for them: they were now all dead. Cancer.

Sanne had been on her own in the Martian colony for now almost two years. All the others had died eventually. The highest mortality rate had occurred after the bankruptcy of the Martian Show Corporation, when the already scarce supplies from Earth stopped coming entirely. The seven children born after the pictures had suffered from lack of bone reinforcement medicines, which were direly needed for this low-gravity planet. And while everybody else had tried to keep out of the solar radiation, the shortage in vitamin D supply had led to a new surge in cancer occurrences. Sanne was now the only survivor.

She went to the desk corner and switched on the main computer. The digital clock on the wall indicated Wednesday 15 September 2094. The time was 20:00 in Amsterdam, Europe, Earth. The ageing computer would take at least ten minutes to start, so that she had time for a shower.

In the shower, her mind drifted. She wondered how the world could have possibly let the colonization of Mars happen in the first place. In the early 2070s, an eccentric Dutch Billionaire, Mr. Vroom (pronounced with a long o like in 'ohm') had decided it was his duty to colonize Mars. He had been disappointed by the cancellation of the exploration program and was convinced that only a true Martian colony would have the resources to efficiently find traces of fossilized life on the red planet.

Before the invention of compact fusion reactors, before the deployment of the first space elevator, before the recent completion of the new orbital station, before the recent deployment of the lunar installation, a private corporation had sent seventeen Dutch couples to Mars to build a colony and find traces of life. Stupid idea. In the end, the colonists had been kept busier with their own survival than with hazardous prospection under an irradiating sun. So far, no trace of life or fossilized life had been found on the red planet.

When she came out of the shower, Sanne weighed herself. The balance showed 27 kg (60 lb). Of course, it was Martian kilos. On Earth, she would weight 71 kg (157 lb). But since she was 2.05 meters (6.7 ft) tall, it was way too little anyway.

Gravity on Earth was three times stronger than on Mars. She wondered an instant how it would feel to walk there. Would her legs be able to carry her at all? They would probably put her in a wheelchair at the beginning, but how long would she have to stay there?

After she had changed to comfortable clothes, she returned to the computer to check her emails. With the coming test, she expected to have received a message from Ralf. And with a bit of luck, she might be on Earth sooner than in her wildest dreams.

She browsed through her mailbox and spotted a message from Ralf entitled "*Good news*".

Dear Sanne,

I know that the test of the Alcubierre-White metric has been postponed thirteen times already during the summer, but this time the test is on. All the preparatory tests of the Alcubierre spacecraft have been conclusive.

The Sino-Russian team wanted to test the Alcubierre drive today, but it has been postponed until Friday 17 September for diplomatic reasons. The new European president was sworn in today, and she didn't want any other event to overshadow her investiture.

The testing procedure will be broadcasted by the Japanese Space Agency (JAXA), and the program is the following (in Coordinated Universal Time):

11:30: start of the broadcast program.

12:00: first warp travel from Earth's orbit to Mars's orbit. The ship will be unmanned. The travel time will be 25 seconds. You will be able to spot the spacecraft's radio signature when it orbits around Mars. You are kindly requested to send a radio signal to Earth when you have spotted it. The spaceship will then return to Earth.

13:15: Second warp travel, with a Russian dog and a Chinese cat onboard. Same procedure as above.

14:30: If the health status of the above animals is assessed to be acceptable, which we all hope, there will be a third warp travel with the following crew:

- *Dr. Alice Fu (China): Commander*

- *Dr. Anatoli Govorov (Russia): Warp drive specialist*

- *Mrs. Nariko Kobayashi (Japan): Pilot*

I will be in New York at the request of the secretary general on that day.

I was told that your rocket was to be assembled by the end of this week. If the test of the Alcubierre Metric is successful, which most people believe it will be, we may be able to welcome you back on Earth during the first half of October.

In the meantime, keep working on your distance courses at Columbia University. You most likely will have the possibility to do the last term of your Bachelor's on the campus in New York, next spring.

Kind regards,

Ralf Åhman
General Director
United Nations Office for Outer Space Affairs
United Nations Office at Vienna
Vienna International Centre,
Wagramerstrasse 5,
A-1220 Vienna
Austria – European Union

02: THE ADMIRAL
IN CIVILIAN CLOTHES
(16 SEPT 2094)

They were always picky at the gate of the White House when it came to security. Hydrogen powered vehicles had been forbidden since a male supremacist sniper had blown up an SUV within the complex. Autopilot-equipped vehicles would not be let in either, as a hacker had once hijacked a self-driving car within the White House compound and chased secret service agents, killing a patrol dog in the process.

Admiral Johnson was not concerned with these two restrictions as he was only leasing a little electric car with no fancy high-tech capabilities. He was told to park by the entrance of the West Wing.

Glover Johnson was a short black man in his mid-thirties with a chest circumference hinting he could take at least 265 pounds on the bench press. Or perhaps rather say 120 kilos. As a junior officer, he had been involved in the conversion of the US Navy to the metric system, and it had not been one of his easiest tasks. He was not at the White House to discuss the metric system, though, but to meet President Fang. He had been summoned by her chief of staff, Mr. Williams.

In the lobby of the West Wing, he was handed a visitor badge and asked to wait on a bench. It was half past seven on the morning of Thursday 16 September 2094.

"Admiral Johnson?"

It was Mr. Williams, a tall and slightly overweight blond white man, wearing an anthracite suite with a black tie.

Glover rose to his feet. "It's me. Pleasure to meet you, Mr. Williams."

"Thank you for coming on such short notice, Admiral. I was looking for a US Navy officer in uniform, not in civilian clothes."

Glover Johnson was wearing a navy-blue suit, white shirt and red tie. He felt he had to explain himself.

"I have been working with nuclear propulsion safety for ten years now. In that branch, it's an asset to wear civilian clothes in order not to intimidate technicians with lower ranks. When it comes to nuclear safety, trust is paramount."

"Well, you will not have intimidated the president, if that's what you think," the aide said as he led the way at quick pace through a labyrinth of corridors out of the West Wing and into the White House's main building.

A moment later, Rear Admiral Johnson was introduced into

the Oval Office, where the president greeted him. Though in her late fifties, President Fang was more athletic than most of her predecessors. She was taller than him, Glover noted, but shorter than she appeared on TV. She wore a grey suit but had light blue sneakers on her feet. This was her trademark.

The president showed him to one of the sofas and she sat down on the opposite couch.

"Madam President," Mr. Williams said as he sat down beside her, "Rear Admiral Glover Johnson here is the US Navy's lead expert on compact fusion reactors. Submarine branch. Master of Science in nuclear engineering. Distinguished himself in the deployment of compact fusion reactors in the fleet in the 2080s and, most importantly, wrote the book: *How US Navy nuclear safety standards could be used for nuclear deployment in space.* He has been consulting for NASA for three years now."

"You told me already," the president cut in. "The Navy man at NASA."

"*Apollo 1, Columbia, Challenger…*" Mr. Williams listed. "NASA's history is paved with disasters. How many nuclear disasters for the US Navy in the past 150 years? Zero. We'd better want more Navy men at NASA."

The president rose to her feet, took a few steps and looked at Glover.

"Admiral Johnson, thank you for being here so early. I have fifteen minutes before my normal schedule begins. You know why I summoned you. Tomorrow, the Russians, Chinese, and Japanese will test a spaceship that is said to go faster than light. The American public is more or less taken aback. I need to know: A, what is the chance of success of this warp test…. B, what would happen in case of failure? What are the safety standards for this ship? Not that I don't trust the Russians… and C, why aren't we first to test a warp drive? How could the easterners beat us in that race? Why is not the first warp spacecraft an American ship?"

The president was insisting so much on the last question that Glover thought he'd better start by answering that one: "If the Sino-Russian test is a success, this will be mostly thanks to us. They did indeed develop the warp propulsion technology, but they could not have had it ready for testing so fast if it hadn't been for us. We did a lot of preparatory work they have built upon. And any eastern success could, in this case, be called an American victory. This is, perhaps, what our fellow Americans should be informed about".

"What do you mean?"

Glover was still sitting on the sofa, looking up at her. "The warp technology makes use of nuclear compact fusion reactors to generate the warp field. NASA was instrumental in the completion of the new international orbital station two years ago. It is powered by compact fusion reactors, thanks to us. NASA was also the first to deploy compact fusion reactors onboard a spaceship, with the launch of the *Manhattan* in May last year and of the *Orion* in January this year. Before these two launches, we played it very openly when setting our safety standards. The United Nations Office for Outer Space Affairs has recommended all National space agencies to use our standards."

"We played it openly… Good." The president went back to the sofa and sat down next to Mr. Williams. "What about the Russians and the Chinese?"

"The Russians and the Chinese are following the rules we set," Glover replied. "They are following the American standards regarding safety, you can tell the public. They also played it openly. They shared the design of the ship with the UN Office for Outer Space Affairs, as we did. At NASA, we went through their design, and they are pretty compliant. They finished assembling their ship, the *Alcubierre*, in June. They started their nuclear reactors in July, following all the safety procedures."

"Excellent," the president said as she raised again to her feet. "I may be able to calm down some congressmen and senators. What about the test tomorrow? What will the outcome be?"

"I am not a warp drive expert," Glover admitted, looking up at the president. "It will, however, most probably be a success. The Russians tested the warp drive in the Black Sea in November 2092, two years ago. You probably saw it, a kind of mini-submarine. They had it warp over ten kilometers. They had mice on board, and they survived. In February last year, they conducted a warp test in space with that same torpedo-like ship. The warpedo, they call it. It was a success again, but they lost the warpedo on the third test, so there was not much publicity. Today, most people in the US believe it was a conspiracy by the Chinese to claim technological advances they hadn't actually made. It was not. It worked. I am not worried as far as their ship is concerned. The main issue will be for the crew's exposure to Hawking radiation when the ship warps spacetime. But they will first test it on a dog and a cat."

"Fine. So, you are positive there won't be any catastrophic outcome tomorrow?" the president asked as she sat down again on the sofa.

"There may be a failure, yes, it can always happen," Glover acknowledged, "But if anything serious happens, it will be during the first warping test, and the spaceship will be unmanned. Anyway, they will warp it away from a spot located at a safe distance of 500,000 km from Earth, so nothing catastrophic will happen. Actually, I think the testing procedure is so safe that we could even involve some American astronauts."

"What do you mean?" the president wondered.

"They are using two Chinese spaceships, the *Yang Liwei* and the *Cheng-Ning Yang,* to transport the testing crew and engineers to the departure position. These are chemically propelled. We could offer them the opportunity to use the *Orion*, instead, and at the same time show the world the value of EM-drive propulsion. We are, after all, the first to have successfully developed the EM-drive technology."

"Please remind me what an EM-drive is?" The president asked.

"Electromagnetic-Drive," Glover explained. "It uses electromagnetic waves to propel itself in space. It works on solely electric power. No need to have huge tanks of hydrogen. The *Orion* can make it to Mars in only eight weeks, and with no propellant. She is now fully operational, and NASA had planned to have her crew observe the warp test."

"Good," The president said as she stood up again. "Mr. Williams, please inform the NASA administrator, and contact the Chinese and Russian space directors. Tell them we are ready to put the *Orion* at their disposal for the testing of the *Alcubierre*."

Mr. Williams left the Oval Office, leaving Glover alone with the president. He, too, rose to his feet, believing it was time for him to leave, but the president instead led him through the garden door of the Oval Office. They stayed under the West Colonnade. The sun was still low in the East at this early hour, and Glover wished he had sunglasses. The September sun was still strong.

The president turned to Glover and looked him in the eyes.

"Admiral Johnson, you know what amendment of the Constitution I am currently struggling with?"

"Yes, Madam. You would like the presidential election to take place on a Sunday, rather than a Tuesday. You would like the US president to be directly elected, rather than through a college of electors. Above all, you would like to make the voter enrollment of US citizens automatic for all types of election. You would like to have it steered by a federal agency that would work closely with the federal tax office."

"34% of American people who are, in theory entitled to vote, don't vote because it's too complicated to get registered on an electoral roll. Most of those people belonging to minorities like you or me, and are almost entirely people from economically excluded backgrounds. In Europe, they have had automatic enrollment of voters for twenty-five years already. Do you see the Washington monument over there?"

The president was pointing toward the Obelisk, south of the White House.

"I see it, Madam."

"How ironically the city of Washington has been built! You know this alignment of Capitol Hill, the Washington Monument, and the Lincoln Memorial. It is as if Congress is constantly pointing George Washington's middle finger at Abraham Lincoln."

The president turned back to Glover and smiled.

"You may think I am a bit rude and cynical. The truth is that Congress is killing me and I have to pass this amendment before the mid-terms in just a month. I can do it, on the condition that I am not bombarded on either my right or my left for the sole reason that the Russians and Chinese are the first with a spaceship that travels faster than light. My only card to play is that of international cooperation. As long as the Russians and Chinese are playing fairly, I am safe. Else I am in trouble. We are in trouble."

"Over the last two years," Glover replied, "I have been rather satisfied with our relationship with them through the UN Office for Outer Space Affairs. I will be at the UN headquarters in New York tomorrow. The UN secretary general wishes to watch the broadcasting of the test together with representatives of the various space agencies of the world. But I will also meet the director of UN Space Affairs."

"What is his position, as to having two eastern powers as the only ones to master warp technology?"

"The usual UN stuff," Glover replied. "You know, like…*such a technology cannot be kept for the self-interests of a few nations but has to be used to serve mankind* and blah blah blah. However, it seems that there is a genuine interest from smaller countries to request that warp technology should be transferred to a kind of a newer International Space Agency. If the test is successful, there may be UN resolutions going that way. Your ambassador at the UN will know more than I do."

"You are right. This is not your job. However, should you have any prior information about any project for increased international cooperation in that field, I would like you to call Mr. Williams. Thank you, Admiral Johnson."

"Thank you, Madam President."

03: V LIKE VAHLROOS (16 SEPT 2094)

The Vahlroos Tower was a 56-story-high skyscraper located in lower Manhattan, in the Financial District of New York City. A large silver painted letter V topped the building, glancing in the sunlight.

Sophie Couillard entered the tower's lobby. She was a tall and athletic blond woman in her mid-thirties. She wore crimson sneakers and carried a red backpack, contrasting with her anthracite suit. However, it was her cap that distinguished her most. She wore a red and white cap with the Canadian flag on it, and she noticed how some of the employees were rolling their eyes in disapproval. She didn't care.

A glance at the lobby's digital clock told her it was Thursday 16 September, 9:06. The meeting would start in twenty-four minutes.

She took her badge and went through the security gates past the reception and made it just in time to catch an elevator bound upward. It was the fast elevator, and it quickly climbed past the floors of the Vahlroos Corporation divisions: Vahlroos Construction, Vahlroos Property, Vahlroos Investment, V-Fusion, V-Lab and V-Space.

At last, it reached the tower's last and 56th floor, where Betalpha Holding Inc. was headquartered. Sophie got out, though her badge clearly indicated she belonged to the V-Space division.

At the floor's reception, she looked for Michael. He was not there. Not surprising after what had happened to his son. She glanced around. Most of the directors had already arrived, including the chairman of the board.

They were grabbing some doughnuts and making it slowly to the meeting room, chatting with each other. There was no woman among them. The directors of the Board of Betalpha Holding, the holding corporation of the Vahlroos Corporation's businesses, were all old, grey-haired white men, most of them overweight. Ah, no, there was one black man, but he was also old and grey-haired. Mike used to joke that it was one of the collateral damages of increased life expectancy. As long as none of them was senile yet, one could live with it. Damn, where was Michael?

She decided to call him from her mobile.

"Mike, are you all right?"

"Yes, Sof'. I'm OK. I will be there five minutes before the meeting of the board starts."

"You are sure you don't want to postpone it? After what happened to Willy?"

"This was tragic. But the culprit has been caught, and I hope he will be sentenced to death. Anyway, it's no use crying over spilt milk. I'm there in ten minutes. See you."

He hung up.

"*It's no use crying over spilt milk.* Obviously, it takes more than what happened to move our good Michael Vahlroos, CEO and minority owner of this corporation."

This was Jim Pattison, the chairman of the board, who obviously had been eavesdropping. He went on: "Four days ago, last Sunday, his five-year-old son, who lives with his divorced wife in Florida, is kidnapped while playing soccer. Mr. Vahlroos is asked to pay a huge ransom. Instead of negotiating, together with the FBI, he thinks he is smarter and offers twice as much to whoever will bring him the kidnappers. A very cowboy-like behavior… "

Sophie was considering the chairman. With his huge belly and white trucker moustache, he looked like a fat walrus. Mr. Pattison went on:

"Of course, the kidnapper panicked and killed the son and tried to get rid of the body. But the bad guy has been caught by some bounty hunters, and this Michael Vahlroos sounds satisfied. He has just lost his son, the bastard! That's none of my business, anyway. As long as he doesn't gamble with this company the way he did with his son's life, I am fine. See you in the meeting room, Miss Couillard."

Sophie lingered a while by the reception and gazed through the windows of the 56th floor. Ten kilometers (6.2 miles) to the south, under the Verrazano-Narrows Bridge, she could catch a glimpse of the large dyke that had been built to protect the Upper Bay and New York City from the rising level of sea water.

"Gentlemen, good morning," said Michael Vahlroos in an emotionless voice.

In the large conference room, the CEO of Vahlroos Corporation was standing by the white canvas screen hanging against the wall. In front of him was a very long table around which the investors had taken their seats.

Michael was a thin, forty-year-old blond man with grey eyes and a Swedish nose. He was wearing a brown blazer, but no tie. Ties were forbidden throughout the Vahlroos Corporation. It was a 200-year-old European invention, and it was about time to get rid of them. Men would not enter the twenty-second century wearing ties like dogs wearing leashes.

Michael started the meeting: "For those of you who don't know her, let me introduce you Sophie Couillard, the new general manager of V-Space. MSc from Toronto University. Previously worked for Bombardier and Boeing. She has worked for us since eighty-eight and was the project leader of the Albaspace, our very successful aerospace shuttle, which is, by the way, not only operated by NASA and ESA but which has also been picked by President Fang to be the new Air Force One."

Sophie, who was standing beside Michael, smiled awkwardly at the Directors. She was used to working with engineers, not with investors. Michael continued his presentation.

"As you know, I was not meant to lead such a corporation so young. I studied nuclear physics at MIT and worked at Lockheed Martin with the development of compact fusion reactors. Thirteen years ago, however, my Father died in the Big Two. Incompetent geologists had failed to predict it. The most devastating earthquake to hit San Francisco. As a result, I inherited the Vahlroos Corporation, and turned an organization that was only making money building and managing properties into something that is meant to serve the destiny of mankind."

Sophie could see that most of the Directors were already bored. Come on, Michael, don't bother them with this ideological stuff, this is off-topic, she thought. But Mike went on.

"When taking over, I founded V-fusion, first to successfully develop and commercialize a compact fusion reactor, or CFR."

"Yeah, using the expertise you stole from Lockheed Martin," someone grumbled in the room.

Michael went on unperturbed: "The CFR has now been adopted by 80% of the US Navy, 70% of the Chinese Navy, and 60% of the European Navy. This is a commercial success. It has now been deployed in space. First in the new orbital station, but also in the two recent spaceships NASA has launched: the *Orion* and the *Manhattan*. And the *Alcubierre*, whose warp drive will be tested tomorrow, is equipped with four of our CFRs. The CFR is one of our success stories, but not the only one. The Albaspace is another one. It is equipped with four CUBIC-R engines and one scramjet. Let me remind you, CUBIC-R engines have modular designs enabling them to alternately serve as Regular jet, Ramjet or Rocket Jet. The Albaspace can reach Mach 22 on the scramjet, and Mach 30 on the rocket jets. With its suborbital capabilities, it can reach any place in the world in less than one hour while being comfortable enough for VIP passengers. Hence the decision by President Fang to use it as Air Force One. Even better, it takes only eight hours to reach the orbital station. Eight hours only to reach an orbit position of 400 km [250 miles]!"

"How long do the space elevators take?" the chairman asked.

Jim Pattison was referring to another kind of atmosphere escape technology, using geostationary space tethers attached to orbiting asteroids to carry electrically driven capsules into space.

Sophie decided to answer and jumped in: "It takes seven hours to reach 400 km of altitude. But there are only two space elevators, the Sino-Japanese one on Tarawa in the Pacific, and the Euro-American one in European Guyana. That means that you need to get to either of these locations. When you have reached the altitude of 400 km, you still have to transfer to the orbital station, which can take an additional ten hours. Of course, the space tethers can carry a payload of 500 tons while the Albaspace is limited to 10. The space tether is fine to put a fusion reactor into orbit, but the Albaspace is much more convenient for passengers, allowing direct and faster flights."

"And this why we must think ahead," Michael Vahlroos resumed. "Tomorrow, the Russians and Chinese will have the *Alcubierre* ship warp spacetime. This means it will transfer from A to B faster than the speed of light. This is the future. Their ship, however, can only warp from one orbital position to another, which is not convenient. First of all, such a spacecraft has to be assembled in space. Since there is a state monopoly on space elevators, as Miss Couillard explained, carrying huge payloads into orbit is kind of problematic. We, at V-Space, believe we can build a ship with warp capacity, which would be able to take off from our atmosphere and land back in our atmosphere while being able to carry a significant payload of 200 metric tons. Such a spaceship would make possible the mining and exploitation of mineral resources of the Solar System. And believe me, when the Earth's population is soon to reach 11 billion people, we need all the extra-terrestrial resources we can get."

There was some whispering in the room and Jim Pattisson, the chairman, finally said:

"The first to be able to build such a ship would indeed have quite a significant competitive advantage. Can we do that? Can we build a warp ship capable of entering the atmosphere?"

"Yes, Mr. Pattison," Michael replied. "Miss Couillard here will explain."

"Warp technology is a term from the *Star Trek* series, from the twentieth century, though everybody uses the phrase today," Sophie started. "However, the exact term is *Alcubierre-White metric*. In 1994, 100 years ago, a Mexican theoretical physicist named Miguel Alcubierre showed it was theoretically possible to warp spacetime, in accordance with the Einstein field equation, provided one disposed of a tremendous amount of negative energy. Twenty years later, Harrold White at the Eagle Work laboratory showed that the required amount of negative energy could be drastically reduced by shaping the field as a cigar and optimizing its thickness and oscillation. Mankind has known how to generate negative energy in quantum physics for quite some time, with the Casimir force. However, as long as the general theory of relativity and quantum mechanics could not be unified in a single theory to explain gravity, it was impossible to even consider constructing an Alcubierre-White metric."

"The unified theory was proposed by Dr. Anatoli Govorov and Dr. Tintin Mutombo from Moscow University in 2091," Michael went on. "A few years earlier, Dr. Alice Fù, from Harbin University in China had discovered how to generate a field of green plasma triggering a Casimir-like force. Successful small-scale testing convinced the Russian, Chinese and Japanese governments to fund the *Alcubierre*."

"While Dr. Govorov and Dr. Fù are considered as heroes in Russia and China," said Sophie, "Dr. Tintin Mutombo was expelled back to Congo when his Russian visa expired. We immediately hired him, and he now works with us at our Bobo-Dioulasso R&D center, in Burkina Faso."

"Why are all our V-Space main installations in Burkina Faso?" A director asked.

"There are no earthquakes in Burkina," Michael answered. "Much safer than the American West coast. It is also well connected to the sea through Côte d'Ivoire and Ghana, and it is close to the Sahara where we can safely test fly our aircraft. Besides, people there are well educated."

"One problem remains," another director said.

It was Sonny Baldwin, the only black director in the room.

"What is it, Mr. Baldwin?" Michael Vahlroos asked.

"Currently, it is forbidden by international treaty to have any fusion reactor closer than 200 km to the surface of the Earth. Despite progress on safety, airplanes are still not allowed to operate compact fusion reactors in the atmosphere."

"Yes, I know," Michael replied. "It is, however, permitted by international treaty to let ballistic missiles fly nuclear warheads in our atmosphere. Sometimes I don't understand anything about international law."

There was some laughter in the room and Michael resumed

his answer:

"However, Mr. Baldwin, your worries are legit. Our ship will not leave or enter the atmosphere in any conventional way, but warp through it. We will just exploit a loophole in the treaties. To be safe, I will also establish closer contact with the UN Office for Outer Space Affairs. I have arranged with the UN secretary general to meet its director this very afternoon. He will stay in New York over the weekend."

04: A GIFTED LITTLE DRUG DEALER (16 SEPT 2094)

While the meeting of the board of directors was ending in New York, it was four in the afternoon in Paris, European Union. At the police station of Sevran, Inspector Nathalie Chautel, a short, but rather hefty, dark-haired white woman, was in a good mood. She was sitting at her desk in front of her computer.

Earlier in the afternoon, a police patrol had arrested a minor drug dealer. He had barely 10 grams of hashish on him, not enough to prove he was a drug dealer, but he also had a smartphone. The "IT expert" of the police station, who was, in fact, a regular policeman with additional training, had quickly copied an image of the mobile phone onto an external hard-drive and handed it over to Inspector Chautel, claiming there was not much to use.

The inspector decided to have a look nonetheless and accessed the phone's mirror image using her computer.

The phone contained almost no pictures, and no contact information, which was rather intriguing. Checking the battery log of the phone, she saw that one of the apps the suspected drug dealer was using most was the spreadsheet app. To her surprise, the last file accessed by the spreadsheet app was an image file (.jpeg). She first tried to open the file with the preview app, but the image was said to be corrupted. She got an idea and copied the image file to her computer, changed the extension and tried to open it with her spreadsheet app. It worked, and she could not help laughing. It was an accounting spreadsheet! The dealer was keeping tracks of all his transactions: how much he had sold to each customer; how much he had purchased from his suppliers (who were referred to with nicknames) and how much he owed to each of them. These were not impressive amounts, though. The business size was rather small, but the books were tidy.

She quickly saw that two thirds of the supply came from the same supplier. It was getting interesting.

She had another idea. There were only a dozen contacts registered on the phone, among which were his father and five siblings. However, when checking the incoming and outgoing calls, there were many more phone numbers. The suspect was smart enough not to save contact information on the device. Examining the ringtone settings, Inspector Chautel realized that two phone numbers were set to specific ringtones. One of these was the sound of a shell falling and exploding. It was set for all incoming calls from his father. The other was the theme of *The Godfather*, an old movie from the twentieth century. She clicked again on the phone number to have the theme played one more time.

"Oh dear, this was a stupid mistake," she thought happily.

The phone number triggering the *Godfather* theme was a European phone number. But there was no contact attached to it. She opened the European Federal Phone Database and entered the number. It belonged to a foreign diplomat. She first thought it was a mistake and checked again. It was not a mistake.

"*Putain de bordel de merde,*" she swore," ('Holy crap!') "I'd better interrogate this guy alone."

The interrogation room was a dark and dirty little room. The suspect was a thin man of average height with black, curly hair. He wore jeans, a green T-shirt, and a brown thick shirt on top of it. He and Inspector Chautel were sitting on two chairs opposite each other, with a dusty table separating them. On the table was a digital voice recorder. She pressed the on-button.

"It's 16:43, starting the interrogation of Samir Benyamina, arrested this afternoon at 13:12 in Beaudottes in possession of 10 g of cannabis. Samir, everything we say will be recorded and available for the justice. If, however, you wish to say something off the record, please tell me, and I will switch off the recorder."

"*Je comprends,*" Samir answered ('I understand').

"No lawyer has arrived yet, and it may take some time before a lawyer be appointed to you. If you wish not to answer a question in the absence of your lawyer, just tell me."

"OK."

"You have been arrested in possession of 10 g of hashish while standing at crossroad known for drug-dealing. We are trying to establish whether you were attempting to sell the drug or if it was for your personal consumption, in which case you would only be liable to pay a fine."

"*C'était pour ma conso perso*," Samir explained ('It was for my personal consumption').

"We'll start with the identity of the suspect," the inspector continued. "Samir Benyamina, born on 21 October 2077 in Marseilles. Your father, Ali Benyamina, is from Algeria and came to France in 2074, is that correct?"

"Correct," Samir answered. "It was after the Qatari flu had killed so many in Europe, and the EU needed foreign manpower."

"Your father used to be a truck driver, but has now been unemployed for four years. Your mother died of cancer in March earlier this year, I can see. You have my sympathy… You have five siblings… You go to a Technical High School and should become a certified cook at the end of this year, if you do not go to jail, of course… Yet you have no criminal record."

"You see, no criminal record! The 10 grams of Hashish were for my personal consumption!"

"Yet the results of your urine sample have just come back, and there is no trace of cannabis in it."

"Of course, I was planning to smoke it tomorrow night. Today is Thursday. I don't smoke in the week."

Inspector Chautel switched off the voice recorder, looked Samir in the eyes, and said in a very weary voice:

"Really? Do you know, Samir, why cannabis is illegal in France? Do you think, Samir, that cannabis is illegal for social reasons? Just to let people from socially challenged suburbs like you have a side business so that you don't starve to death? If it were legal, after all, big corporations would have all the cannabis market, and there would be no market share left for you. Do you think cannabis is illegal just to buy social peace in areas like Sevran-Beaudottes? That we just catch a drug dealer once in a while to pretend we do something?"

"Yes, that would seem very logical to me," Samir answered impertinently.

"It's illegal for health reasons: a regular cannabis smoker under 26 will lose six points of IQ in ten years, and our society cannot afford this. Six points of IQ! That's quite something. And yet, you look like someone rather intelligent."

Samir smiled and gave the inspector an arrogant look:

"I guess I started with a very high IQ, and I can afford to lose 12 points of IQ and still be smarter than you."

Chautel sniffed twice and replied:

"That's very possible. And yet, you are sitting on the

wrong side of this table at this very moment. And yet, you are practicing to become a cook, and you will probably never make it to university. But I know you are smart, very smart. Did you know that juvenile gang leaders are often very gifted kids who could have turned out differently, had they been coached properly?"

"Isn't that obvious? Being a gang leader requires a certain set of skills."

The inspector smiled:

"Don't you want to know why I know you are so smart? Well, I will tell, you. No worries, the recorder is off. I know everything, Samir. You had a spreadsheet on your phone with a list of all your transaction."

"No, I don't know what you are talking about."

"Yes, you do. This spreadsheet was disguised as an image file. Our IT guy missed it. I didn't. I also saw that none of your business contacts is saved on your phone. Yet you had set a ringtone to a specific phone number."

From her smartphone, she played the theme of the *Godfather*.

"Does it remind you of somebody?"

Samir turned pale.

"Hassan Benkirane. You are familiar with that name?" the inspector asked.

Samir did not answer.

"He is the cultural attaché of Morocco's embassy in Paris.

He is also a close friend of the Prince of Morocco. You have been calling him on average six times a week over the last four months. Do you have such good relations with fancy people?"

"I will not answer this question, in the absence of a lawyer," Samir answered coldly after pulling himself together.

"And this is your right. But relax, Samir. The recorder is off. Don't you want to know why?"

"Why have you switched it off, then?"

"Listen, Samir. Everybody knows the Royal family of Morocco is one of the major importers of cannabis in Europe. Everybody knows, but nobody wants it to be on the public record, me least of all. As of yesterday, we have a new president in the EU. Under the whole presidential campaign, she has been blaming Morocco for jacking-up the prices of phosphate, which in its turn trumps fertilizer prices and, indirectly, food prices. She has privately joked several times of having the European Union invade Morocco. What would you think of it?"

"I don't care. My father would even like it, he hates Morocco."

"So typical for an Algerian," she commented, rolling her eyes.

Samir went on: "My grandfather even fought in the Summer War. He was a war hero. He rose from the rank of private to major under the four months of fighting."

"The Summer war…" the inspector said. "It was in 2040. As the income from oil started to shrink dangerously, Algeria attacked Morocco, allegedly to obtain the independence of

Western Sahara, but most certainly to gain the exploitation rights of phosphate mines in that region. The Algerians got their asses kicked, pretty much. Quite a waste of human lives. Would you really want a war between Europe and Morocco?"

"Perhaps not…"

The inspector looked Samir in the eyes and said:

"I really want to avoid any misunderstanding or pretext that may lead to unnecessary conflict. And for that, I need intel. I want information that I can pass along to people with the same goals as mine. The question is; what do you want, Samir? Do you want to spend some time in jail wasting your youth, or do you want to put all this behind you, graduate high school, and do your European Civil Service in a place far from your father? I think you do not like him much? Your ringtone for his number is a mortar shell exploding"

Samir was quick to ask: "If I want to avoid jail, what do you suggest?"

"You decrease the scale of your business. Only one provider, the cultural attaché. You don't sell to people in the street anymore, so that you don't get caught. I buy the cannabis from you. No spreadsheet on your phone. You pass me all relevant information concerning him. In June next year, after you graduate high school, you will do your Civil Service in a decent place."

"Do I get no criminal record?" Samir enquired.

"Not even a single line."

"Then, it's an offer I cannot refuse, I believe."

"It is indeed," the inspector smiled.

05: THE GIRL WHO WANTED TO BE BATMAN (16 SEPT 2094)

At five o'clock in the afternoon, the sun was still twenty degrees above the sea, in Casablanca, Morocco. In one hour, though, it would plunge beneath the horizon, Deng Huang knew it. He had gone out to buy some alcohol at one of his contacts' places, and he was now back home in his villa, located very close to the École *Américaine*. Aisha was already there, out in the backyard.

The sixteen-year-old girl was wearing shorts, a sport bra and boxing gloves, her dark hair tied behind her head. She was punching and kicking the punchball hanging over the terrace, just in front of the swimming pool.

"Good evening, Aisha," Deng greeted.

She did not answer and only acknowledged his presence with a glance, too busy with her workout session. He was always impressed by her muscular body. If she had been born in a less poor area, she could certainly have competed in athletics.

On the terrace table, Deng noted an open notebook. Aisha seemed to have been doing her homework. Mathematics. Derivative functions.

Finally, Aisha took a break in her boxing, catching her breath.

"Hi Deng," she finally said, while grabbing a bottle of water nearby. "Is it true, your ex-girlfriend is the commander of the *Alcubierre*?"

"This is correct. Alice has been appointed mission commander for the testing of the warp drive. I have understood it was because the Chinese Agency considered the Russian guy to be rather immature."

Aisha took a few sips from her water bottle and said: "Don't you regret being a businessman? Look, you were a combat diver during your military service, and now you just sit behind a desk, while your ex is exploring space. Aren't you ashamed?"

"We all contribute to the world in different ways. I am still the general manager of the Moroccan affiliate of Wong-Hò. That's pretty good, I would say. Furthermore, I would not have met you, if I had stayed in China."

"I like your villa for sure," she said, and resumed her training session.

He gazed at the short Aisha, her dark, tied-back hair and the sweat dripping along her muscular body. He liked her legs most. These were real Batman legs, packed with muscles and without a single gram of fat. She had often joked that she had long wanted to be Batman when she was a young girl.

It was still damn hot, even though it would soon be the evening. Deng let Aisha pursue her boxing and took off his clothes, grabbed his bathing suit and dived into the swimming pool.

It was where it had all started: in this swimming pool. Aisha's mother was Deng's housemaid. One day, before the summer, when he had come back earlier than normal from work, he had caught her watching her daughter in the pool. She had explained awkwardly that her daughter wanted to learn how to swim, to become a police officer. Most public swimming pools were in a very poor maintenance state, in Casa. Deng knew that. The result was that, though Casablanca lay by the sea, 70% of the Casablancan kids couldn't swim. That didn't stop the Moroccan king from sleeping well at night, though.

Deng had told Aisha's mother there was no need to apologize. He had done his military service in the Chinese Navy and was himself a good swimmer, so he had promised to teach Aisha how to swim over the summer. She would come to his place on Fridays and Saturdays.

This could just have remained innocent, but it didn't, Deng thought as he front-crawled back and forth in the pool. It was just biology. All species are genetically coded to ensure their survival. That was the sole purpose of each species, including mankind. No other meaning in life. Biologically speaking, it meant that each species was programmed to reproduce. In crude terms, it meant that a man was genetically coded to have an erection when he was aroused by a girl. Damned be the biology

Muslim North-Africans had understood this. That was why women used to be concealed behind a veil. So that men just wouldn't be tempted to assault them. That was what Aisha would ironically declare when he was complaining she sometimes walked naked in his garden.

Aisha was going to the *Lycée Fatima Mernissi*, named after the famous Moroccan sociologist, and their religion teacher had a very feministic view of Islam. As a result, Aisha often made fun of any male supremacist interpretation of Islam, which was still a very dominant interpretation of that religion in Morocco.

Nonetheless, it was so his affair with Aisha had started. As he had been standing in the pool and teaching a bikini-clad Aisha how to crawl, he had had an erection. As she had been swimming back toward him, she had seen it. And what had she done? She had dived, drawn down his shorts, and he had felt himself being orally stimulated. Ten minutes and a condom later, they had been lying in his living room, and they had decided to start a relationship.

Not that it was unusual for expats in Morocco to engage in this kind of practice. Many, be they from China, India, Europe, or America, would have a sexual relationship with a younger girl or boy and provide financial support to their family in exchange. This was, of course, something the Moroccan government would firmly deny.

He really liked Aisha, though. She was smarter than she thought. She was the first in her family to have ever made it to high school. She now wanted to be a police officer or a firefighter. He believed she should even try to make it to university. He really saw potential in her.

06: Diplomat of Outer Space Affairs (16 Sept 2094)

High above the Atlantic, Ralf Åhman was sitting at the rear of the Austrian Airlines flight 87 to New York. One of his occasional co-workers had been this admiral from the US Navy who was so focused on safety. The admiral had made such an impression on him that Ralf would now only sit on the next to last row in a plane's cabin, even if it meant he had to fly in tourist class.

He glanced at his watch. It was 13:30 in New York. He went back to his tablet-laptop hybrid, on which he was reading *Feedback of the Earth*, written by the famous geologist Dr. Sheldon Cooper. The thesis of that book was that, though global warming had had well-known geophysical consequences, such as the rise in sea-level and the increase in tropical storms, it would probably trigger geological feedback with consequences far more severe for mankind.

The melting of ice caps and the thermal expansion of the oceans were reallocating the mass at the surface of the Earth. It had in its turn an impact on the speed of the rotation of the Earth. Even if these speed variations were not more than a few milliseconds a day, it was enough to dramatically increase the magmatic convection within the mantle of our planet. This had already led to an increase in earthquakes and volcanic eruptions. That was fact. The Big One that had occurred in San Francisco in 2033 had been expected, but not the Big Two in 2081.

Large volcanic eruptions at regular interval could have an impact on the climate, like under the Little Ice Age, six hundred years earlier. Dr. Sheldon Cooper thought that the next five decades would gradually be marked by the start of a global cooling era. This indirect consequence of global warming may have far more severe consequences for mankind. For how to feed a population of 11 billion, which it was soon to be? And that was only the most optimistic scenario, according to Dr. Cooper. At worst the feedback from the Earth may trigger the eruption of super-volcanoes, like the one in Yellowstone. This would probably mean the extinction of most mammals on Earth, including mankind.

"Well! He is not pessimistic, this guy," Ralf thought.

He was invited by a steward to switch off his tablet-laptop and put it under the seat in front of him for the landing. He took his newspaper instead: *The Chained Palmiped,* one of the last few newspapers still printed on actual paper. It was a sarcastic European weekly paper specializing in unraveling political gossips and scandals. It was often seen as the sibling of the French counterpart, *Le Canard Enchaîné.*

Its headline read: '*Eugénie's evil genius*' It was about the newly sworn-in European president, Eugénie Bonavita. In her entourage was an advisor who seriously advocated a war against Morocco to control the phosphate mines. Ralf cast an interested glance at the article, as the plane made its final approach.

At the US customs, Ralf Åhman showed his UN diplomatic pass. The customs official looked at it interestedly, while considering the UN Director. The Director of the United Nations Office for Outer Space Affairs (UNOOSA) was an overweight man of intermediate height in his late thirties. He had dark brown afro-hair and a pale brown skin. His right eye always seemed half shut.

"How do you pronounce your name?" The customs official finally asked him.

"Åhman…, it's pronounced 'Oman', with an open O," Ralf replied.

"What is this weird letter? An A with a circle on top of it?"

"It's an Å. It's a Swedish letter. Å like in an Ångström. You know the Ångström unit? It's a ten-billionth of a meter."

"Never heard of it. I don't like the metric system anyway. So, you are Swedish? Yet you sound like a Scot when you speak."

The nationality was never mentioned on a UN pass, but it was not unusual for bored customs officials to try and guess.

"My mother is Scottish. My father was Finnish, of African descent, and I grew up in Sweden. Say I'm European."

"Have a nice stay in New York, sir."

It was 16:30 when Ralf arrived at the UN headquarters, by the East River. He had had to queue for a chauffeured taxi, as the UN internal policies forbade its staff to use unmanned taxis since a Chinese diplomat had been kidnapped by a group of hackers.

He reached the 35th floor, where the Office for Outer Space Affairs had two small rooms at their disposal.

Why did the secretary general have to book him a meeting with this Michael Vahlroos? He had jet lag and was in no mood for meeting a lobbyist.

He went to the Office's room to leave his luggage and found out that Michael Vahlroos was already there, sitting on the room's little sofa adjacent to the two working bureaus. An intern had brought him in, though visitors were not supposed to see this very unofficial room. Posters of *Star Wars* and *Star Trek* were hanging on the walls.

"Good afternoon, Mr. Åhman," the CEO greeted him, as he quickly stood up to shake Ralf's hand, "An intern told me no conference room had been booked for our meeting, I took the liberty of being brought in here."

"Good day to you, Mr. Walrus."

"Vahlroos, Michael Vahlroos.," Michael corrected.

"Sorry, sir. I blame it on the jetlag." Ralf put his trolley bag under one of the desks and opened his blazer. He wore a black suit with a white shirt and dark grey tie. His black shoes were perfectly polished. He briefly considered the tall blond CEO who wore no tie and had dirty brown shoes. At least Michael was lucky enough not to be persecuted by the UN secretary general for not polishing his shoes.

Michael smiled and said apologetically: "I am afraid we will have less than fifteen minutes to spend together. I have to travel to Florida tonight. My son… He was murdered last Sunday. I have to see his mother."

"I'm sorry to hear that."

Ralf briefly wondered what kind of a father would arrange a business meeting just after the murder of his son. He was a UN diplomat, however, and had been witness to more peculiar behavior.

As he looked around the room, Michael went on unperturbed: "Well, not much to be done against fate, or destiny… And the world does not stop at the loss of one life, even if it's your child's. What a cozy office you have here. I see all these posters of Star Wars on this wall, and pictures of… Eisenhower and…who is this one?"

"Henry Kissinger," Ralf answered. "He was a US State

Secretary during the Cold War. And there you have de Gaulle, a French president, and there, McMillan, a British prime minister."

"Fascinating. And over there, on that wall, you have posters of Star Trek, and other people I don't know, except perhaps Eleonore Roosevelt, here."

"This person is Woodrow Wilson, the US president behind the Leagues of Nations, which was founded after the Great War. This one is Dag Hammarskjöld, the second secretary general of the UN. There, this is Ralph Bunche… a UN diplomat… Nobel Peace Prize in 1950."

"Intriguing," Michael commented. "And why are these hanging together with *Star Trek* posters, while the others are together with *Star Wars* posters?"

"I guess this is a joke from the interns… On that wall, the Kissingers and Eisenhowers are the so-called *Realists*. They believe the primary goal of every nation is to demonstrate power. For them, chaos is the natural order of things in geopolitics. This suits very well the *Star Wars* franchise. On the other wall, you have the *Idealists*, the ones who believe that nations can cooperate to reach a common goal and achieve peace. Of course, this suits the *Star Trek* philosophy."

"I see." Mr. Vahlroos sat back on the sofa he had been sitting on when Ralf had entered. "And what about someone, like me, who believes that private corporations have a key role to play to make the world a better place? What would you call me?"

Ralf grabbed a chair and sat down opposite Michael. "A liberal. Liberals believe in the leading roles of individuals, NGOs and Private Corporation in international relations."

"Then I am a goddamned liberal, Mister the Director of the UN Office for Outer Space Affairs. The Vahlroos Corporation is a key player in the current space race. All the nations owe us. The compact fusion reactors used by NASA, by the orbital station and the new *Alcubierre* ship are all made by us. The new Albaspace aerospace shuttle is also ours."

"I am aware of it, Mr. Vahlroos, and I am grateful," Ralf said.

"In the future, you cannot let a single state have a monopoly on the manufacturing of spacecraft with warp capabilities. This would lead to diplomatic chaos. If only the Russians and Chinese possess the technology, it will increase the tension with the West and the South. A private company, on the other hand, is neutral. At Vahlroos, we believe that, within five years, we can provide the world with a new warp spaceship that could even enter the atmosphere. These spaceships would be available to all states, companies or even private individuals who could afford it."

"I appreciate your concern for the world's peace, Mr. Vahlroos," Ralf replied. "However, what would happen if private companies equipped with your spaceships started exploiting resources in outer space, as you advocated it in *The Wall Street Journal* a few weeks ago? Under the current international legislation, any private person or company can claim a natural resource they have found in space. Would it mean that a big corporation could claim a planet in a remote system?"

"That's not what I meant."

"But it could be one of the implications. In the current legal framework, warp technology can have tremendous consequences for all of mankind. More regulation will most certainly be needed."

"You are right," Vahlroos admitted. "We need regulation. We have always needed regulation. However, keep in mind that too much regulation can discourage private initiative. It is often privateers who dare boldly go where no one has gone before."

Ralf rose to his feet. "Privateers? Like Cortez and his conquistadors who sacked Latin America in the 16th Century? Private initiative, like the Martian Show Corporation? Seventeen couples sent to Mars and left there with no hope of return, and for what? For the sole purpose of entertaining a bunch of stupid followers on Earth: what was the added value of this for mankind? All of them dead, except for one daughter. Who took care of her when the Martian Show Corporation went bankrupt? Your private insurance, perhaps?"

"No, this is not what I meant," Michael replied calmly, looking at Ralf from his sofa.

"My department, here at the UN, has taken care of it. UNOOSA. We helped the Martian girl sue the European Union, which had approved *The Martian Show*. They were convicted of complicity in slavery. Technically, a girl born on

Mars to work for free for a digital show is called a slave."

"Oh, please…"

"With the indemnities, we organized a rescue mission. A Burkinabe engineer designed robots that we shipped to Mars on board a European probe. Using Martian minerals, these robots built a rocket. This was not the work of private insurance, but of an international organization which had to clean up after the failure of a private corporation."

"Please, Mr. Åhman", Michael Vahlroos said as he stood up. "I guess you are tired because of the jet lag. I will leave you. However, you should know that at V-Space, we have now hired that Burkinabe engineer."

Michael left the room. Ralf reflected that he had perhaps just been an undiplomatic diplomat. Michael Vahlroos was the CEO of Vahlroos Corporation. They were the main private actors in the space industry. As the director of UNOOSA, Ralf knew he would most certainly be compelled to work with them in the coming years.

But he was indeed tired. He decided to go to the hotel and hoped, on his way down the UN building, he would not stumble upon the secretary general. He was in no mood to talk to anybody important.

As Ralf checked in at the Radisson Blu, he met the 'admiral in civilian clothes' as he used to call him. He had spotted him at the desk already, on entering the hotel. At first, he wanted to avoid him. He was tired, and those damned Americans had a habit of being too socializing for his Nordic taste. He was, however, a diplomat and could not just behave like a shy Swede or a distant Finn.

"Good evening, Admiral Johnson."

"Good evening, Ralf," Glover replied. "Nice to see you."

"What brings you to New York, Glover?"

"Same as you. Your SG's office invited other representatives of various space agencies including myself to watch the broadcasting of the *Alcubierre* test at the UN building."

Ralf's face displayed a weary smile. "To be there at eight in the morning. Not a decent time for a diplomat."

"That's what happens when the Chinese get to choose the broadcasting time. Well, it was nice seeing you, Ralf. I was thinking about going to the hotel's gym. Do you want to join me?"

"I would be glad to," Ralf lied, "but I have some work to do. However, can we meet for breakfast at 7:00, tomorrow morning?"

"As you wish. Have a good night."

"Likewise, bye."

As they parted, Ralf felt relieved he would not have to spend the evening with the American. He wanted to be left alone. When he entered his room, he glanced at the hall mirror and wondered briefly if he shouldn't have followed Glover to the gym instead. He was only 38 years old but was at least 20 kilos

(44 lbs) overweight. He guessed he liked his job too much.

He sat down on the couch in front of the broad, flat screen and clapped his hands. A computer voice answered.

"Room butler, at your disposal. May I help you?"

Ralf did not like the idea of having a microphone constantly listening to his movements in the room. Some people at the UN were even claiming that intelligence services from most of the great powers were just hacking these digital hotel butlers to spy on them.

Since Ralf was not planning to reveal any secret, he thought he may well have fun with the device.

"I would like to watch a movie," he replied.

"What kind of movie?" the computer enquired.

"Happy ending movie."

"Do you wish to see a Walt Disney movie?"

"Why not?"

"Would you like to watch Star Wars – episode 26?"

"Hell, no! Something old, older than Star Wars."

"Would you like to watch The Third Man on the Mountain?"

"Never heard of it, why not?"

The flat screen on the wall opposite the bed turned on to play the movie. But before the movie started, a notice message was displayed: *The story of this movie is set around 1860. Back then, the world population was about 1.3 billion. In 2094, the world population is about 10.4 billion.*

Since the middle of the 21st Century, the UNESCO had

made it compulsory to set the demographic context of each projected movie in relation to the present time. The purpose was to make the world population aware of the untenable demographic growth.

The movie that followed was about 19th-century alpinists attempting the climb of a difficult mountain called the *Citadel*. As he was falling asleep, Ralf decided that the *Citadel* looked very much like the *Matterhorn* in Switzerland.

07: TINTIN FROM CONGO
(17 SEPT 2094)

The village of Kodala was located southwest of Bobo-Dioulasso, the second largest city of Burkina Faso, Western Africa. On this early morning of Friday 17 September 2094, two young men were lying on mattresses on the floor of a classroom of the village's primary school. They were rolled in individual mosquito nets.

Thierry Diakité had been awake for quite some time, now. Sleeping in this village was impossible. It was not because of the mosquitoes. The rainy season was over. It was because those villagers were just as goddamned religiously zealous as they were in Bobo. First, there had been the local Mosque's muezzin calling for the Morning Prayer and singing loud *"Allah-wa-akbar"* and other things in Arabic. Then, there had been the evangelists turning on some loudspeakers shouting *"Jesus loves you"* in English. And, as if that had not been enough, the little Catholic church had started ringing its bells. As far as Thierry was concerned, all religions were equally noisy.

Moreover, the mattress on the floor was not as comfortable as the one on his bed back home. Thierry regretted he had not spent the night in his room in Bobo-Dioulasso and come here only in the morning, but his former schoolteacher Lenka had insisted. And he owed her so much.

He got up from underneath his mosquito net, took his clothes and went to the bathroom, where he got dressed after a quick shower. Thierry Diakité was a well-built young black man of average height.

He decided to go to the village. Older houses built in earthen bricks and more modern concrete buildings stood beside each other in what could be perceived as anarchy. However, and this was the Burkinabe miracle, every single house had access to running water with a tap installed. The villagers were already up, cooking outside their houses.

This was the village where he had been born and spent most of his childhood. He still knew some of the inhabitants, and he talked with a few of his acquaintances on his way to the cemetery. In the graveyard, he stopped beside the tombs of his parents, lying next to each other. His father had been a Maliki Muslim and his mother a Catholic Christian, and they had slightly different tombstones. When he looked where he had come from, he could not help thinking how lucky he had been. It was mostly thanks to Lenka.

He had barely known his mother. She had died of malaria

when he was six. He remembered going to the school to find the teacher, and Lenka just telling him to stop crying and be a man now. Four years later, his father had been killed in an anti-Chinese riot. A Chinese farming corporation had been trying to extend their culture onto the lands owned by the villagers. There had been violent demonstrations. The Chinese had paid armed guards to protect them, and the latter had opened fire at the crowd. It had been a sad day for Kodala.

His schoolteacher, Lenka, though, had seen how intelligent and brilliant Thierry was in class. She had ensured that he would be able to go to high school in Bobo-Dioulasso. This had opened up for him the way to university and eventually to a PhD in robotics at the University of Kigali, Rwanda, during which he had won a competition organized by the UN. Under their patronage, he had developed the robots that had now been used on Mars to build a rocket to repatriate the last Martian survivor. This had landed him a job at the space subsidiary of Vahlroos Corporation shortly after his PhD defense.

At twenty-four years, three months and nineteen days, he was a Doctor in robotics working at V-Space. Not bad for an orphan from Kodala.

A quick glance at his watch told him it was already past 10 o'clock. The first test would be at 12 o'clock Burkina time, but the TV program would start at 11:00. He decided to go back to the school.

Lenka Sawadogo was standing in front of the school talking to Tintin, who had been sharing the classroom for the night. Lenka, a dark-skinned middle-aged lady, was wearing a light pink suit and a straw hat. Tintin, a thin, tall young man with a lighter skin complexion, was wearing a white cap, green but too short trousers and a white T-shirt with a blue lettered text reading: "*With great brains come great possibilities.*"

They were discussing something animatedly in English, rather than in French, which was their mother tongue.

"So, Lenka, if I understand correctly, you are here for your campaign," Tintin summarized. "Do you really think that you have a chance to win the seat in the parliament?"

"Well, I hope so," Lenka answered. "Isn't Burkina called the 'Republic of teachers'? The last four presidents all started their careers as school teachers. I only aim for a seat in the parliament."

"And you are using us to do your private PR" Tintin asked provocatively.

"It's mostly for the kids," Lenka objected. "It will be an honor for them to meet Thierry Diakité, born here, and the main engineer behind the Martian robots, and Tintin Mutombo, co-inventor of warp propulsion. By the way, I have to ask: is it Tintin, like in *Tintin in Congo*?"

"Tintin, like in *Tintin* from *Congo*," Tintin retorted. "I'm proud of my name. In Congo Kinsha, if you call someone 'Tintin', it means they are funny. And people do like Tintin in

Congo. My grandfather, a white man of French origins, has been nicknamed *Capitaine Haddock* since he moved to Kinshasa. So, it's not surprising my Mother wanted to call me Tintin."

Thierry jumped in to their conversation: "I've heard his family is pretty rich, back there in Kinsha," he said. "They own several restaurants and a nightclub called Le Moulinsart. They are all nuts about Tintin."

"Yes, but still," the former schoolteacher objected. "*Tintin in Congo* is rather racist. Look how Hergé drew Congolese people!"

Tintin laughed and retorted: "And look how Hergé caricatured white people. With their big noses and all. Pretty mean, too. You would probably not believe me, but when the Belgians stopped publishing *Tintin in Congo*, it was the Zairian dictator Mobutu who asked them to reissue the album. True story."

"Ok, I won't insist," Lenka gave up. And, changing the subject: "So how do you like your new work at V-Space, both of you?"

"Hard to say," Thierry said. "So far, it has not been much work. Mostly coffee drinking. And the air conditioning in the premises is enjoyable when it's too hot outside."

"I am here at V-space by default," Tintin admitted. "The Russians refused to renew my visa at the end of my PhD, driving my supervisor crazy. Anatoli wanted me to do a Post-Doc in Moscow, but instead I was shipped back to Congo."

"Anatoli Govorov?" Lenka wondered.

"Yes, precisely. He who will be the propulsion specialist on board the spacecraft for the warp test. Luckily, the Chinese insisted he wouldn't be the commander. And believe me: it was very wise of them! Anatoli is a good supervisor when it comes to theoretical physics, but when it comes to being practical, don't rely on him!"

Lenka looked anxiously at her watch. "Let's go back inside the school and see how the kids are doing. I hope the social workers are soon done with their sex education class."

In the schoolyard, there were a lot of teenagers, younger kids and a few parents sitting on the floor or standing. A few had secured some chairs. In front of the school building, the social workers had set a whiteboard on which a penis and a vagina had been drawn with various arrows naming the different parts. Beside it, they had placed a table, on which were many carrots and condoms, and they were now demonstrating how to put a condom on carrots. The kids were mostly laughing. The two social worker ladies, two very attractive black women, were assisted by the Catholic priest and the Sunni Iman who were also trying to put protections on vegetables.

They were obviously less gifted than the ladies. Thierry noted that the evangelist pastor was nowhere to be seen, but then remembered that he belonged to the few who still believed that using a condom was a capital sin. "Getting AIDS was a capital sin, literally, you prick," Thierry thought.

"And remember," one of the social workers concluded. "Having a baby before graduating university equals greater likelihood to poverty. Always use protection and contraceptive means."

With a sign, she invited Tintin, Thierry and Lenka to join them by the whiteboard. As Lenka was delivering a short introductory speech about the coming test of the warp drive, which the kids would be able to watch on the school's TV, Thierry erased the penis and vagina on the whiteboard and, instead, drew the sun and the four first planets of the solar system. In the meantime, Tintin got an idea. He grabbed a condom, inflated it with his mouth, tied it with a knot and started to draw on it using a marker pen.

The kids started laughing more and more, not listening to Lenka, which irritated the latter.

"Tintin from Congo, what are you doing?" she asked.

"Explaining physics, Mistress," Tintin answered, moving forward to the children, holding the inflated condom in his left hand.

"*Les enfants, une question s'il vous plaît: est-il possible d'aller plus vite que la vitesse de la lumière?*" He asked the kids, switching to French ('Kids, one question please: is it possible to travel faster than light?').

Half of the kids answered *oui* (yes), and the other half

answered *non* (no).

"Well kids, it is *impossible* to go faster than the speed of light. Never say it is possible. It's a big no-no. The planet Mars is currently located 78 million kilometers [43 M miles] from Earth, one of the closest positions it can be to our planet. This means that, at the present time, light takes 4.2 minutes to reach Mars from Earth. And, of course, so do radio waves."

Tintin went on: "Today, the *Alcubierre*, a spaceship currently in orbit around the Earth, will be able to reach Mars in 25 seconds. Ten times faster than it takes for radio waves to reach the red planet. But let us be clear, the *Alcubierre* will never go faster than the speed of light.

"*Mais alors, comment c'est possible*?" a kid asked ['So how is it possible, then?'].

"We physicists do what you kids are best at: we cheat!" Tintin said, and the children started laughing.

"Time and space are actually combined as a single system, called spacetime. The *Alcubierre* is equipped with warp propulsion. The principle of a warp drive is, as given by its name, to warp spacetime. By contracting spacetime in front of her and expanding it behind, the *Alcubierre* can reach a speed which we, from a fixed observation point, may consider is faster than the speed of light. But it isn't. Look at this inflated condom."

The children who had just had a sexual education class started laughing again, but Tintin continued his exposé: "Well, I am using this condom for something even better than sex: physics. Look at the condom's surface. It is in only two dimensions. Should you be an ant crawling on it, you would have only two dimensions for your travel: forward and backward, as well as left and right. Look at these two black spots I have drawn. They are currently 17 cm apart."

The kids laughed again.

"Well, by warping the extra dimension, that is to say, the air inside the condom, I will have the two black spots kiss each other."

With his hands, Tintin started contracting the condoms between the two black spots and air expanded to the other extremity of the contraceptive device

"You see? Easy peasy. When you master an extra dimension, insolvable problems become solvable."

"Well, after all, perhaps he is 'Tintin' as they say in Congo Kinsha," Lenka said to herself.

08: THE PARTY IS ON
(17 SEPT 2094)

At the Martian colony, Sanne van der Maas had installed herself as comfortably as possible on the sofa. She had moved the whole radio set to the sofa's side table and had laid her digital tablet next to her on the sofa. It was soon to be 12:35 in Amsterdam. The program would start at 13:30.

She switched on the TV. Because of the transmission delay, it was showing a 4-5 minutes late broadcast. On the second channel, a movie was starting. It was called *A Bridge Too Far*. The introduction text read: *The story of this movie is set in 1944. Back then, the world population was about 2.4 billion. In 2094, the world population is about 10.4 billion.*

She switched to the first channel. They were discussing the upcoming tests. She rose to her feet and went to the kitchenette. As she was cooking some rice and frying tomatoes, half an eggplant and green peppers, she tried to listen to the news broadcast.

When she made it back to the sofa with a plate, the news anchor explained that on this day, 17 September 2094, it had been 150 years exactly since *Operation Market Garden*, one of the greatest allied failures of World War Two.

She switched to the second channel. Two British officers with their para red berets were standing and talking in a room with a projector.

"But, sir, we keep getting reports from the Dutch Underground," said the low-ranking officer.

"I've read them," replied his superior. *And so has Field Marshall Montgomery. Now, look here. There have been thousands of photographs, from this sortie and all the others. How many of them are showing tanks?*

"Just these, sir."

"And you are seriously considering asking us to cancel the biggest operation mounted since D-day, because of three photographs?"

"No, sir."

"Sixteen consecutive drops have been cancelled in the last few months for one reason or another. But this time the party is on. And no one is going to call it off. Is that fully understood?"

"Yes, sir."

Sanne turned the TV off. That was how absurd decisions were taken in the first place. When high-ranking dominating people were refusing to listen to the divergent opinion of their subalterns. That was how *The Martian Show* had been started in the first place. That was how she had ended up being born on Mars with no way of returning to Earth.

She felt suddenly nervous. What if the *Alcubierre* ship had not been properly tested and everybody had failed to see it? What if the warp test failed? Could it happen?

And then she relaxed slightly. The *Orion* was now ready, since it had been used to tow the *Alcubierre* to the test area, according to the news. The *Orion* would take only eight weeks to come to Mars. So, if the warp test failed, but NASA gave their thumbs up to a Martian mission, she would be on Earth by the end of January, at the earliest. That was Plan B.

But still, she would rather see a successful warping of spacetime and be on Earth by the beginning of October.

09: THE FIRST WARPING OF SPACETIME (17 SEPT 2094)

It was seven in the morning on that Friday in New York City, when a still sleepy Ralf Åhman emerged in the breakfast room of the Radisson Hotel. He was wearing sneakers, white jeans and a UN blue polo with the insignia of UNOOSA on it. He went for the coffee machine like a cruising missile, helped himself to a cup, added a cloud of milk, and took a few sips. He immediately felt his mind sharpen. Glancing around, he spotted the admiral in civilian clothes, sitting alone at a table, drinking some juice and absorbed in the reading of his tablet. Glover Johnson was wearing a black suit and a white shirt, though no tie. Always wearing a kind of uniform, Ralf thought. Perhaps he was not aware it was casual Friday at the UN?

Ralf refilled his cup of coffee, took a plate he filled with salmon, cheese, dark bread, butter, crescents and chocolate bread and made it to the admiral's table.

"Good morning, Glover, interesting news?" Ralf asked, putting his plate on the table and sitting down in front of the admiral.

"Very uninteresting. On *Tox news*, they are mostly talking about how disappointed the Chinese are not to be able to be represented by a panda for the second test."

"It was also their main concern on *Bollox news* when I was shaving this morning. A shame this species has gone extinct."

By the end of the twenty-first century, Fox news had become the largest media group on the North American continent. Because of its tendency to severely bias its news reports, it had been nicknamed *Tox news* by web surfers, with a '*Tox*' like in intoxication. In Europe, the Bolloré group was the leading media corporation, and its one-sided coverage of events had it nicknamed *Bollox news*.

"Never cared about pandas," the admiral went on. "They were ugly and stupid plantigrades. They deserved to die out. Look at polar bears: they have become more enterprising. They are hunting reindeers, catching dolphins and killing walruses. They deserve to live. Speaking of which, you've got a polar bear's ration here." Glover was looking at Ralf's plate.

"I ate nothing yesterday evening, and I will skip lunch today," Ralf defended himself.

He hated to be lectured about his unhealthy food habits. Ralf had indeed quite a prominent belly, while the admiral had no extra fat. Even worse, he was well trained, and his muscular breast, shoulders and biceps could be guessed through his suits.

"So, today is 17 September 2094," Ralf said to change the subject. "17 September is not always a good day for UN Swedish diplomats. Luckily, I am also Finnish and Scottish."

"What do you mean?"

"17 September 1948, Folke Bernadotte. 17 September 1961, Dag Hammarskjöld. If the *Alcubierre* test fails badly today, I will be the next UN Swedish diplomat to crash."

"The Russians and Chinese shared with us their safety protocols," Glover replied. "Both the American and European space agencies have agreed to the test procedures. I don't see what could go wrong. And if something goes wrong, it will be at the first, unmanned test. No lives are at risk."

"You don't believe in fate or bad luck?"

"Of course not," the admiral answered. "I am a nuclear engineer. I only believe in the random functions of the universe, and their corollary: We should do everything to land on the right side of the statistics."

"What do you mean?"

"Each event has a given probability to occur in a certain environment. As engineers, you just want to increase the probability of occurrence of good events and decrease that of bad events. In the case of the *Alcubierre* test, the probability of failure is ten times less than that of a woman dying in labor. Nobody talks about maternal death anymore. It's all about being on the right side of the statistics."

"Well, Glover, you are not reassuring me. Every year, there are too many women dying in labor, and I find it sad, if it was just because they were on the wrong side of the statistics."

"The statistics are not static. We all strive to pull as many people as we can to the right side of them."

"It's twenty over seven," Ralf said. "I'm done with my breakfast. Perhaps we should get going. We could borrow the hotel's bikes."

The Radisson, like most hotels in New York at the end of the 21st Century, had bikes at the disposal of their customers.

"Why not?" Glover replied. "It's a ten-minute bike ride there. Shall we meet in the lobby in ten minutes?

"OK."

When Ralf met Glover in the lobby, the admiral had already grabbed two bikes. He handed over one to Ralf.

It was a sunny morning, and as they biked eastward, Ralf was happy he had his sunglasses. Glover complained that the Radisson hotel had no helmets left for them and mentioned that the probability of them having a biking accident on their way to the UN headquarters was higher than the probability of seeing the warp test fail later that day.

They followed East 33rd Street to 1st Avenue, where they turned left until they reached Ralph Bunche Park, opposite the UN headquarters.

After passing security control, they made for the cafeteria, where a huge canvas projection screen had been installed. The UN secretary general, Jarek Janowski, was already there. The US representative took Glover apart and introduced him to other members of the permanent US delegation.

Standing beside a short, thin, but muscular man casually wearing mountaineering pants and a T-shirt was the representative of the South Asian Union, a slim woman of intermediate height in a perfectly pressed purple skirt-suit. Hira Dorjee-Sherpa was blind, and therefore she wore so-called 'earGlasses'. These were special digital glasses connected through two wires to her earlobes, which helped her brain picture a 3D-image of her surroundings in bad resolution. Ralf greeted her, and she introduced her husband Temba, who worked as a high-altitude mountain guide in Nepal during the spring but as a climbing instructor in New York during the rest of the year.

Ralf was then greeted by Esko Punainen, the representative of the European Union. He was much taller than Ralf, had grey eyes and grey hair but was equally overweight.

"Terve, Ralf. Onko sinulla minulle Koskenkorvan pullo?" he asked in Finnish ('Hi, Ralf. Do you have a bottle of Koskenkorva for me?'). "It's not always easy to get hold of a bottle of Koskenkorva in New York."

"Sorry, Esko, I have just arrived from Vienna," Ralf replied, also in Finnish. "Moreover, it would not be wise for a UN official to hand over a gift to the representative of a Member State."

"You are so Swedish, after all," Esko joked in English.

People had started to sit down on various chairs across the cafeteria. Esko and Ralf sat close to each other.

The first test should have started at 8:00 New York Time. But it was delayed twenty minutes, for reasons that were unclear. In the meantime, the studio was broadcasting a live interview from Luleå University, in Sweden, where two PhD students, a man and woman, had worked on the set-up of the Alcubierre metric.

The young man, a certain Mikko Andersson, had a T-shirt on which there was an inscription in Swedish together with a picture of a mosquito and the Lapponian flag. The young woman, whose name was Valeriya Limonov, had a T-shirt with an inscription in Russian together with a picture of a panting husky dog and the Russian flag. Ralf made a note of their names.

The amount of negative energy necessary for the warping of spacetime could be reduced considerably by having the right thickness and the right oscillation of the field. Both PhD students had worked on the optimization of the field generated by the green matter.

Of course, this was something else about them that amused Esko, so Ralf got distracted and could not understand all the technical explanations.

"Come on, Ralf, you speak Swedish, and so do I," Esko whispered to Ralf in Finnish, to be sure no one would understand. "And I also happen to know enough Russian to understand what is written on her T-shirt."

"They are kids, studying physics; they have humor, that's all," Ralf replied in Finnish.

This did not hinder Esko from adding: "On his T-shirt, it's written: '*In Lapland, mosquitoes are so huge it's nice when they suck you*'. On her T-shirt, it's written: '*In Siberia, husky dogs have such huge tongues, it's nice when they lick you.*'

"I had guessed it. Luckily, none of the *Tox* news commentators understands Swedish or Russian. But it's gonna be on the web later today."

At 8:15, the broadcast switched to the *Orion* ship, which had towed the *Alcubierre* to a safe position, half a million kilometers from the Earth. The anchor woman insisted that the test was only possible in such safe conditions because of the active cooperation of NASA, which had not only had the Russians and Chinese benefit from their expertise in terms of nuclear safety, but also made possible the towing to the current safe location in a shorter time than chemically propelled ships would have done.

While the *Orion* was a larger conventional spacecraft with an orbital ring around it, the *Alcubierre* looked entirely different. It was nothing but a cylinder, a 49 m (161 ft) long cylinder with an 18 m (59 ft) diameter. The front and the rear were mere flat disks, the main entry hatch being at the center of the rear one. The design was certainly not appealing to fans of science fiction. However, it was necessary to generate the cylindrical, green-matter-induced warp field around the ship.

The *Alcubierre* was now twenty kilometers (12.4 miles) away from the *Orion*. The test was about to begin. A green flash suddenly swallowed the spacecraft, and the *Alcubierre* was gone. There was an exclamation in the room. It was 8:22.

So far, so good. It should take twenty-five seconds to reach the vicinity of Mars, an additional five to ten minutes to turn around and another twenty-five seconds to come back to the *Orion*. The ship should be back before 8:33.

Ralf was nervous, and thought about Sanne, on Mars, who would broadcast a message to Earth, when receiving the arrival signal of the *Alcubierre*. Esko was talking about his summer house he had purchased in Northern Finland. It took an eternity to get there. With warp technology, he could perhaps be able to spend a weekend in Finnish Lapland while still working in New York.

At 8:26, everybody turned silent, and a ticking clock on the screen showed that there were 45 seconds left before the reception of any radio message from the red planet was expected.

At 8:27, there was no message.

At 8:28, there was a radio message, and Ralf was relieved to recognize Sanne's voice:

"Martian colony to Earth, radio signature received from a

spaceship identified as the Alcubierre, *today at 12:23 UTC. The spacecraft has commenced its turnaround maneuver.*"

There were some cheers in the room. People started chatting so much that everybody missed the new green flash on the TV screen at 8:31, marking the return of the *Alcubierre*.

When the people in the room realized the spacecraft had come back, there was even more thunderous applause, and the secretary general, like a 'Mr. Obvious', commented that the first test was encouraging.

The *Orion* had now reached and begun docking to the *Alcubierre* to prepare the second phase of the test.

Ten minutes later, the broadcast program was showing two astronauts boarding the *Alcubierre* from the hatch docked to the *Orion*. They were a man and a woman, a Russian and a Chinese person. Or rather, an Afro-Chinese person, as Alice Fù's father was from Senegal. Anatoli Govorov, the tall, hefty Russian, was holding the camera while floating behind Alice Fù, who was carrying two small pets under her arms, a cat and a dog. Both pets had electrodes patched on their bodies and these were linked to a transmitter strapped to their backs.

They went through the airlock and found themselves in a 20 m (66 ft) long cylindrical operation room with an 8 m (26 ft) diameter. In front of the airlock's hatch, equipped with the only window of the spacecraft, were three seats behind computer screens and advanced control panels. This was the secondary flight deck. It was solely meant for docking or close-range flying-by maneuvers.

The primary operation room was located in a compartment revolving around the cylindrical room at a constant speed to create gravity. The two astronauts floated their way to the middle of the cylindrical room, where smaller ladders were spinning around the cylinder's axis. They led to the gravity department. Alice gently grabbed one, putting her feet on the ladder steps, and started spinning with it, feeling the gravity effect immediately.

As she climbed down the ladder into the gravity department, the pets became much heavier, and she had difficulty keeping them under her arms. The small brown dog jumped down to the floor of the gravity deck, and it was immediately attacked by the black and white cat which had managed to set itself free. In less than a second, the cat had set his claws on the dog's back, messing with the electrodes. Alice quickly interfered, caught the cat and lifted it away, but the dog was already mewling.

Anatoli, who had been filming the event from the top of the ladder, commented that they would have probably to put the two animals in two separate rooms. This was not a problem as the ship was rather spacious, as he would show the viewers.

In fact, two gravity decks, each 2.1 m (7ft 11 in) high, were revolving on magnetic rails around the cylindrical 0-G room. Of course, on each deck, the floor were concavely and the ceiling convexly curved, but one would get used to it. The total gravity area was 1,734 m² (18,664 ft²). The control room and the lab were on the inner deck, while the eight rooms, living room, gym and kitchen were on the outer deck. As the ship was initially meant for only 15 crew and passengers, it was rather spacious.

As they were placing each pet in separate sleeping rooms, Alice explained that though the spacecraft was 49 m long, the habitable section was only 20 m long. This was because all the front of the ship was occupied with the compact fusion reactors as well as the hydrogen, oxygen and water tanks.

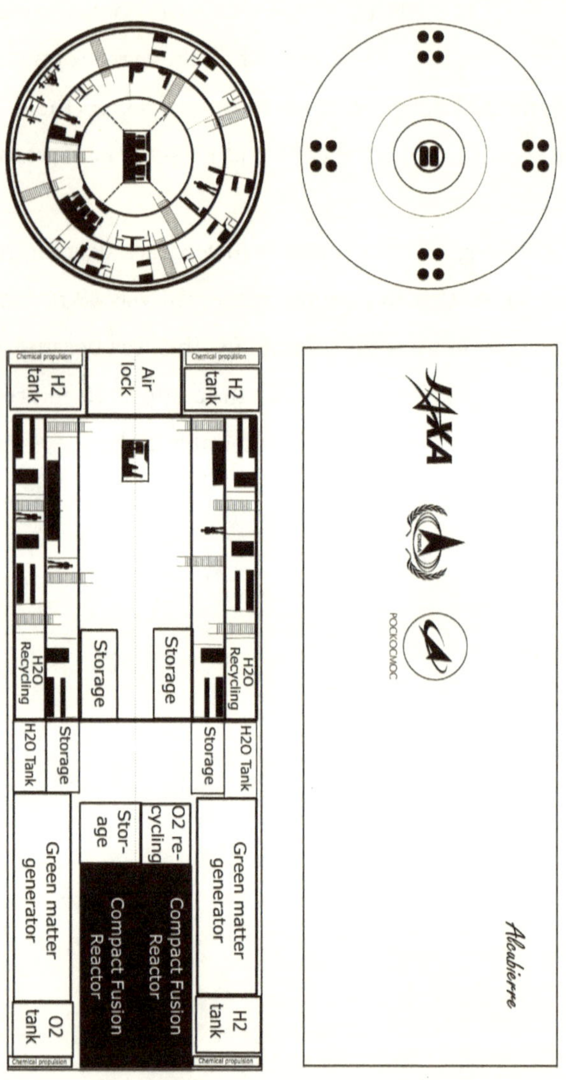

Figure 1: Drawing of the Alcubierre spaceship designed by the Japanese, Chinese and Russian space agencies.

At 9:02, the two astronauts were back in the *Orion,* which undocked itself from the *Alcubierre.* At 9:16, the second phase of the test started: there was a green flash, and the spacecraft disappeared again. At 9:22, a radio message from the Martian colony confirmed the reception of a radio signal sent by the *Alcubierre* at 13:17 UTC. At 9:26, the spaceship was back in the vicinity of the *Orion.*

Within a few minutes, the broadcast program was showing recorded images of the dog and the cat in their separate rooms under the warp travel. They seemed barely to have noticed anything. The dog looked particularly bored, while the cat, though more alert, was not displaying any sign of advanced intelligence.

"*The dog is a Moscow street dog,*" the male anchor person commented. "*According to our information, it's a kokoni dog.*"

"*Never heard of a kokoni dog before,*" the female anchor person replied.

"*Kokoni… it means the daughter's dog in Greek. These are perfectly useless small domestic dogs.*"

"*And hence the degrading term daughter's dog,*" the female anchor person inferred. "*I would only assume that Greece used to be a very male supremacist nation.*"

"*What I find more interesting to wonder about is how a small Greek domestic dog found itself as a street dog in Moscow. Anyway, we are told that we will be given a briefing about the two pets' health in just half an hour so, now, some advertising.*"

Ralf wondered briefly how many were watching the broadcast of the test worldwide. Five billion? Six billion? More? At 10:12, viewers were informed that data recorded on the dog's and cat's bodies had been reviewed and that the Chinese, Russian, and Japanese space agencies were meeting with each other, in order to decide whether the warp test with a human crew would be done within the next hour or postponed.

Ralf decided to help himself a cup of coffee while waiting for the joint decision of the space agencies. At the coffee machine, he met Glover:

"Let's hope that the agencies will not rush into a stupid decision," the admiral said. "I trust the Chinese and the Japanese, but I have doubts about the Russians…"

Years after the first warping of spacetime, people all over the world would still have very sharp memories of what they were doing during the test broadcast. In the Paris suburbs, Samir Benyamina would remember being released from the police station, going home, opening the door of the paternal apartment and seeing his fat, bearded father lying on the sofa with a bottle of coke in his hand and his eyes glued on the TV. Fat Ali would not even scream at him for having spent the night in jail. That was unexpected.

In Casablanca, Aisha Barjaoui would remember Deng Huang constantly talking in Chinese, barely paying attention to her, and mostly focused on his ex-girlfriend Alice Fù.

Ralf Åhman and Glover Johnson would forever remember the FBI and the US secret services suddenly show up inside the cafeteria of the UN headquarters and calmly but firmly head for Jarek Janowski, the UN secretary general. The Polish diplomat who had been in office for the last two years was suspected of rape of a minor the previous night and was therefore deprived of his liberty.

The UN staff and diplomats present were so taken aback that they missed the thumbs up given for the first warp travel with a human crew onboard. As the final test was about to be broadcasted, almost everyone had gone to their office or various meeting rooms to deal with the crisis.

Ralf had never liked the SG very much. He was the kind of diplomat who put more weight on properly polished shoes than actual diplomatic works, but he was nonetheless shocked and outraged to see that the UN secretary general was most likely a pedophile. Just at the time when sexual assaults by UN Blue helmets in peacekeeping missions across the world had reached an all-time low!

As Ralf entered the UNOOSA office on the 35th floor he noted that Glover was behind him.

"You almost lost me," the admiral said. "Ah, I love this room, with the posters."

"We should add a wall of shame with the picture of UN

sexual predators," Ralf said sarcastically.

"There is nothing we can do about this crisis," Glover said very matter of factly. "I am only a NASA employee, and though you are the director of a UN office, you have no say in this crisis."

"True," Ralf admitted. "The Security Council and the General Assembly will take care of it."

"So, at least we can watch the end of the test on your tablet-laptop," Glover suggested.

Ralf took it forth and resumed the broadcast. The *Alcubierre* and her crew had just warped back from Mars. They could hear the voice of her commander, Dr. Alice Fù:

"It has been a giant leap for the crew, but only a first step for mankind."

"You wrote that line for her, did you, Ralf?" Glover asked.

Ralf nodded.

10: THE 149TH SESSION OF THE UN GENERAL ASSEMBLY (SEPT 2094)

On this morning of Friday 24 September, Ralf Åhman was exhausted. Since he had landed in New York a week earlier, he had had the feeling of being caught in an avalanche. However, he now felt that the avalanche had lost momentum while he had managed to remain on the surface.

It was a sunny morning, in sharp contrast with the previous four days of heavy rain falls. The streets were covered with smaller water pools, in which sparrows were splashing about. It was a good sign, Ralf thought, as he was biking from the Radisson to the United Nations Headquarters. Or perhaps it was only the result of the random functions of the universe, as the admiral would say. Anyhow, the sunny weather was boosting his morale, and that was the most important thing.

He parked his bike in Ralph Bunche Square, in front of the UN building, sat down on a bank and grabbed a newspaper from his backpack. It was the latest edition of *The Chained Palmiped*, which was issued every Thursday morning.

The front page's main headline was '*Sherpa summits the UN*'. It was better than *Bollox news*, which had titled "*Blind Nepalese to lead the UN*" earlier that week.

All had happened very quickly. On Saturday, as the FBI had taken the secretary general into custody, there had been many contacts between the American, Chinese, Japanese, and Indian delegations. The secure phone lines between the White House and most of the Asian capitals had certainly been overheating. When the UN Security Council had met at 21:00 on that 17 September, Hira Dorjee-Sherpa, the representative of the South-Asian Union, had been surprised to see that all other members of the Council, with the notable exception of the representative of the European Union, Esko Punainen, who had been kept out of the loop, had been suggesting that she would act as the UN secretary general until the Council and the General Assembly would agree on a successor to Jarek Janowski.

At 48, Dr. Dorjee-Sherpa was a skilled Nepalese and South Asian diplomat. Though she had been born blind, she had excelled at her studies and obtained a PhD in International Affairs from Dehli's university. She had first worked for the Nepalese Foreign Office for three years, before officials from the South Asian Union (SAU), whose headquarters were also located in Kathmandu, noticed her, and decided to use her diplomatic skills.

In this South Asian Union, which united, among other States, India, Pakistan, Nepal, Bangladesh, and Sri Lanka in a sort of federation similar to the European Union, Nepalese personnel were much appreciated, as they were perceived as most neutral. After working for seven years at SAU's headquarters in Nepal, she subsequently had served as the SAU ambassador to Russia and Japan. She had now been the SAU representative to the United Nations for a year.

She had a flawless record, and it was not surprising that the members of the Security Council had unanimously proposed her to serve as acting secretary general until the next one be appointed.

The front page of *The Chained Palmiped*'s second headline was '*Bonavita, bad life at the UN*'. This was referring to the first speech of the European president at the UN. On the previous Monday, the 149th session of the UN General Assembly had opened. During the first four days, each of the 236 member states of the UN, including the regional unions such as the European Union, the South Asian Union or the Western Asian Union, were given the right to give a ten-minute speech in front of the General Assembly. This kind of exercise was usually done by Secretaries of States or Foreign Ministers, but it was very common for heads of state to have a go at it. On Tuesday, Mrs. Bonavita, exactly six days after she had been sworn in as president of the European Union, had given her first speech at the UN. It had been a confused and unstructured speech, tackling issues from warp travel to global phosphate supply and alleged pedophilia among UN personnel. It was meant to last much longer than the allocated time slot and, after ten minutes, her microphone had been cut off, as was the rule. She had reacted by grabbing one of her high heeled-shoes and agitating it menacingly to the chairman of the General Assembly.

Ralf was still laughing, remembering the incident.

Another headline entitled '*Space bitch under cat attack*' was referring to the Chinese cat aggressively attacking the Russian female dog under the warp test and concluded that 'cats could be real bitches.' Ralf turned the paper around to check the headlines on its back page. The one that caught his eyes was entitled '*Lethal earthquakes warped away in the news*. It was referring to a major earthquake of a magnitude of 8.4 on the Richter scale that had hit the Bihar province in India in the night of 18 September. There had been over 80,000 dead and missing, but this had largely been overshadowed in the media. The first successful warp test and the arrest of the SG charged with child abuse were monopolizing the headlines.

In this article, *The Chained Palmiped* mentioned how an angry mob in the town of Sithi accused five Dahlit women of witchcraft and how these were burned alive for having allegedly caused the earthquake. Ralf pondered briefly over the book he was reading, *Feedback of the Earth* by Dr. Sheldon Cooper.

It was true that the frequency of earthquakes and volcanic eruptions had been increasing.

It was now quarter to nine. Ralf decided it was time to go. He was to meet the new acting SG at nine. He grabbed his bike and made it to the UN building.

On the 38th floor of the UN building, Hira Dorjee-Sherpa welcomed Ralf into her new spacious, but not over-large, office.

Half of it was occupied by a large bureau in mahogany wood and three chairs, the other half by a set of black leather sofas. On the desk were two glass flower vases with an amaryllis and orchids and on the wall behind it was a large bookcase covered with books. On the wall by the sofa was a large painting with Nepalese motifs. Behind the sofas was the window and its view over New York.

"Welcome in, Dr. Åhman."

"Thank you, Dr. Dorjee-Sherpa."

Ralf Åhman was wearing a black suit with a blue shirt and a yellow tie, while Hira Dorjee-Sherpa was wearing a light grey suit and holding a white stick.

"My earGlasses are charging on the desk," she explained. "The battery life is less than four hours. Anyhow, I can focus more easily without them. Please, we can sit on the sofas."

Ralf and Hira sat down on two sofas opposite each other.

"The introduction of the 149th session is now over," Hira said. "This is time-consuming, but necessary, as each nation, regardless its size, should have the right to express itself."

"Yes, but as the acting SG, you were probably the only one to listen to all the speeches," Ralf retorted. "There were not many people in the room when Grenada was holding the chair. I hope you are feeling in great shape for today's task."

"Yes, the Fourth Committee."

"Do you want me to summarize?"

"Yes, please, Ralf."

"The UN Office for Outer Space Affairs," Ralf Åhman started, "of which I'm the director, serves currently the Committee on the Peaceful Uses of Outer space, which consists of only 98 member states out of 236 Nations. With the development of warp travel, outer space affairs must become a more central part of the United Nations."

"Agreed," the new secretary general said.

"Ideally, we would need at least a new international treaty on space exploration, exploitation and colonization. However, to be able to enforce anything, a real International Space Agency would be required. The current office for outer space, with just a coordination role, could not, for instance, impose a quarantine on a commercial starship coming back from an unknown star system."

"Indeed."

As he was talking, Ralf noted how Hira kept her eyes shut as if to be more focused. He went on. "The Fourth committee of the General Assembly passes resolutions related to outer space and colonization. It was originally meant to handle colonization issues on Earth, but space colonization may soon become relevant as well. We would, therefore, like them to pass a resolution to set up a special committee, here or in Vienna, to draft a new treaty about space exploration, exploitation and colonization. Ideally, we should also be mandated to draft a treaty for the set-up of a new International Space Agency. My office could be the facilitator for the drafting of these new treaties."

"OK," Hira said, opening her eyes. "We will meet the Fourth committee in two hours. What is our strategy?"

"First step," Ralf replied, "give them a picture of the consequences of unregulated space exploration. We highlight the risk of space conflicts for access to resources, the risk of bringing diseases from a remote system, if life should exist somewhere else than on Earth. This leads us to the need for regulations, hence the need for a new treaty. Last but not least, since a treaty is worthless if it cannot be enforced, the need for a proper International Space Agency becomes obvious. Since all nations on Earth are equally exposed to risks stemming from breaches in space regulation, all should share the financial burden of enforcing it, depending on their financial resources."

"OK, that makes sense. After we have exposed our position, do we have a country that would propose a resolution draft going our way?"

"The USA made a very good draft," Ralf answered. However,

the US president, President Fang, didn't want to submit it, lest it may damage her attempt to pass an amendment to the US constitution. However, I have convinced the representative of Kirghizstan to propose the US draft in their own name. So, it should be OK."

"OK, good. By the way, how is the Martian doing? When can we get her down to Earth?"

"Sanne van der Maas is ready on her side. The rocket has been fully assembled on Mars, and its tanks have been filled. The *Alcubierre* has now made several low orbit-passes around Mars. The issue is for the rocket to dock into *The Alcubierre*, once in orbit."

"Why is that an issue?"

"Since the rocket's space module can only dock the *Alcubierre* from the rear, the procedure is quite complicated, no need to go into details. They are currently devising procedures to make the docking fail-safe, but also to be able to retrieve Sanne, should the docking operation fail after all. The Chinese told me they should be ready by the middle of next week."

11: DISCOVERING
A NEW PLANET
(OCT 2094)

In the Martian colony, Sanne van der Maas had cleared up the whole compound. She had washed her sheets and towels, done the dishes, vacuumed and washed the floor, cleaned the kitchen and the bathrooms and removed the dust from all the shelves and racks. As she was packing her hard drives, digital tablet, a few clothes and her green Martian suit in a special case, she suddenly wondered why she had cleaned the compound so well. She was about to leave it forever. No one would ever come here. While had she bothered?

For the rocket launch, she had to put on a cumbersome fully pressurized white space suit. If she had to evacuate the space module once in orbit, the green Martian suit would not cope with the total absence of atmosphere. Besides, when in orbit, green was not as easy a color to spot as white. Surviving in space was all about following protocols and procedures. She had trained half a dozen of times already over the last four weeks to put on the white pressurized suit, but it still took her two hours to be ready. The space suit was pressurized with a third of a normal atmosphere for her to be able to move and, as a result, had a very high concentration of oxygen. Her body therefore needed a whole hour to adapt to the pressurized suit. After the acclimation period, she checked the pressure and oxygen level. All was fine.

She put a coiled rope around her shoulder, took the case and made it to the airlock. In the airlock, she put the case on her mountain bike's baggage rack and led it out. She typed a code on a control panel to turn the colony into idle mode. All the plants in the colony's greenhouses would progressively die, but the colony would still run at a low regime, to keep the compound from freezing. The colony was to be usable as a shelter, in case a spaceship had to make an emergency landing there. This had been required by all space agencies involved in her rescue.

Her cumbersome space suite made it impossible for her to bike and she had to walk the 2.7 km (1.7 miles) to the launch pad. Luckily, one of the insect-like robots helped her carry the bike and the case to the rocket.

She uncoiled the rope and tied it to the bike and case at one end, and to her suit on the other end. Next, she went up the ladder into the space module. A few minutes later, she had pulled up both the case and the bike into the module and sent the robot away. She felt sad for this robot: out of the compound, it was not protected from Martian sandstorms. It would probably 'die' out there in the next few months.

She closed the module's hatch, sat down on the pilot seat and, using a control pad, started to follow the ignition checklist.

It was Friday 1st of October 2094. When the APU was on, she plugged a cable from her suit in to the control panel. She now had access to the rocket's radio. The frequency was 121.5 MHz.

"Rescue Mission, this is Martian 1 calling… over," she called. No answer.

"Rescue Mission, this is Martian 1 calling… Do you read me? Over," she called again.

Still no answer. The *Alcubierre* was certainly currently orbiting on the other side of the planet, and the radio waves could not reach her. She decided to wait another five minutes.

"Rescue mission, this is Martian 1. Are you there? Over."

"Martian 1, this is Rescue Mission, we read you. Current orbit time is 10 minutes." She recognized the voice of the pilot, Nariko.

"Martian 1, you can initiate take-off. We will pick you up whatever orbit you reach." She recognized the voice of Alice Fù, the commander of the Alcubierre.

"Rescue mission, copy that. Initiating take-off sequence. See you up there."

That was it, Sanne thought. She had done the checklist, everything looked fine. She started the engine. The computer commenced the count-down loud in her ear-phones. The take-off was to be automatic: "*7…6…5…4…3…2…1…Take-off*"

Sitting back, Sanne felt heavier and heavier. The take-off acceleration was programmed so that she would weigh no more than three times her Martian weight upon take-off. Three times her Martian weight was what she would weigh on Earth. Damn, it would take time for her to get used to the Earth's gravity. Through the window, the Martian sky was getting darker and darker as the rocket was leaving the planet's atmosphere. A moment later, she felt as if she was falling, constantly falling. She had escaped Mars' gravity! She was in weightlessness. Another fifteen minutes and she was in orbit around Mars.

It took six hours for the *Alcubierre* to succeed with the docking maneuver. Sanne had to switch oxygen bottles twice, and she started to be worried. But in the end, her space module docked onto the warp ship.

It was Anatoli Govorov who opened the airlock's inner hatch and helped her into the spacecraft. He was a tall, solidly built man in his late twenties with short brown hair and blue eyes. He wore a suit with the Roscosmos insignia, the insignia of the Russian space agency.

"What the hell? Are you bringing a mountain bike with you?" he asked.

"It's a souvenir from Mars," Sanne explained. "And I guess it may be useful on Earth."

A moment later she was in the long 0G cylindrical room she had seen on TV.

"Let me help you out of your space suit," a woman's voice said.

It was Alice Fù who had floated from the commander's seat. She was a slim, dark-haired Afro-Asian lady of medium height, also in her late twenties. Her dark blue suit wore the insignia of the Chinese National Space Administration (CNSA). She asked Anatoli to get Sanne's inner suit and a moment later, Sanne had changed into it. Her suit had the badge of the European Space Agency on it. It fitted her length.

Beside Anatoli, Alice and Nariko, Sanne was introduced to a medical astronaut from the Japanese space agency, and to two astronauts from the European and American space agencies respectively, who had been invited to follow the navigation procedures onboard the *Alcubierre*.

"If you get tired of weightlessness, you can come to the gravity decks," Alice said. "The inner deck simulates a gravity of a quarter of that on earth. The outer deck's gravity is a third of that on earth. Almost the same as on Mars."

Alice led the way to the ladder to reach the first gravity deck revolving around the cylindrical room. Anatoli followed both of them. On the inner gravity deck, or deck 1, Sanne felt that she was indeed lighter than on Mars. A pity the gravity deck had so low a ceiling, though. Her head was almost brushing against it. They obviously had not thought about Dutch people, when designing the ship.

She had barely stepped off the ladder in to the gravity compartment when a little brown dog trotted toward her and started to jump at her. Sanne kneeled down to fondle the dog. It had bad breath.

"That's the space bitch," Anatoli commented after joining them on the gravity deck.

"Cute. What's her name?" Sanne asked.

"Calypso."

"What kind of breed is she?"

"She's a Moscow street dog. Vets assume she's a kokoni. I'm not an expert."

"There was also a cat, for the test. Where is he?"

"The cat is back in China," Alice explained. "Anatoli's girlfriend has adopted the dog, but she can't take care of her. That's why Anatoli keeps this brown beast onboard the ship."

"Girlfriends are all the same," Anatoli grumbled. "You stay together for two years, and she will ask for either a pet or a baby. I guess that a licking little kokoni is still better than a screaming little human being."

Both Sanne and Alice laughed.

"The Doctor from the JAXA is going to check on you and give you a series of vaccines," Alice said. "When this is done, we will warp back to Earth. Anatoli and I are going back to the cylindrical room. We have to undock from your space module."

"One more thing," Anatoli added, "The doc will certainly give you some chocolate bars. Don't give any to the space bitch."

Sanne had not had anything to drink for 9 hours, so she was thankful when the Japanese medic came and gave her a bottle of water and some chocolate bars, after installing her in the living room. After the exam was completed and she had received four vaccines, she was asked to strap herself to her seat. On the loudspeakers, she heard Alice say:

"Out-warp coordinates confirmed by the pilot, the engineer and the commander. Checklist completed. Ready for warp at three. 1…2…3… warp."

The warp journey lasted only 27 seconds. Sanne was a bit disappointed. She was confined in a room with no window and could not even feel any kind of acceleration that would tell her the ship was indeed warping spacetime. There was only a clock on a screen showing the time remaining before the arrival at the out-warp point.

"Sanne, welcome to our home," Alice said over the loudspeaker. "We are currently 420,000 km (261,000 miles) from the Earth, and 36,000 km (22,300 miles) from the Moon. We used a lot of hydrogen and oxygen for the docking of your space module. We will first head for the fuel station on the Moon's orbit. We have to refill our tanks."

Sanne unstrapped from her seat and went back to the secondary operation room, in the 0G cylindrical room and floated her way to the flight station. Alice was sitting in the middle, between Anatoli, the engineer and Nariko, the pilot. The flight station was equipped with numerous screens but past it, on the wall, was hanging a huge screen.

"It gives you a view of what is in front of the ship," Nariko explained.

On the screen, she immediately caught a glimpse of the Earth, in the background far behind the Moon. She first felt a thrill. But then she realized that it was still at quite some distance, and it would probably be some time before she could walk on it.

It took two hours for Nariko to bring the *Alcubierre* to the Moon's refueling station. As they were making their approach, they flew over the Moon's south pole.

"You see, this is the south pole of the Moon," Alice said, showing the images on the screen. "You see the crater? This is the Shackleton crater. It is more than 4 km [13,123 ft] deep. Inside it, there is ice."

"This is our source of energy," Anatoli added. "There is a mining installation inside it, melting ice and hydrolyzing it. The lunar elevator consists of two space tethers attached from the Moon to the asteroid beyond the Lagrange L1 point."

Lagrange L1 point? Sanne had no idea what he was talking about.

Alice explained: "The Lagrange L1 point is just the balance point in the Moon Earth system. It just means that the lunar elevator is steady, and not orbiting around the Moon, else it would not work."

"One tether is attached to the Lunar equator, where there is some mining for Helium 3, which is used to fuel the compact fusion reactors," Anatoli went on. "But the other tether is attached to the south pole of the Moon. 200 kilometers [124 miles] above the Moon, there is the station for us to refill our tanks with oxygen and hydrogen."

"It was completed three years ago, in 2091," Alice continued. "The mining installation is operated only eight weeks a year by astronauts from all the respective space agencies. But the refuel station is operated all year long."

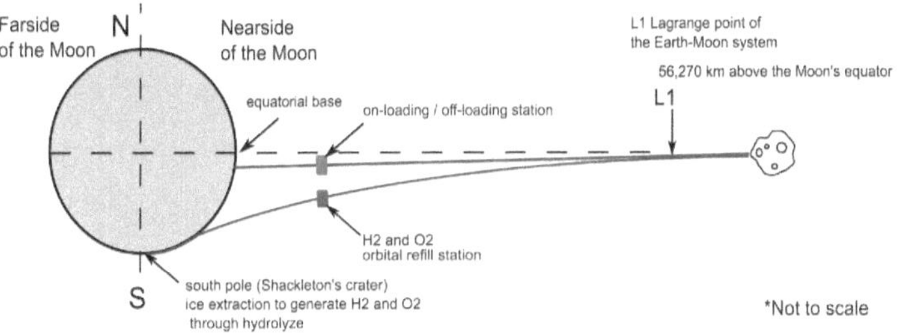

Figure 2: The lunar installation with the space lunar elevator and the refill station. Based on the work by Wikipedia user Bryan Derksen, but adapted to the story of this book.

After refilling her tanks, the *Alcubierre* headed for the Earth.

"We will go directly to the Tarawa space tether, which will bring you to Earth," Alice said. "Though it will take sixteen hours to get there."

"If we had an EM-drive, like the American *Orion*, we would make it in only five hours," Nariko said.

The Electromagnetic-Drive developed by the Americans used electromagnetic waves to propel itself in space, thus only requiring electric power. The *Alcubierre* had only chemical propulsion for approach maneuvers.

"Ice supply on the Moon is not unlimited so we cannot just waste fuel just to arrive faster," Alice added.

The ship was now on autopilot and they all went to the gravity compartment. After an unhealthy dinner, Sanne went to bed. She did not sleep well. Not only was the bed too short for her, but she had been overwhelmed by the events of the day, leaving the red planet, boarding the *Alcubierre*, warping to Earth, meeting actual humans. She reflected on how it felt to physically meet healthy human beings. She had been completely on her own for two years, and before that lived ten years with sick and dying people. She had even laughed at Anatoli's comments on girlfriends wanting pets. She did not remember when she had last laughed.

She also thought briefly about Ralf Åhman, the UNOOSA director. The Fourth Committee of the UN General Assembly had voted a resolution asking his office to facilitate a conference for the drafting of two new space treaties.

Sanne had been taking distance courses in economics at Columbia Economy and was currently writing her Bachelor thesis about 'survival economies', with a strong focus on space colonization. Now, the UN was mentioning the need of regulating space exploration and exploitation. She was, of course, deeply interested in it. Not only as a student in economics, but also as the sole survivor of the Martian colony.

She was briefly wondering if she may have a chance to attend the coming Vienna conference, but eventually fell asleep.

The following morning, as she was eating breakfast, she could follow the progress of the *Alcubierre* from the TV screen in the kitchen.

They were now flying past the orbital station, a large structure made of two rings, each 40 m (131 ft) thick and 100 m (328 ft) in diameter, around a 25 m (82 ft) wide and 120 m (398 ft) long cylindrical core.

"There are seven gravity decks in each ring. It was completed two years ago," Alice explained. "The construction work started in 2087, two years after the world's respective national space agencies agreed to it. The introduction of compact fusion reactors and space elevators made that possible."

"We will dock on the Tarawa Space Elevator in two hours," Naruko stated.

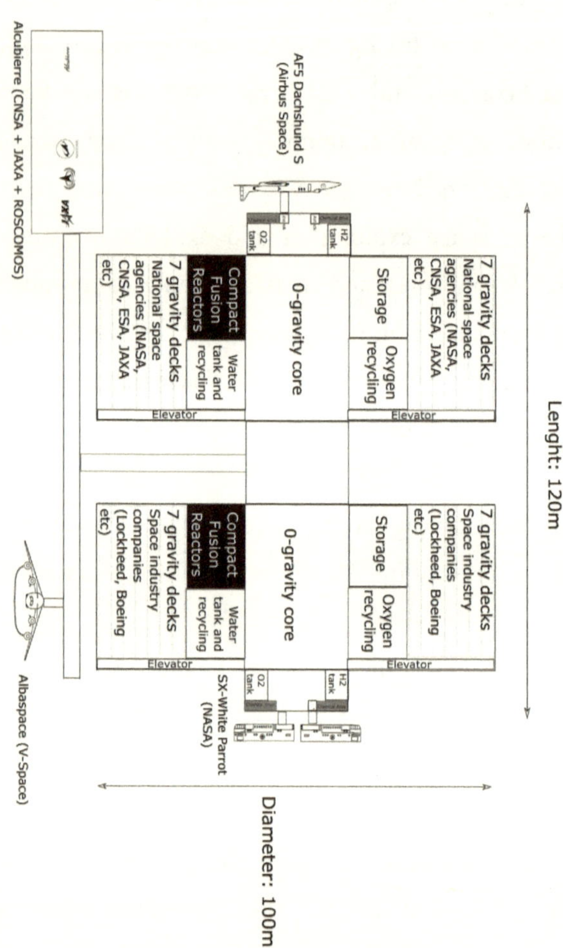

Figure 3: The orbital station in 2094. At that time, the Albaspace from V-Space and AF5 Dachshund S from Airbus Space were the main aerospace shuttles. Most of the Earth to orbit transit, however, went through the space elevator.

Space tethers, or space elevators, were 50,000 km (31,000 miles) long cables made of nano-carbon fiber. They were anchored on Earth at the Equator and attached to a captured asteroid orbiting beyond the geostationary point. The key was to keep the elevator's gravity center beyond the geostationary orbit at 36,000 km (22,400 miles) of altitude.

By 2094, there were two space tethers, the Americano-European one, in Guyana, in South America, and the Sino-Japanese one on Tarawa in the Central Pacific. The *Alcubierre* was heading for the latter one, whose loading station was orbiting 400 km (250 miles) above sea level.

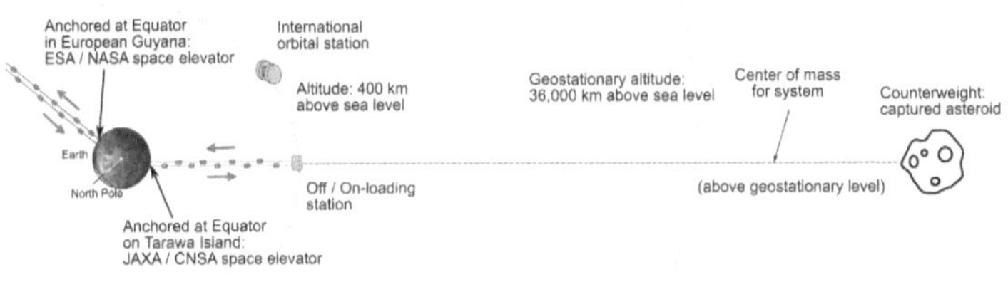

Figure 4: The space elevator / space tether used to bring payload into orbit. Based on the work by Wikipedia users Skyway and Booyabazookan, but adapted to the story of this book.

Sanne was given a red landing suit, which she was to wear in the space elevator on her way down to Earth. Alice and Nariko helped her into it.

A moment later, the *Alcubierre* was docked at the space elevator's unloading station.

"Enjoy the sushi, when the JAXA takes care of you," Anatoli told Sanne.

The Japanese doctor led Sanne into the airlock and helped her float with her case and bike. In the loading station of the space tether, the other astronauts looked curiously at the tall Sanne from Mars who insisted on bringing a Martian bike with her to Earth.

There were two cables linking the loading station to Earth. Space lifts were coming up into orbit on one of them and used the other one to return down to Earth.

They had to wait nearly one hour before the next lift Earth-bound was ready to embark passengers. But Sanne did not mind. It was nice, in a way, to wait in weightlessness watching the glowing Earth beneath her. When at last the time had come, the doctor helped Sanne shut down her spacesuit, and led her through the station's airlock to the space lift that had just been unloaded.

There were another seven astronauts, most of them from the Chinese and Russian space agencies, to follow Sanne and the

Japanese doctor into the space lift. When everyone was ready, the space lift operator tapped on a command screen and the space lift started falling toward the Earth.

The lift took one hour to come down to the altitude of 150 km (93 miles), as it was traveling on the magnetic section of the cable. The next section was, however, a chain-like cable which the lift climbed down using a set of pinions at the exasperatingly low speed of 25 km an hour (15.5 mph). They would need another six hours to reach sea level. Being confined to the little space lift with nine other people for a seven-hour descent to Earth was one of the worst experiences Sanne had ever had. The space lift operator, who wore the insignia of the Japanese Space agency on her shoulder, noted that Sanne was worried.

"Don't be nervous," she said, "It's quite safe. If we have to bail out of the line, the space lift still has three parachutes."

"Has it happened before?"

"Many times," the operator replied. "The lift is powered by electricity provided by the cable. If there is a too violent thunderstorm, they have to shut off the power, down there, and the lifts on the lines cannot hold themselves, hence the parachutes."

"Has it ever happened to you?" Sanne asked.

"Yes, once. It was quite shaky on the way down, because of the wind. But the worst was once we had ditched into the raging sea," the operator laughed, "We had to wait 23 hours for rescue and everybody was seasick. We were puking on each other."

Most of the other astronauts started laughing as well.

"And what if the cable breaks?" Sanne interrupted. "Doesn't it fall on people underneath?"

"It has never happened before. However, the chain-like section is designed to dismantle into small parts, if not under tension. It would just fall into the sea. The upper section of the cable and the loading station will still remain in orbit. It's quite safe, I'm telling you. Designed by Japan."

"But financed by China," a Chinese astronaut added.

Sanne was not feeling any better. She wanted to urinate. She considered briefly using the diaper she wore under her spacesuit like all astronauts. She decided she would hold herself.

The descent was not made easier by the falling night over the Pacific. It was pitch dark when they were still in the mesosphere. There was nothing to watch through the window. She had nothing to do than sit in silence while other astronauts were talking in Chinese, Russian or Japanese.

It was 22:25 local time when the space lift landed on Tarawa. It had once been an atoll and the capital of the Kiribati islands, in the central Pacific Ocean. It was now only a set of concrete cubic structures. As the sea level had risen five meters (16 ft) during the 21st century, the islands of the atoll had disappeared below the surface. The inhabitants had relocated to other Pacific nations as climate refugees, most of them now in New Zealand. The atoll would certainly have been allowed to sink completely into the sea had it not been for its geographic location: it was on the Equator, in the middle of an ocean. As such, it was an ideal spot for a space elevator.

When all the passengers in the lift had opened their red landing suits, she felt a quick moment of anguish when the operator opened the hatch. Then she remembered that no oxygen bottles were needed to breathe on Earth.

All the astronauts rose from their seats and left the lift except Sanne, who was unable to get up. Weighing three times her Martian weight was way too much. The Japanese doctor arranged a wheelchair to be brought forth. Sanne remembered being pushed and pulled in a bus that drove for quite some distance. Only the space tether was shining in the dark, with blinking lights to warn airplanes. Behind dimmer lights, she remembered seeing the fusion reactor that was powering the island complex. They arrived at a kind of floating airport, where she was helped out of her red landing suit and, a moment later, boarded a plane with the rest of the astronauts.

The plane landed on a smaller airport that had a Japanese name. She was transferred to a helicopter with the doctor, while the plane took off for another location, probably in China. The helicopter landed on a hill by the sea, as far as she could guess, and she was transferred to what she thought was a hospital. She fell asleep as soon as she had been carried to bed.

The next day, she was told she was in the infirmary of the

Uchinoura Space Center, not far from Kagoshima, in the south of Japan. UNOOSA had convinced the Japanese space agency JAXA to keep Sanne for a while in a remote location so that journalists would let her alone. The UN space office would just issue a brief communiqué stating that Sanne van der Maas had safely arrived on Earth.

She was told that she was in good health, but she would simply need to follow a two-week training program to be able to stand and walk. An official from the European Embassy in Tokyo came to help her fill in a form so that she could get a European passport and obtain a European tax number, a must, she was told, for all European citizens.

The Japanese personnel were very nice and always caring. They made sure she had enough to eat. Because of her length and lack of muscles, they joked that she would need to eat like a sumo. She got to love Japanese food, from ramen to sushi. It was the first time she had tasted fish and she liked it, though it had become rather exceptional due to the strict quotas to preserve fishery resources.

The physiotherapists had her do some exercise to build up the muscles in her legs. They also put electrodes on her muscles during the night. She could already walk on all fours like a baby, but it took five days before she was able to walk with a rollator. After another six days of training, she was able to walk 200 m on her own without stopping.

Under her rehabilitation program, she very much enjoyed

the warm and sunny weather, as well as the scenery, with the green hills and the volcanoes in the background. It was quite a contrast to the red, barren landscape at Elysium Planitia. She still felt it was unreal, though. Especially the fact of being able to walk outdoors without any specially designed suit.

What worried her, on the other hand, was that she had heard that the Earth was had become more active lately, tectonically speaking. She had to take part in an earthquake drill and was secretly afraid that the nearby volcanoes would have a major eruption under her stay in the region. It did not happen.

Two weeks after her arrival in Uchinoura, the official from the European Embassy in Japan came back. He had brought a European passport in her name as well as a few clothes in her size. The clothes were courtesy of UNOOSA in Vienna. The director of that UN Office would soon arrive in Tokyo. They were expected to meet him the next evening in Tokyo, at the JAXA's headquarters.

The following morning, Sanne said farewell to the staff of the Uchinoura Space Center and left with the embassy official, who complained she had to bring a bike with her. A long taxi drive took them to the Kagoshima central station where they boarded a high-speed train to Tokyo.

At Tokyo's central station, Ralf Åhman and the director of the Japanese space agency were waiting for them. Sanne received a warm reception at the JAXA's headquarters. She was not used to so many people and kept silent most of the time.

They made her taste saké, and Sanne decided she didn't like alcohol, after all. They had booked her at the Radisson hotel, but the next day, it was already time to leave Japan.

She and Ralf were to take a direct flight to Amsterdam, in the Netherlands, where she would meet her grandmother, who had been unable to come to Japan with Ralf. Sanne wished she could have stayed longer in Japan to do some sightseeing. It would have to be another time.

The flight to Amsterdam happened to be more enjoyable than the night flight from Tarawa. It was daylight, the weather was excellent and she could enjoy the scenery. She also felt in much better shape. As they were landing in Amsterdam, Ralf pointed to the impressive dykes that had been built all around.

"The sea level is rising," Ralf said. "Even though carbon emissions have been cut dramatically since the 2050s, and the temperature rise is starting to stabilize, thermal expansion will continue for another thousand years."

"Thousand years?"

"Yes," Ralf confirmed. "As the famous Dr. Sheldon Cooper once said: *Geophysics can be a real bitch sometimes.*"

In Amsterdam, she was disturbed to see that cars were driving on the right, rather than on the left like in Japan. She also noted that the Dutch were much taller than the Japanese and that she didn't stand out so much despite her 2.05 m (6.73 ft).

Ralf took Sanne to her grandmother's house in a taxi.

"Well, Sanne," Ralf said. "It was a real pleasure to meet you, and I am happy you are now safely home. If you have any issue related to your arrival from Mars, just give me a call. You have my number."

Sanne made a note of it. She was about to stay with her grandmother, with whom she had never had any contact, while Ralf was soon to chair an international conference in Vienna that may decide the future of space exploration. She wished she could stay with him instead.

12: THE MINORITY PROJECT (OCT 2094)

It was still dark on that October morning, when Thierry Diakité went out to do his jogging in the streets of Bobo-Dioulasso, Burkina Faso. The heat was still bearable at that time of the day. As he was running, he thought about his first two months at V-space.

He had first been very happy to get a job in the Vahlroos Corporation's subsidiary. He was working with space engineering while being back in his home country. That was the dream. Perhaps not as great as working for Airbus Space in Toulouse, but still.

At first, it had been exciting. He had been appointed as a senior specialist in the Tool Department. His job was to assist any department in developing algorithms and solving their issues. In a way, it was enriching to work with everybody, from R&D to manufacturing.

Things started to go wrong when the new director of V-Space

moved to Burkina Faso, the week just after the warp test. Why couldn't she have stayed in New York? Sophie Couillard was a respectable, experienced manager, but she was a Canadian, a French-speaking Canadian who would of course speak French in Burkina Faso. Except that Canadian French was not really French.

He still remembered the first speech she had given in front of the French-speaking employees. With her strong *Québecquois* accent, she had first complained about the Burkina's *maringouins* that were allegedly worse than in Canada. *Maringouin* was the French-Canadian word for mosquitoes. At first, nobody had understood, but then, suddenly, Tintin had burst out laughing, followed by all the attendees. Including Thierry.

"Ah, Tintin, you stupid boy," he said aloud, remembering the incident.

If laughter was contagious, it was also treacherous. As a result of this first incident, Thierry had felt Sophie Couillard would simply ignore any comment or suggestion coming from Tintin or him.

"*Allah wa akbar,*" a muezzin started singing from a minaret nearby.

"The public alarm clock goes off again", Thierry thought.

The sun was now rising over Bobo-Dioulasso, and as soon as the muezzin was done calling Muslims to prayer, some Evangelist church turned on loudspeakers broadcasting the *Jesus-loves-you* kind of song, and a moment later it was the turn of Catholic church bells to disturb the morning peace.

Thierry sprinted the last 800 m (0.5 miles) to his home, running in the middle of the *Place de la Femme*, which was decorated with a golden statue of a lady pointing firmly at a vacuum cleaner for her husband to use it.

Thierry lived on the third floor of a workers' house built for V-space employees. His room was a so-named corridor room, and he was sharing the kitchen and lavatories with nine other colleagues, among whom was Tintin.

As he walked in, he came across Tintin, who was leaving his room and heading for the shared kitchen. He was grumpy:

"*P'tain, quand est-ce que vous allez devenir athéistes dans ce pays? La religion c'est mauvais pour le sommeil.*" ('Damn it, when are you gonna become atheists in this country? Religious is harmful for one's sleep.')

"Is it better in Congo?" Thierry wondered.

"You want an honest answer? No. But since your former teacher Lenka is now a Member of Parliament, perhaps you could write to her? Ask her to prohibit any religious sound before 9 in the morning. That would be nice."

"Why don't you write to her yourself?" Thierry replied, as he headed for the corridor's bathroom.

After a quick shower, he met Tintin in the kitchen for breakfast.

"Sincerely?" Tintin commented. "You think that Sophie will

listen to us because you put on a white shirt? Come on, she wears sneakers at the office!"

Thierry had indeed put on a white shirt and beige trousers, making him look like a University Student in Kigali. He glanced at Tintin's clothes. "That's certainly better than jeans and a T-shirt with Einstein's field equation."

"Come on, Thierry. We both have a PhD. She has only a Master of Science. Graduates perhaps wear suits and shirts. Doctors don't."

"This is not the attitude to convince them of their mistake," Thierry remarked.

"We will convince her all right. It's the other idiots I'm worried about."

The V-space premises were located in an industrial area, south of the *Avenue de l'Indépendance.*

On Friday 22 October 2094, shortly after lunch, Sophie Couillard had scheduled a meeting with all the Business Unit directors concerned.

They had all gathered in a large conference room around a long central table. Chairing the table was a TV screen: Michael Vahlroos was attending via video-conference, even though it was still early morning in New York.

Sophie was wearing a white polo shirt with the V-Space insignia printed in dark blue on her right shoulder. "Michael, let me first introduce you the executive committee," she said.

"It's a very global team. The V-liner's project leader is Brice de Robien, from the EU."

"Hello, Mike," the project leader greeted with a heavy French accent. He was a sun-tanned white man in his forties wearing a Hawaiian shirt.

Sophie pointed at a fat grey-haired man wearing a pink shirt and with visible sweat halos under his arms. "Vladimir Gerasimov is our warp propulsion BU director. He worked with the design of the *Alcubierre* before joining us."

She pointed at a thin dark-skinned man with a little moustache. "Abhineet Singh, from the South Asian Union, is our BU director for structure and material. He did an excellent job for the development of Albaspace."

"Ana Luiza Messerschmitt, from Brazil, is the head of conventional propulsion," Sophie continued, "and also a veteran from the Albaspace."

Ana Luiza was a sun-tanned brunette wearing a short blue dress. She smiled at the screen and the camera above it. "I believe the V-liner is a more interesting challenge."

Sophie then pointed at a black woman with a colorful dress and a golden necklace. "Finally, we have Nafissatou Kondé, from Senegal. She is the new head of Manufacturing."

"It's a pleasure to meet you all," Michael Vahlroos's image said on the TV.

"And sorry, I forgot to mention…" Sophie added, "We also have with us Dr. Tintin Mutombo, from Congo Kinshasa, and

Dr. Thierry Diakité, from… here. The only local in the room, as a matter of fact."

Sophie suddenly regretted she had said that. As she looked around, she realized that despite the fact they were in Africa, there were only three Africans in the room. On the other hand, diversity was a winning factor, and V-Space could not be all African.

"Well, as you know," Sophie continued, "the purpose of this meeting is to assess the feasibility of the current design proposition of the V-liner. Brice will first present the current concept. Tintin, our warp propulsion senior specialist, and Thierry, our senior tool specialist, have been selected as Devil's advocates: they will heavily question the concept until we all agree to approve it or reject it."

"Until you reject it," Tintin corrected, smiling. "There is not a single chance in the universe that you will approve it."

"Tintin, you are so arrogant and so wrong," the Russian warp director corrected. "Our concept is fool-proof."

"Please, gentlemen," Brice said, "Let's start the presentation."

The French Project Director tapped a few times on the touch screen of his tablet, and a hologram started displaying over the conference table.

"We have a 3D-animation," Brice said proudly, looking at Michael Vahlroos on the screen.

The hologram started flickering, and the animation did not seem to start.

"Damn it," Brice cursed. "There is a problem with the holographic projector."

The Project Director tapped a few times on his tablet's touchscreen. Nothing happened. He looked embarrassedly at Sophie, and then at Michael on the screen. "We should call someone from IT to fix it."

"I'm not gonna wait for an IT technician to come and fix it," the CEO yelled from his TV screen. "Do you know what my hourly salary is? It's out of the question that we wait a single second more of my life for the holographic image to be fixed. Can't you just show the animation on 2D screens?"

"Sure, we can," Brice said sheepishly. He tapped a countless number of times on his touchscreen, and the animation eventually started on the white canvas screen hanging on the wall opposite the video-conferencing screen.

Sophie had already seen the film, but she pretended to be interested so as not to upset Brice, who looked in distress for having been yelled at by Michael.

The animation showed how a cylindrical ship, very like the *Alcubierre,* was standing vertically on a launch pad. Rocket engines were started underneath them, and the cylinder slowly took off straight up. On the screen, the ship's altitude was displayed, and at 40,000 m (131,000 ft), it started its warp drive, disappearing in a flash of green. On the next scene, the V-liner was seen to warp out in orbit of the Earth, and from there it warped to Mars and back again. It then placed itself in orbit and warped itself into the atmosphere. It came out of warp at 60,000 m (197,000 ft) above the ground and started its rocket engines to brake and land vertically on the launchpad.

The next sequence of the film was to show how the V-liner could be directly assembled vertically to speed up its production time and reduce the manufacturing cost. Another sequence zoomed on safety: The gravity compartments were smaller than on the *Alcubierre*, to give space for the crew and passenger to sit on seats built in special pods for take-off and landing. Should an accident occur at take-off or landing, these pods would be ejected and land safely back on Earth with parachutes.

The five directors, Sophie, and Michael, on the screen, all applauded at the end of the animation movie. Tintin and Thierry were, however, not impressed. The CEO noticed it through the video-conferencing system.

"Tintin, Thierry," Michael Vahlroos said. "What are your reservations?"

"I have three," Tintin replied. "One, it won't work. Two, it's a low intellect concept. Three, it is not adapted to the current market situation, so it won't sell."

The fat, sweating Russian warp director became red. "How arrogant you are! You–"

"Let him expand his arguments, Vladimir," Sophie cut him off. "One, it won't work. Why is that?"

"The take-off part is not an issue," Thierry jumped in. "The V-liner can safely warp out of the atmosphere and make some faster than light journeys in space. However, the vertical landing in the atmosphere is bound to fail."

"Why?" Michael Vahlroos asked from his TV screen.

"On its start position, in orbit, the V-liner will have a tremendous relative speed in relation to the Earth's surface. The stress upon warp-out would be gigantic if you furthermore add the atmospheric pressure."

"Two years ago," Michael objected, "The Russians tested a warpedo in the Black Sea."

"Yes, we did," The fat Russian warp director said. "It was mythic."

"It was not as glamorous as he said," Tintin retorted. "I was there. Besides, the warpedo was eventually lost under some test in space the following year. Anyway, in this case, the configuration is different. For the Black Sea test, both the start and end points had the same speed relative to the rotation of the Earth. This is not the case for the V-liner atmosphere re-entry."

"Even if we believe the structure can resist the test," Thierry continued, "the spaceship will not have the time to stabilize and land vertically on the launch pad. I did a simulation: it would require at least 150 km [93 miles] of free fall for a computer to stabilize the ship, without killing all the passengers due to an excessive G-force. The atmosphere gives us maximum 80 kilometers [50 miles]."

On the screen, Michael Vahlroos looked perplexed. He

looked at the Brazilian Director for Conventional Propulsion. "Ana Luiza, what is your view on this?"

The attractive brunette sighed and said: "The current tests have not been conclusive. However, I am confident that with proper artificial intelligence we will solve that."

The French Project Director in a Hawaiian shirt suddenly rose to his feet and looked at the camera of the video-conferencing system. "Ana Luiza is right. Currently, the simulation is unsatisfactory indeed. However, we have several leads, and I can guarantee it will be solved within two years." Brice de Robien sat back on his seat.

Sophie turned to the Congolese theoretical physicist, looked him deep in the eyes and said softly: "Your second reservation, Tintin: It's a low intellect concept. Please expand."

"In the current V-liner concept," Tintin explained, "We only take existing concepts and put them together: *Alcubierre* plus conventional rockets equals the V-liner. Nothing challenging in that. This lack of intellect also causes us to miss the current market need, my third reservation."

This aroused Michael's interest, who, from his screen, said: "Tintin, you are a brilliant theoretical physicist. You are co-author of the article presenting the new and now accepted theory unifying quantum theory and general relativity."

"I am the primary author," Tintin corrected "Anatoli was my supervisor at the time. He is the secondary author."

"Indeed," Michael went on. "What the hell do you know

about the market need?”

“A lot,” Tintin replied. “I am the most brilliant mind in this room, do not forget it, and I can tell you, this is not the right time to push for the V-liner.”

Sophie saw how Vladimir’s and Brice’s faces were turning crimson. She signaled them to hold their anger.

“Why is that?” Sophie asked Tintin politely.

The Congolese physicist looked at his hands and then smiled at the V-Space CEO on the screen.

“The V-Liner is a big ship designed for mining activities on celestial bodies, we are all clear about that.”

“Yes,” Michael replied. “It’ a ship for mining activities and that’s going to become a huge market anytime soon.”

“That’s where I disagree,” Tintin replied, smiling at everyone in the conference room. “Space mining activities won’t become a huge market anytime soon. Perhaps in twenty or thirty years, but not anytime soon.”

“Why is that?” Sophie wondered.

The Congolese physicist seemed to think a moment, and said:

“There is the Vienna Conference coming. The UN will be regulating space travel within a year or two. And when they do, their first step won’t be to encourage space mining activities, but to promote space business in our immediate orbit, by developing the orbital station, for instance.”

“Then, that’s good for our Albaspace,” Ana-Luiza

commented.

"That's good for the Albaspace," Tintin admitted. "But our aerospace shuttle takes eight hours to the orbital station and can't even reach the Moon. Yet, this is where there will be an immediate market: fast travel within our near orbit."

"What do you have in mind?" Michael Vahlroos asked on the screen.

Tintin looked at him. "What if you could go anywhere in the world in less than fifteen minutes? Would you pay for it?"

"Sure, I would," Michael replied. "But we already have the Albaspace, and it can already reach any place in the world in less than an hour. Even the new EU president has expressed interest to acquire one to serve as her 'Euro Flight One.'"

"Would you pay more to travel anywhere in fifteen minutes rather than one hour?" Tintin went on. "Would you also pay more to be able to go to the orbital station or the lunar base in less than 15 minutes?"

"Sure, I would," Michael answered without hesitation.

"Then, please let me show my and Thierry's concept: the V-craft. A warp ship with atmosphere entry for the near-orbit transportation market, rather than the space mining market."

Tintin tapped a few times on his touchpad, and another animation commenced on the room's white canvas screen. It featured a black cylinder lying on two dozen wheels on a runway.

"It is thinner, as there is no gravity deck," Tintin explained. "Its purpose is to travel fifteen minutes, not to set up a mining installation on a moon of Saturn."

The animation showed how two modules slowly deployed out of the cylinder, one at the front and one at the rear, and turned into two sets of wings and jet engines.

"Cubic-R engines," Tintin said. "Four at the front, and four at the rear. They can rotate so as to enable vertical take-off and landing. This is how you want to land on the Moon, or on Mars, for what matters."

Next, the V-craft started its engines and took off from the runway. As it was gaining speed, it retracted its front and back wings, and only the rear rocket engines remained on, while both the front and rear modules slowly retracted into the cylindrical fuselage.

"It reaches an altitude of 12,000 meters (40,000 ft) in four minutes only. From there, it warps, straight above the horizon."

On the screen, the V-craft warped away in a flash of green.

"Brilliant," Nafissatou commented, "By warping horizontally, no need to go as high as 40 km."

"The V-craft will now go through a set of warp flights and warp back horizontally in the atmosphere. It comes out of warp at 15,000 meters (49,000 ft) of altitude and glides from there before starting its landing maneuver. It takes maximum ten minutes. It comes pretty fast."

On the screen, the animation showed how the V-craft

deployed its front and rear wings again as it was braking by flying in an S like the 1980s space shuttle. Finally, it had lost enough horizontal velocity to execute a vertical landing on the runway.

"Of course, this concept is not fully developed either," Tintin admitted. "The deployment of the front and rear wing and jet engine modules will not be easy, but it will be manageable. Anyway, much easier than programming a successful landing for the V-liner."

Sophie was actually quite impressed by Tintin's concept. He was an arrogant scientist, but he was intelligent, she had to concede. However, most of the directors were showing strong disapproval.

For Abhineet, it would require developing some much lighter material, and it would not be easy. Nafissatou conceded that the manufacturing would cost much more, as it could not be vertically integrated as the V-liner could.

Eventually, after long debate, Sophie decided to stop the meeting and send everybody away. Only Michael remained on the TV-screen.

"What do you think, Sophie?" Michael asked.

"I like Tintin's idea very much," Sophie admitted. "But I seem to be the only one."

"Seriously?" Michael objected. "His concept is a regression from the V-liner. Quick travel around the Earth. There is nothing interesting anymore about it. Besides, it may compete against our own Albaspace. The market we want to be in is extraterrestrial mining."

"But what if Tintin is right? What if we are twenty years too early on that market? Then we will go bankrupt. Focusing on the near orbit travel is not silly after all. 15 minutes to the Moon, that counts for something. Tintin is perhaps right— There will be sightseeing on the Moon, or even on Mars a few decades before corporate mining within the solar system. At least, if the UN has its way."

"Well, let's prove the UN wrong," Michael replied. "Tintin's project has too little ambition and will result in more costly spaceships. This will lead us nowhere. We shall create our own demand. That's how we will be remembered as visionary entrepreneurs. We will create the V-liner, and promote space mining."

Sophie was, in a way, happy Michael was only on a TV screen. Otherwise, she would have slapped him in the face to bring him back to reality.

"This is your decision, Sophie," Michael went on. "You are the GM of V-Space. I am only a minority owner of Betalpha and the CEO of Vahlroos Corporation. But if I were in your shoes, I would just drop Tintin and Thierry's ideas, and go ahead with the initial plan. I have a good feeling about the V-liner. It's gonna be a great success."

Right now, Sophie hated Michael Vahlroos. She had,

however, made her decision.

The V-Liner was conceived for a hypothetical huge future market, while certainly confronted with an unsolvable problem according to Tintin and Thierry: its atmosphere re-entry. She trusted their opinion more than that of her Project Director.

Meanwhile, the lighter V-Craft was technically achievable within five years but would be more expensive to manufacture and would have to be confined to the near-orbit transportation market, rather than used in hypothetical mining ventures.

The choice was easy, but she had to be careful not to offend Michael Vahlroos.

That evening, Tintin and Thierry went out for a beer at the *Thomas Sankara*, their favorite bar in downtown Bobo. They were both having a Sobebra, the locally brewed beer. Tintin raised his glass.

"To our tiny, modest success," he said.

"You call that a success?" Thierry wondered. "They decided to go ahead with the V-Liner nonetheless."

"Truly," Tintin admitted. "But Sophie Couillard also decided to support the development of our V-craft until the next assessment stage. She called that 'risk mitigation'. She did not have to, but she did it nonetheless. She is not too bad a GM, after all."

"The V-craft remains called *the minority project*," Thierry objected.

"Better than *zero project*," Tintin retorted.

"It sucks anyway," Thierry replied. "I'm feeling I am wasting my time here. The goal of each human being should be to make the world a better world. The V-Liner, promoting corporate mining, may well serve corporate-kind, but not mankind. And what about our V-craft, our minority project? To get anywhere in the world in fifteen minutes? What's the added value of this for humanity? It will only serve the super-rich."

"You think too much, Thierry," Tintin replied. "Humanity does not matter. It's too imperfect, it's bound to go extinct anyway. The great programmer of the universe does not give a damn about animal species, be they humans or ants or dinosaurs. It's that simple."

"You are always so positive," Thierry grimaced.

Tintin took a few sips from his beer and smiled. "What I mean is that the goal of life is not to understand the meaning of mankind, but the physics of the universe."

"You are really not a humanist!" Thierry joked.

"Of course not, I'm a physicist," Tintin replied. "My grandfather is a humanist, though. You should meet him. Why not come to Kinshasa for Christmas and visit him? He used to be French, but is more intelligent than that Brice of a project leader we have at V-Space."

"Come to Kinsha for Christmas?"

"Why not? You have done a three-year PhD in Rwanda, and never set foot in Kinshasa! We have to remedy it!"

13: THE DRAFTING OF INTERNATIONAL TREATIES (OCT-DEC 2094)

After accompanying Sanne from Japan to Amsterdam, Ralf Åhman had been back in Austria on Wednesday 20 October, and immediately began catching up with his work in the United Nations Office for Outer Space Affairs, located in the Vienna International Center. He was rather pleased with the latest developments.

The Vienna Conference was to start the following Monday, and two-thirds of the participants had already agreed to his proposed layout of the treaties as well as the arrangement of the task forces. UN secretary general Hira Dorjee-Sherpa herself would be in Vienna for the kick-off. Even better, the US president had insisted on lending the admiral in civilian clothes to the United Nations Office for Outer Space Affairs for the six weeks of the Vienna conference.

It had to do with domestic politics, Ralf had understood.

President Fang's Amendment for automatic enrollment of voters had been approved by the Congress by a whisker. She was now hoping to have all 51 States of the US Federation ratify it before Christmas while trying to keep a majority in the Congress after the mid-term elections. To that end, she wanted to show her fellow Americans that the US was playing a leading role in the negotiation of the new space treaties, by detailing Glover Johnson to the UN.

Ralf was hoping to use Glover to scare all the representatives into accepting his proposals. A former US Navy safety concerned submariner was an excellent asset to have.

Glover had arrived in Vienna already on Friday to do some sightseeing, accompanied by his girlfriend, Laura. Ralf invited both of them to the restaurant the next evening. Laura Martinez was a short but athletic Hispanic-American, and Ralf assumed that going to the gym was their only hobby. It was the first time Ralf had seen Glover not wearing a suit.

"You two met in the US Navy?" Ralf asked Laura after they had ordered.

"Already at Annapolis," she replied. "We both studied nuclear propulsion. I also served in the submarines. After Glover was promoted to an office job, I joined the merchant fleet to have more time. I work for Maersk, a Danish shipping company."

"Do they have nuclear propulsion, at Maersk?" Ralf

enquired.

"They have twelve super tankers equipped with compact fusion reactors," Laura replied. "They plan to get more."

They were served some giant schnitzels with fries and a very little salad.

"Wooha so big rations!" Laura exclaimed. "No wonder Austrians are so fat. I hope this Vienna conference won't make you fat, Glover. And me trying to lose weight…"

Ralf, who himself was at least twenty kilos (44 lbs) overweight, was slightly embarrassed by Laura's comment, all the more since other overweight Austrian customers in the restaurant were now all looking at Laura.

She went on: "When you are at sea, you always go up in weight. I gained nine pounds on my last mission."

Glover suddenly looked irritated: "You went up four kilos, Laura. Pounds belong to the past."

Laura cast an annoyed glance at her boyfriend and turned back to Ralf: "Being a sailor is about gaining weight when at sea and losing it when on land. I am currently in my diet phase."

Ralf looked at his rather over-dimensioned abdomen, stroked it with his hands and said: "I should also go on a diet. I am at the head of an office for Space affairs, but I am clearly not in as good shape as the astronauts from all nations I regularly shake hands with."

"It's easy," Laura said. "As Glover usually jokes, losing weight is as easy as launching a nuclear strike. You just get a checklist, and you follow it."

Ralf laughed, but Glover looked embarrassed as if his sailor girlfriend was clashing with his diplomat friend.

"There is quite a good gym at the Vienna office," Ralf said. "Perhaps I should start going there."

"If you wish, Ralf, I can design a program for you," Glover offered. "If you can spare forty-five minutes or one hour a day, and be careful with your diet, I can help you be in better shape."

"Oh, what the hell! Why not?" Ralf said resigned, grabbing his pint of beer and drinking it up.

The next day, Glover had mailed a program to Ralf. Rule number one, no breakfast. Did polar bears wake up and say, "Oh I'm hungry, let's have breakfast before hunting"? No! Polar bears went hunting hungry. Breakfast was a useless meal. Rule number two: no food before 11:00 and after 20:00. Every day, either in the morning or at lunch, he was to follow a 45-minute training program at the gym in the UN Vienna office. Since he was living less than five kilometers (3.1 miles) from the UN office, he would also walk home rather than take the subway.

These would be intense weeks ahead, Ralf thought: losing weight and drafting important international treaties.

The following day, Ralf went earlier to the UN office, to spend some time at the gym. He somehow felt more relaxed for the rest of the day. It was Monday 25 October, and the first day of the Vienna Conference.

The UNOOSA premises were so small that Ralf had got access to some of the forum rooms belonging to the International Atomic Energy Agency in the same building.

In the large aula, the UN secretary general Hira Dorjee-Sherpa, who had just flown in from New York, opened the conference with an introduction speech to all the representatives. It had been exactly 149 years and one day since the United Nations had first existed as an international body. She laid the emphasis on what the UN had accomplished so far but also on the challenges laying ahead. Space exploration and colonization could be seen as both opportunities and threats and needed to be better regulated.

Now, the General Assembly had given its consent for the reunion of an extraordinary Committee on the Peaceful Uses of Outer Space, in Vienna. This Vienna Conference would be tasked with the drafting of two international treaties. One would be related to the regulation of space exploration, exploitation and colonization, while the other was to establish an international organ to enforce these regulations.

When Hira was done, Ralf was invited to take the floor.

"Two treaties, totaling fourteen chapters," he started, showing some slides on the large white canvas screen behind him.

"The first treaty will be the Treaty on Space Exploration, Exploitation, and Colonization, already called T-SEEC. It will, among other things, close the loopholes of the 1967 Outer Space Treaty and of the 1979 Moon Treaty. It will contain nine chapters, listed here on this slide: *1) Humanity and Space, 2) Space Exploration, 3) Exploitation of Space Resources, 4) Colonization of Celestial Bodies, 5) Space Transportation, 6) Space Labor, 7) Space Hazards, 8) Safety Principles* and, last but not least, *9) Enforcement of Space Regulations.*"

Ralf paused. So far, no reaction from all the national delegates sitting in the vast auditorium in front of him.

"The second treaty is the one establishing a UN Space Agency, whose name we have still to find and agree on. It will have five chapters, as listed on this slide: *1) Missions and Prerogatives, 2) Bodies and Instances, 3) Resources, 4) Relations to the Existing Space Agencies*, as well as a fifth chapter amending chapters 7 and 77 of the UN Charter."

"As a result, you have been divided into sixteen task forces. One task force per chapter, plus one coordination task force per treaty. My staff and I will provide counselling and serve as facilitators. Every Saturday will be wrap-up day. I am confident we will draft realistic and acceptable treaties within the next six weeks."

The representatives of each delegation were then dispatched into sixteen working rooms, and the drafting began.

The first week went rather well. Not only had Ralf managed to stick to his program to lose weight, but he had noted that by working out in the morning, he was less stressed and had a clearer mind during the rest of the day. By abstaining from eating too late in the evening, he slept better despite his increased workload.

Every day, he was visiting each of the sixteen task forces, dispensing his advice and helping participants to find a compromise. In each of the task forces, he had at least two of his UN personnel actively mediating between the parties.

Glover Johnson was assisting with both the '*Space Hazards*' and the '*Safety Principles*' task forces that were in two adjacent rooms. Ralf was amused to hear him constantly refer to the 'random functions of the universe' and the need for mankind to decrease our exposure to them. Glover had certainly succeeded in planting a seed in the brains of the diplomats of the two task forces, and a few weeks later, the term was being used by most newspapers.

By the end of the first week, the task forces had drafted the outlines of each chapter, underlining what was consensual and what was controversial. The first wrap-up session on Saturday 30 October went fine, as no major disagreements had occurred.

When he went back to his office at the end of the day, he realized he had 13 missed calls from the same Dutch number. Intrigued, he decided to call back. It was Sanne van der Maas. She was in Vienna, in front of the UN Office. She could not stand staying at her grandmother's anymore. Ralf was the only other person on Earth she had the phone number for. Since Ralf had told her she could call him anytime, she wondered whether she could crash on his couch.

"No worries, Sanne," he replied. "I am still at the office, but I am almost done. I'll see you in ten minutes."

Ralf was sore. Of course, he had told her he would be happy to help her with anything. That had never meant he was offering his couch to Sanne, though. This was certainly the first blatant case of a misunderstanding between a Martian and an Earthling. But he could not let her sleep on the street either.

Ralf met Sanne in the square in front of the Vienna Office. She looked less skinny than when he had left her in Amsterdam. They went together to the U-Bahn and took line 1 to Schwedenplats, where Ralf had his flat, a three-room apartment, a bachelor's apartment.

"I have a spare room, where you could spend a few nights," Ralf said, "I will have to remove some stuff, but you could sleep there. Sorry if the flat is messy, but I've had no time to clean it."

There was indeed some dust on the floor and on the furniture. The spare room was furnished with a bunk bed. There were pictures of two kids, a girl and boy.

"Do you have kids?" Sanne asked.

"Two. Dag and Eleonore. They now live in Norway with their mother. We are separated."

"You mean divorced?"

"We never were married. I will remove my clothes and suits

from the spare room. Just one moment."

Ralf used the spare room as a utility room where he could easily iron his shirts. He would have to do it in the living room or in his own room now. As he took his suits to his room, there some dust flew up, and Sanne coughed.

"Sorry, Sanne. Welcome to a bachelor's home. I bought a service robot to help me clean up the flat, but it worked for less than a year. It's over there, besides the sofa."

"You use robots to clean up flats?"

"It was popular to buy or lease them a while back. But I think people have grown tired of them. They always get out of order. In the end, you spend more time fixing the robots than it would take to do the cleaning yourself."

Ralf went to the kitchen after ensuring Sanne was interested in a cup of tea. He started the water boiler, while Sanne glanced around in the adjacent living room. She expressed an interest in two cactuses by the window.

"The only plants I've got that have survived so far," Ralf explained. "I'm always traveling, but the cactuses are not too demanding. So, what are your plans, Sanne?"

"Well, in January, I am going to New York to finish my bachelor's degree at Colombia University. I'm basically spending the money I have left from the indemnities paid by the EU. Most of the indemnities were used to finance my rescue mission from Earth, you know."

"I know. What do you plan to do until January?"

Sanne looked embarrassed.

"Well, US universities are so expensive. I don't have much money left… And I don't know anybody on Earth…"

Ralf had an idea. "Would you be interested in helping me with the ongoing Vienna conference?"

"How?"

"As a former Martian, you may add local color to the conference. And perhaps help me convince those who are still reluctant to admit the needs of better regulations for private initiative in space."

"I would be happy to."

"Good. I will try to see if I can give you a position as an intern. It may take a week or two. If so, you may be able to get a temporary flat. In the meantime, you could stay here."

"Really?" Sanne said as her face lit up. "Thank you so much."

"I hope you do not get bored in the meantime."

"No worries, I have to work on my bachelor's thesis. But the conference is indirectly linked to it."

"What is it about?" Ralf wondered. The water had now boiled and he poured it into two cups, adding tea bags to them.

"*Economic models in space colonies.*" Sanne replied. "On Mars, it was rather a survival economy: an economy in which all efforts were pursued in view of a single goal: survival. A parallel can be drawn with war economy: an economy in which all efforts are pursued with one purpose: war."

"Like under the first and the second world war… Interesting."

Ralf noted. "What do you plan to do after your bachelor's?"

"I would like to do a Master's in Economics at Cambridge University, in England. But in between, I will do my European Civil Service. I have to do only one year, though, since I am considered as an immigrant coming to Europe after the age of 18."

As Sanne had been talking, Ralf had led them to his living room and a moment later, they were drinking tea on the couch.

On a dusty shelf, Sanne spotted a picture of a young Ralf in a sailor's uniform. "Where did you do your service, if I may ask?"

"In the submarines, France, two years."

"Submarine? Did you apply for it?" Sanne wondered.

"I had applied to do the military service rather than the civil one. I wanted to serve as an Arctic ranger in northern Scandinavia, but they sent me to the submarines in France."

"Why?"

"I said I was claustrophobic and Francophobic. They said that serving in the French submarines would be the best way of being cured of these two diseases."

Sanne laughed.

"That's part of the integration," Ralf explained. "The goal of the European Service is not only to dispose of cheap labor to do public service tasks. It is mostly to safeguard an integrated society rather than a congregated society. That was the topic of *A European Dilemma*, ever heard of that book?"

"No, what is it?"

"Of course, you are too young," Ralf smiled. "*A European Dilemma: Integration Versus Congregation in Liberal Democracies*, published in 2036."

Ralf put his cup of tea on the side table and went up to the bookcase surrounding his TV, in front of the sofa.

"Who wrote it?" Sanne asked.

"It was a comprehensive sociological study. There were many authors. One of the lead authors was a Cambridge Professor, a certain Gareth Fraser. He is still alive. You may meet him in Cambridge if you do your Master's there."

Ralf retrieved a thick book from his bookcase and handed it over to Sanne before sitting down again on the sofa.

"What is the book about?"

"According to the authors, modern societies can be categorized in four different ways, depending on how the different groups within them interact with each other. The four ways are *segregationism, assimilationism, congregationism* and *integrationism.*"

"*Segregationism, assimilationism, congregationism* and *integrationism,*" Sanne repeated.

Ralf went on: "In a segregationist society, a dominant group will impose a separation between each group by force. There will be a limited and asymmetric interaction between these groups, for instance, the white community separating colored people in the American southern states, prior to 1965.

"In an assimilationist society, a dominant group will deny

the existence of the other groups and force these to adapt in order to blend in with the main group, for instance, France until the 1960s. In both segregationism and assimilationism, there is a dominant group that imposes its will."

"What about congregationism and integrationism?" Sanne asked.

"In a congregationist society, people are free to interact with each other the way they want. However, when people are totally free, they usually interact in such a way that they seldom really mix with each other. They congregate and the result is a 'salad bowl'.

"In an integrationist society, on the contrary, people from different background and origins will interact with each other, and in the end blend and form a completely new integrated group, a 'melting pot'. The problem is that people from different origins don't naturally mix with each other. This is the paradox that *A European Dilemma* outlined."

"What paradox?" Sanne wondered.

"In liberal democracies, people may do what they want. And when they do, they choose to live with the people who are most like them. They congregate. At the beginning of this century, this trend got even more reinforced by online social media."

"How?"

"Until the early 2000s, TV had an integrationist effect, forcing society to watch the same limited offer of programs. Then came the social media, like Facebook, which was the leading social network until the Qatari Flu. They had algorithms imprisoning their users in their restricted bubble of thinking. It made people more narrow-minded, even though at first everybody thought the Internet would make people more open-minded. Social media only fostered congregationism and its by-products such as intolerance, racism, and so on."

"I see."

Ralf took a few sips from his cup of tea and went on: "If congregationism is rather a natural behavior, from an anthropological perspective, it still tears apart the fabric of society and, in the end, threatens democracy. On the other hand, a society can only be integrationist if it abolishes prejudices and forces people from different backgrounds to work and live together, without any attempt at domination from any of the groups."

"That's the difference from assimilationism," Sanne noted.

"Exactly, but it still requires its citizens to do things they would not naturally do. That's the paradox. Liberal democracies foster congregationism, which may lead to their own downfall, while a more integrationist policy may be considered as not liberal enough. By mixing young Europeans from different backgrounds and forcing them to live away from their family for two years, the European Service is the integrationist institution by excellence. When it was introduced in the 2040s, there were huge demonstrations and protests. But today, nobody questions its purpose."

Ralf took the book from Sanne's hands, found the page he wanted and showed it to her:

"Here, this drawing is what best summarizes the group dynamics I just talked about."

Sanne looked at it and said: "Have you read *Red Mars* by Kim Stanley Robinson?"

"No, I haven't," Ralf admitted. "I perhaps should, as the UNOOSA director."

"In it, people congregate all the time, and the resulting colonization process is rather nasty."

Ralf smiled. "Well, if I get my way, I will ensure that integration prevails over congregation even for space colonization."

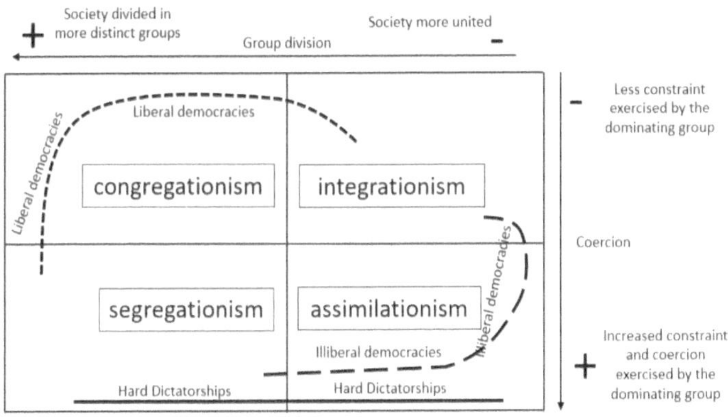

Figure 5: The four different ways of aggregating the sub-groups within a society, as described in 'A European Dilemma: Integration Versus Congregation in Liberal Democracies' (published in 2036)

The following week, Sanne stayed at Ralf's home. Ralf had promised he would try to obtain the authorization for Sanne to join the conference as an intern, but it took more time than expected. Sharing a flat with Ralf was, however, easier than sharing with her grandmother, who was constantly at home, and almost harassing her.

At least Ralf was not judging her all the time for not looking people in the eye. He was not strongly recommending her to have sexual intercourse with a male prostitute to lose her virginity. He was not forcing her to become part of a Calvinist church, she who was an atheist anyway. After spending ten days with her grandmother, she could totally understand why her own mother had applied to be part of the Martian colony project.

Sanne had cleaned the whole apartment the first day and worked on her bachelor's thesis the following few days. As she was pondering how to best compare a 'survival economy' to a 'war economy', she smiled at the thought that she would soon have a taste of what she wanted to do later. She was far from being done with her university studies and had not even done her civil service, but she would soon be an intern in Ralf's office and attend the Vienna Conference! She would have an insight into the creation of the new UN space agency that would regulate space exploration. The very UN agency she hoped one day to work for.

However, it seemed to take more time than expected to

get the authorization to work as an intern. Was not Ralf the director of UNOOSA? Were they background-checking her? How could it take such a long time? As the only survivor of *The Martian Show*, Sanne had certainly one of the most public backgrounds on Earth.

Meanwhile, life went on in Ralf's flat. Sanne had realized that Ralf had a brand new modern kitchen but never used it. He was constantly bringing take-away home. Sanne offered to cook herself instead so that it would be cheaper, but they had a disagreement: while Ralf was now trying to lose some weight, Sanne was still trying to gain some. Each evening, Ralf would come home with a light take-away salad, while Sanne would have cooked pasta dishes, risotto, quiches or even baked pizzas. Ralf was tempted every time but managed to hold off.

Though people mostly read digital books at the end of the 21st Century, Ralf had a few printed books in his bookcase. Sanne noted that three of them were written by a certain Brian Urquhart. There was a blue one, a black one, and a red one. Sanne grabbed the red book and opened it. It was about a certain Ralph Bunche.

"Ah, Ralph Bunche," Ralf noted when he came home. "The first black person to receive a Nobel Prize. My parents named me for him. But since I was born in Finland, it had to be spelt with an f, rather than ph."

"Your mother is from Scotland, you told me," Sanne said. "But your father, where is he from?"

"He was born and grew up in Finland. On his side, my grandmother was a Finn of Somali descent while my grandfather was from Eritrea, though he changed his name from Ahman to Åhman after emigrating. Both my parents met in Bulgaria during their civil service and my mother moved to Helsinki with my father. Living in Finland was, however, too hard for my Scottish mother, who could never quite learn Finnish very well. When I was a teen, they moved to Sweden. Swedish is easy to learn. Even for senile Americans."

"Do they still live in Sweden?"

"My father died of the Qatari Flu, in 2072. He was a nurse. Sadly, most of the healthcare personnel were overexposed to that disease. After his death, my mother moved to Scotland."

"I've read about the Qatari Flu," Sanne said. "One billion dead in three years."

"Yes. It was horrific. I was fifteen when it started and seventeen when it ended. Schools were closed and turned into dispensaries. Luckily, we had distance classes… The only funny thing was that the Qatari Flu did not actually start in Qatar. It first broke out in Saudi Arabia. However, it was first covered by Qatari media, hence the misleading name."

Ralf suddenly changed the subject:

"By the way, I got you a seven-week internship at the Vienna office. You will be my intern."

"Thanks! I will be able to follow you at the conference?"

"Yes. On the other hand, it seems that there is no guest flat available at the moment. You can keep using the spare room, though, my kids will not be visiting me before Christmas."

From the second week of November, Sanne was able to follow Ralf at the conference. She did not like having to interact with so many people and held herself as a distant observer. Perhaps it helped her to quickly understand his negotiation and persuasion strategy.

He had found the common denominators all parties had in these talks: it was called *sovereignty*. Most countries were afraid to see their sovereignty at risk if two great powers, Russia and China, were the only ones to have warp technology at their disposal. Russia and China were in their turn afraid that a major corporation with huge capital funding would get its hands on warp technology and start claiming exoplanets in remote systems without being held accountable to anybody on Earth. This could also threaten their sovereignty.

And what about Earth customs, as it was being joked about at the conference? If a private company was importing extraterrestrial resources to Earth, who would check that these imported goods could not threaten the ecosystem on Earth? If life were to exist in a remote system, even as a primitive form, there was a risk of imported diseases. Who would impose a quarantine on spaceships coming from these systems?

What about intelligent life? Could the nations on Earth let a private company make contact with civilizations in another system? When Europe had let privateers explore South America in the sixteenth century, it had led to a massive plundering of that continent. Could private companies pursuing their own space agenda start an interstellar war? Though this was of course far-reached, UN diplomats had to consider such an eventuality.

Glover Johnson, the US Navy admiral, was doing everything to remind them of risks incurred by mankind due to the random functions of the universe. All the delegates were progressively convinced that when it came to space, solidarity was the best policy.

And, slowly but surely, the drafts were taking form.

Space exploration was to be strictly regulated. Interstellar exploration would be the sole prerogative of the United Nations. However, once a star system had been previously explored by the UN, the UN may license to other private or public organizations the remaining exploration of that system.

Space resources would no longer belong to the first private entity to lay a hand on it. Any exploitation of resources from celestial bodies would have to be authorized by the new international space agency which, and it was a complete novelty as far as the UN was concerned, would be able to levy a tax on it.

Colonization of a new celestial body would only occur under the control of the UN as part of the International Trusteeship System, which had been created after World War Two to accompany the decolonization of Asia and Africa. As such, the treaties planned to add a *d)* to article 77 of the Charter of the United Nations mentioning 'newly colonized celestial bodies' as territories to which the Trusteeship System should apply.

Space hazards such as meteorites, diseases, or even extraterrestrial invasions were listed, and the need for a UN agency to enforce space regulations was recognized.

The missions of the new UN space agency would not only be to lead the interstellar exploration, to regulate the exploitation of space resources and to supervise the colonization of new celestial bodies, but also to protect the Earth and the human species from any space hazards. To this purpose, the UN space agency would be granted a budget financed by a contribution from the member states, but it would also be able to levy a tax on all space activities, from commercial satellites orbiting the earth, to resource extraction on celestial bodies.

The importance of the new agency was to be asserted by the fact that it would be listed as one of the key UN organs in article 7 of the Charter of the United Nations.

14: THE VIENNA TREATIES OF 8 DECEMBER 2094

After the wrap-up session of the fifth week, Ralf Åhman called Glover Johnson and Sanne van der Maas to his office. It was much smaller than that of the UN Secretary-General in New York, but it had an ergonomic desk, under which stood a little fridge, and four chairs around it. One of the corners of the office held a little sofa, and a white board hung on the wall in front of it. No plants, no flowers, and no paintings.

"No major disagreement left," Glover said as he sat down on the sofa. "The treaties may be drafted in time."

Sanne grabbed a chair and sat down opposite Glover. "I've started to understand Ralf's persuasion technique," she said. "Hammering the same message over and over again: the only goal that matters is the survival of mankind, not as a species, but as a civilization. Human civilization can only be with human rights and democracy at its core. Private corporations are not democracies, but autocracies, ergo we must have these two treaties as currently drafted."

"You are simplifying a little bit, but you are very close," Ralf replied as he was looking for marker pens. "However, we have one issue left."

"The name of the UN space agency," Glover admitted. "Nobody liked UNSA for *United Nation Space Agency*. *International Space Agency* becomes ISA and half of the delegates laughed at it."

Ralf had grabbed four marker pens from his desk and turned to his colleagues: "Yesterday, the Russian ambassador in Vienna told me seriously that he wanted the name of the organization to be *Star Fleet*, and now there are forty-seven idiot diplomats who support his idea. It's like we are in a kindergarten."

"You want us to make a counter proposal?" Glover asked.

"Yes," Ralf replied. "Let's have a little brainstorming session."

Sanne moved to the sofa next to Glover, while Ralf started writing down words on the whiteboard facing them: Space, Interstellar, Organization, Agency, Authority, Exploration, Exploitation, Colonization, Regulation, Transportation, Humanity.

Then, Ralf returned to his desk, opened the fridge beneath it and brought forth a bottle of *vodka* and three shot glasses.

"Do you keep that in your office?" Glover asked with wide-open eyes.

"And why not? That's *Koskenkorva*," Ralf replied, "Finnish vodka. While Russian vodka contracts the brain, Finnish vodka expands it."

"Ralf, you don't want us to drink, do you?" Glover objected.

Ralf put the three shot glasses on the side table by the sofa and filled them up.

"When I was a student in Uppsala and was out of inspiration, I would just go to the student parties and got drunk," he said. "In the morning, I often had the solution – provided I had not got laid."

One of the few advantages of not getting laid, Sanne thought to herself while accepting a shot from Ralf. She remembered not liking the saké in Japan but could give the Finnish vodka a try.

"Now, Glover, this is an emergency," Ralf went on, as he was handing a shot to Glover. "We must come up with a counter proposition to this stupid *Star Fleet* by Monday. We will be more creative with some Finnish vodka in the brain."

Glover took the shot reluctantly and Ralf added: "Come on, Glover. You are not monitoring a fusion reactor right now. You are drafting an international treaty. Alcohol is perhaps banned in a submarine, but it's not in an international conference."

"You know, I like *Star Trek* very much, so *Star Fleet* would be fine for me," Glover said.

"And sometimes you are too much like Spock," Ralf retorted. "Come on; bottoms up."

The three drank their vodka shots and resumed their brainstorming. Thirty minutes and two vodka shots later,

Sanne had coined the perfect name: WARSEC. It stood for World's Agency for the Regulation of Space Exploration and Colonization.

"Not bad," Glover said, "It may reconcile *Star Wars* fans with 'Trekkies'. In WARS-EC, you have 'Wars' like in *Star Wars*, and the sound *'eck'* like in *Star Trek*. It could be a good selling name in terms of public relations."

Ralf pondered a short time. "I like the martial tone of it. Ad-hoc UN institutions or missions always have weak sounding names like UNAMIR, UNA-blah, UNA-blih and are consequently weak. This WARSEC name will send a strong signal: we are here to regulate, and we come in force."

That Saturday, Glover, Ralf and Sanne decided to spend the evening together to celebrate their success. After eating some bugburgers made of insect paste in a fancy restaurant, they went to the movie theater to watch a thriller movie set in the mid-2020s: *Hipsters Don't Eat Oysters*. Before the start of the movie, they were reminded: "*The story of this movie is set in 2024. Back then, the world population was about 8 billion. In 2094, the world population is about 10.4 billion.*"

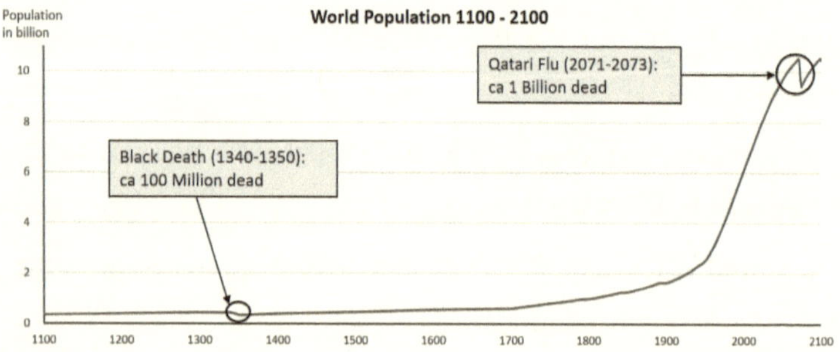

Figure 6: Evolution of the world population between 1100-2100. At the end of the 21st Century, everything has been made to make the world aware of the untenable population growth. The Qatari Flu has previously been mentioned by Ralf Åhman and has had a dramatic impact on the demographic evolution.

The drafts were finalized during the following week. By Saturday 4 December, all the delegations had agreed on their contents, and the final versions were sent to their respective governments. The signature date was set for December 8th.

UN secretary general Hira Dorjee-Sherpa had flown to Vienna for the occasion. She had now been nominated by the General Assembly as the new secretary general for five years and was not simply an 'acting' secretary-general.

On Wednesday 8 December, under the patronage of the UN secretary general, the two international treaties related to outer space affairs were signed in Vienna by the 235 members of the United Nations.

They were the Treaty on Space Exploration, Exploitation and Colonization (the T-SEEC) and the Treaty establishing the World's Agency for the Regulation of Space Exploration and Colonization (T-WARSEC).

That same day, Ralf was informed by his press attaché of the following day's issue of *The Chained Palmiped*. The main headline would be '*UN = Union of Nerds*'.

Anatoli Govorov and Alice Fù, who had both been part of the first crew to travel faster than the speed of light, had been invited for the occasion. That same evening, Ralf had arranged a dinner with them, Glover, Sanne and the secretary-general. They were at the Sofitel restaurant.

"Ralf, I have to say you have lost quite some weight, since last June," Anatoli complimented.

He had indeed lost nine kilos (20 lbs) in seven weeks, and had been quite pleased to be forced to buy the new navy blue suit he was wearing, as his other suits were now too large.

"And you, Sanne, you look much stronger now," Alice said. "When we picked you up from Mars, you were so weak."

Sanne had also spent some time at the UN gym. On Mars, she had had the discipline to do her daily work-out session and had kept the habit. With proper nourishment and a gravity three times stronger than on Mars it had been quite easy to build up some muscles.

"I've heard you will spend the next spring in New York,"

Hira said.

The secretary-general had removed her earGlasses, which were being charged on a side table.

"Yes, Madam. I will finish my bachelor's degree at Columbia University."

Hira turned to Glover: "And you, back to the States as well?"

"I will be back in Washington," Glover said. "Not that I wouldn't like to work for the UN. But so far I belong to the US government."

"If you are interested, I could talk to President Fang," Hira said. "When we set up the new agency, we will need people with experience there, and of course, the best would be to have all of you, Glover, Alice and Anatoli. And perhaps also you, Sanne, one day, when you are done with your studies."

"WARSEC will take over the UN Office for Outer Space Affairs when at least 158 Members out of 236 have ratified it," Ralf said. "It may take some time."

"All the more since President Fang has lost her majority in the Senate," Glover added. "The Republicans are against the ratification."

Hira Dorjee-Sherpa closed her eyes for a short moment and said: "Most of the budget for WARSEC will come from the United States, the European Union, China, Russia, Japan, and the South Asian Union. Even if other countries ratify the treaties, WARSEC cannot function without the ratification by these key members. The South Asian Union will ratify it before

March, I was told."

Alice Fù jumped in: "Russia and China would like to ratify the treaties before Christmas. That's why we are here. We would like to ask you, Ralf and Mme secretary general, to attend the debates at the Duma and at the Chinese parliament prior to the ratification."

Anatoli Govorov acquiesced: "The MPs in both our countries may want to ask questions directly to the UN. So, if you are there, it may speed up the process."

Ralf sighed and said: "You mean, we have to travel to Russian and China in the next two weeks?"

Ralf had mixed feelings at the prospect of these Russian and Chinese excursions. He had hoped to have some time to catch up with his regular job and rest a bit after the conference. On the other hand, it would give a major boost to the overall ratification process if the two nations behind warp technology would be the first to ratify the Vienna treaties.

15: FAMILY BUSINESS
(DEC 2094)

Six months and twelve days to manage in this place, Samir Benyamina thought. The place was his father's three-room apartment, in the Parisian suburb Beaudottes. Fat Ali, as usual, was lying on the sofa and watching TV. Now, he was yelling at the kids to bring him a new bottle of coke.

He had asked Samir. Samir had asked Karim, his younger brother by three years. Karim had asked eleven-year old Abdelkader. The youngest always had to do all the chores. Samir had the advantage of being the most senior boy at home. His older brother Yacine had done his European Service on a farm in Germany, and had been living in Augsburg ever since.

His older sister Fatima had not done her European Service, as she had studied to become a nurse (medical students were not obliged to do their European Service, as they performed public duties throughout their studies). Though she was working part-time, she was still living in the parental flat.

His other older sister, Soraya, had done her service in the military. She had served as an Arctic ranger in northern Norway. She was now studying engineering in northern Sweden, in what Samir would call a shit hole, Luleå. However, that week, she was there for the Christmas holiday, which meant Fat Ali was calmer and milder than usual: He would not beat the children, lest Soraya would beat him back.

Besides, Soraya's boyfriend, a Swede called Anders, was also staying a few nights in the flat. Ali did not want to give him too bad an image of himself.

That evening, all of Samir's siblings and Soraya's boyfriend were packed into the tiny children's room, equipped with two sets of bunk beds. They wanted to be left alone by their authoritarian father and were talking English for the Swedish boyfriend's sake.

Anders was sitting next to Soraya on one of the lower bunk beds. "Why is he such an ass?" he asked. "In Sweden, he would get his ass kicked by any woman for not getting his own coke out of the fridge."

"He did not have such an easy childhood either," Soraya said. "Though that does not change the fact that he is an ass."

Samir's father Ali had been born in Algeria and was the first son of a war veteran. Samir's grandfather had fought in the 2040 Summer War when Algeria had tried to liberate Western Sahara from the rule of Morocco. Algeria had lost, as all the western powers and China had sided with the Moroccans and imposed an embargo on Algerian arms importation. Samir's grandfather had somehow managed to rise from the rank of corporal to that of major under the three-month-long conflict. When the Algerian army had run out of ammunition, he had, however, disobeyed orders and pulled his whole battalion out of the front line.

Samir's father had been quite badly bullied at school for being the son of the most decorated Algerian soldier, who, in the end, had just abandoned his position. Samir's grandfather was an atheist nationalist and his father had therefore reacted to that by becoming deeply religious.

"He claims he is religious," Soraya said, "but I'm pretty sure he does not believe in it at all. Mom used to be truly religious, but she was not very intelligent. He is smart. He has just understood that religion is a way of oppressing women."

"Too bad you went in the army," said Karim, who was sitting on the other lower bunk bed. "Now, he cannot even pretend to be a male supremacist."

Once, after her military service, Soraya had beaten the shit out of their father, after he had beaten their mom. After that Ali had told everybody at the mosque he had fallen down the stairs.

"He came to Europe after the Qatari Flu," said Samir, who was lying in one of the top bunk beds. "Back then, it was easy to get a job as a truck driver. But he's grown fat. Never grow fat, it's bad for your career."

Young Abdelkader, who was already more mature than most adults sighed and said: "Trucks have autopilots so you can drive them even if you have sleep apnea. But then, when you have to load or off-load the truck, you still have to be able to handle that. He can't."

"He's smart enough to get another kind of job, though," Soraya said, "but he's lazy, and most of all, he is an ass. Nobody will ever want to hire him because nobody will ever want to work with him. At least, as a truck driver, he was only pissing off customers. When you start pissing off all your colleagues, then you can't get a job. That's sad but so understandable."

"We just have to wait until he dies," young Abdelkader said, resignedly.

"Say that to yourself, Abdel," Samir replied. "Soraya lives in Sweden, Yacine lives in Germany. In six and a half months, I will be living in the UK, and I am never planning to come back."

"No, don't leave me alone with Fat Ali," Abdelkader said laughing. "I still have another seven and a half years of hell. I hope he dies before that so I can be placed in a foster family."

"So, you will be doing your civil service in the UK?" Anders asked Samir.

"He's gonna change the diapers of senile Englishmen," Abdelkader said. "Good riddance, he deserves it."

"*Je t'emmerde, Abdel,*" Samir told his youngest brother ('Fuck you, Abdel'). "To answer you, Anders. It is only plan B. Plan A is I join the Foreign Legion in June."

"Plan A is not even in your dreams," Soraya replied. "Look at you. You can barely do more than three pull-ups. You barely run two and a half kilometers [1.5 miles] in twelve minutes. I run faster than you. Besides, you have sold drugs."

"But never got caught."

"You got busted," Karim said. "You just got away with a fine, since the police were too stupid to understand it was not for your private consumption."

"Are the French police as incompetent as the Swedish ones?" Anders asked.

The French police were in fact very competent. Samir would not admit it. And he would never tell anybody that he had been more or less forced to cooperate with them. That was why he wanted so badly to join the Legion, to disappear. Civil Service was fine, but come on! It was in the UK! Perhaps the only European country worse than France. He would have preferred Cyprus, or Croatia, or Italy, or Spain, or any place in Europe where girls were attractive.

He had been sentenced to two years in the fucking UK. All the more in a posh city, in Cambridge, a place populated by ill-fucked dudes in suits. It was certainly Inspector Chautel's doing. Yet, he had helped her.

He had participated in her set-up of the Moroccan cultural attaché. It had occurred two weeks earlier. As he had been buying some cannabis from the Moroccan diplomat, a Malinois dog had suddenly appeared and jumped at the attaché.

"*Assis, Sarko, assis!*" a feminine voice had said ('Sit, Sarko, sit'). It had been Inspector Chautel.

"*Excusez moi, Monsieur* ['Sorry, sir'], my dog is always getting crazy when he smells good stuff. Do you have good stuff?"

"What do you mean?" the attaché had retorted.

Then, five young men in sports clothes had come jogging along the pavement in very close formation. They had surrounded Samir and the Moroccan diplomat, who had been dragged along by the flow. A minute later the two of them were sitting in a mini-van in front of Nathalie Chautel, while the joggers had vanished.

"What are you doing? Is this a kidnapping? Who are you?" the Moroccan diplomat had asked.

"Inspector Nathalie Chautel," the inspector said.

"Then you have no prerogative to arrest me, Inspector. I am the cultural attaché of the Moroccan Embassy in Paris."

"I know who you are, Mr. Hassan Benkirane. I'm not here to arrest you. I'm here to talk."

"What do you want?" the attaché had asked.

"I want you to stop importing drugs through Orly Airport," Inspector Chautel had replied. "You want to import drugs, you go through Russia or the Netherlands, but you don't take the direct route through Orly airport."

"I'm not importing drugs."

"I've been following you for three months. I know you are. Orly Airport is very convenient. It has been built so that you can easily avoid the customs if you have only hand baggage. Everybody knows that. Historical reasons. French politicians needed to smuggle blood-diamonds from Africa to finance their political parties."

"What do you want from me?" Hassan had asked again.

"You are well aware we have a new European president. She wants to obtain a reduction in the price of phosphate, in which Morocco has a monopoly. Your monopoly on phosphate is good for you. It's not for our farming industry. Mrs. Bonavita is a hawk. You give her an excuse to start a war with Morocco, she will do it. And it won't be like in 2040. This time, nobody will support you."

"You are stupid!" Hassan had exclaimed, "Nobody would start a war about a little drug trafficking."

"Who is being stupid?" Inspector Chautel had retorted.

While Samir was spending his Christmas holiday in Paris, the two V-Space colleagues Thierry Diakité and Tintin Mutombo had decided to spend their break in Congo Kinshasa.

At their arrival at Kinshasa airport, Thierry and Tintin were met by the latter's parents, who took them directly to the Capitaine Haddock, one of the restaurants they owned. There, they were welcomed by all of Tintin's cousins, uncles, aunts, and friends. The entire restaurant had been privatized for the evening. Tintin really was a star in his family. They were given a seat at the table of honor, with Tintin's parents and grandfather.

Tintin's grandfather, Patrick Desforges, had been nicknamed Capitaine Haddock by the Congolese, because of his beard and white skin. At the table, Thierry was sitting next to him.

"Are you really French?" Thierry asked him.

"I was born in France, at least," Patrick replied slowly. "In 1993, 101 years ago. But I have been living in the Congo for most of my life, so I am Congolese."

"Why Congo?" Thierry wondered.

"Why not?" Patrick said. "It's a long story. When I was a kid, both my parents worked as doctors for the democratically elected government, in Congo Brazzaville, or little Congo. But in June 1997, there was unrest in the country. French soldiers came to our house and asked us to meet at a rallying point to leave the country. My parents were really mad at them. They accused the French soldiers of supporting a *coup d'état* and refused to evacuate with them. Later that summer, all hell broke loose. I was four at the time. We had to follow a flow of refugees through the jungle, and over the Congo River. My first time in Congo Kinsha."

"And you've stayed here ever since?" Thierry wondered.

"No, of course not," Patrick replied. "In 1997 Congo Kinsha was not a nice place to stay either. My parents refused to return to France. So instead we lived in the Netherlands and later in Germany. It was after I had studied hydrology that I moved into

Congo as an aid worker. I met Divine, Tintin's grandmother. Back then, I was black-haired and had a sailor's beard. She gave me the nickname 'Captain Haddock'. She was very enterprising, and she built our little empire: the nightclub, the restaurants and so on."

"Tintin told me his family was rather wealthy."

"You will see the nightclub Le Moulinsart," Patrick replied. "Tintin will take you there tonight, but I'm too old for that."

After dinner, the cousins and friends took Tintin and Thierry to the family's nightclub, the Moulinsart. Thierry almost died of laughter when going to the bathrooms. There, in the urinals, male customers were given a choice to pee on three European historical figures: French Emperor Napoleon, for re-establishing slavery; King Leopold II of Belgium, for plundering the Congo; French President François Mitterrand, for sponsoring the genocide in Rwanda.

It was a hard choice, but Thierry finally urinated on Napoleon, for his re-establishing slavery. He decided he would have more beers, in order to be able to urinate on the other two as well.

Meanwhile, in Austria, Ralf Åhman had got back from China on Wednesday 22 December. He was tired but quite satisfied. Russia and China had ratified the Vienna treaties, much faster than he had ever dreamed of.

When he entered his flat, he found a happy Sanne. She had

received the answer from the European Service Agency: she would do her European Service in Cambridge as a mathematics tutor.

Since his kids would not come to Vienna for Christmas, he suggested she stay in his flat until she flew to New York, just before New Year's Eve.

On Thursday the 23rd, Ralf spent some time in his office catching up with his work and took a plane for Finland in the afternoon. He spent Christmas Eve with his grandfather and cousins in Jyväskylä. On Saturday 25 December, he took an early flight to Oslo and the connecting flight to Trondheim, in Norway. He had to pick up his children at his ex-girlfriend's house.

In the taxi, Ralf was contemplating the snow through the window, when the driver asked:

"Where are you from?"

"It's complicated, but you could say I'm Swedish."

"*Er du svensk*? the driver asked, changing to Norwegian ('Are you Swedish?').

"*Ja, det stämmer*," Ralf replied in Swedish ('That's correct.').

"You work here in a hotel or a restaurant?"

"Not quite. I'm visiting my ex-girlfriend, just picking up the kids."

"I see. By the way, have you seen how we beat the shit out of the Swedes in the biathlon last weekend?"

"No, I'm afraid I missed that."

The only thing that mattered for the Norwegians was to beat the Swedes. If a Norwegian should come ninth out of ten in a race, the Norwegians were happy as long as the tenth was a Swede.

The spiral of prejudices, Ralf thought. Norwegians despised Swedes, who had prejudices against Finns, who were racist against Eritreans, who hated Ethiopians, who loathed Somalis. Stupidity was certainly the most fairly shared attribute on Earth.

At last, the taxi stopped at his ex-girlfriend's house. He stepped out and rang the bell.

A blond woman with grey eyes and wearing sports clothes opened the door. It was Solveig, Ralf's ex-girlfriend. She complimented him on the kilos he had lost and invited him in for a coffee, but he declined:

"Listen, Solveig, I would really like to stay, but I have to be at my mother's in Scotland tonight, I need to leave now with the kids. I have to take two connecting flights in Oslo and Amsterdam before I reach Edinburg."

Ralf remained outside, as he did not want to take off his shoes to come in, while Solveig stood in the doorway

"The kids are almost ready," she said. "You are happy with the outcome of the Vienna conference?"

"Yes, rather satisfied. And you, are you still happy teaching mathematics to Norwegians?"

"They are indeed not as bright as students in Austria.

But at the university, there are many students from France and Germany: they compensate for the poor level of the Norwegians."

"*God jul, papa,*" said the two young kids that popped out of the door, a girl and a boy ('Merry Christmas, Daddy.').

"Merry Christmas, kids."

"*Har du presenter til oss?*" the boy asked ('Do you have presents for us?').

"Yes, Dag, but you will get them at Gran's place. Come on. We have to go."

Back in the taxi, Ralf realized he had forgotten to buy any presents for the kids, or even his mother. Damn it. He had been in China and Russia and didn't even buy a souvenir. His mother would understand, though. He had to text her so that she could fix something for both Dag and Eleonore.

16: THE ONLY GOAL
OF THE UNITED NATIONS
(JAN 2095)

As the US Senate was debating whether or not to ratify the Vienna treaties, Ralf Åhman, as the director of UNOOSA, had been summoned to a hearing by Congress.

He flew to Washington DC on Monday 17 January 2095. The hearing was the following morning. Cold rain was pouring over the city, and despite his umbrella, Ralf was quite drenched after walking the one kilometer (0.6 mile) from the Capitol Hill hotel.

In Congress Hall, he was greeted by some lobbyists.

"Sir, a glass of champagne on behalf of the US Hydrogen Industry Association?" said a white man in a blue suit.

Ralf politely showed he was not interested but a black lady wearing an anthracite skirt suit went on:

"We want to inform you about the new safety standards met by the latest hydrogen engines. Hydrogen powered vehicles should not be banned anymore from transiting through very long tunnels. They are now completely safe."

Ralf stopped and smiled politely at both lobbyists: "Sir, Madam. You are whining to the wrong master. I'm not even a US citizen."

But the male lobbyist insisted: "Hydrogen is the cleanest source of energy. It's cleaner than electric batteries. Carbon-based batteries discharge their energy too fast and the manufacturing of lithium batteries causes terrible environmental damage."

Ralf considered the lobbyist. His shoes were shinier than his. He decided to challenge him:

"Please, sir, tell me: how much energy to you need to obtain one kilogram of hydrogen?"

The lobbyist hesitated and Ralf decided to answer.

"To obtain one kilogram of hydrogen, you need to hydrolyze nine liters of water. It requires 33 kilowatt hours of electricity. However, the consumption of one kilo of hydrogen will give you much less energy. You should know that. Hydrogen is clean only if there is a clean primary source of energy to hydrolyze water."

"This is not a problem," the lady replied, "Nuclear fusion gives us clean and cheap energy. The remaining issue is the safety standards, and that is what we want to inform decision-makers about."

"Good luck with that," Ralf said, and he went looking for a bathroom to dry his face.

Ralf should not have even talked to the lobbyists. But he could not help himself. He was forced to be so diplomatic all the time, that at some point, it felt good to lecture a few lobbyists wearing suits and shiny shoes. Eventually, he found his way to the Senate's hearing room.

The hearing committee was sitting behind a long table on a rostrum. Ralf was to sit down in front of the large bureau in front of them. The chairperson of the committee, a grey-haired Republican lady, led the hearing:

"Mr. Åhman. Under the negotiations of the Vienna treaties, the main argument put forward for the establishment of WARSEC was the preservation of the sovereignty of the UN member states. For me, the Vienna treaties imply a transfer of sovereignty in terms of space affairs to the new agency, WARSEC. What is your position on that?"

Ralf started to thank Madam Senator for asking the question. That was standard, it gave him time to think how to phrase the rest of the answer:

"No state on Earth has ever had any sovereignty rights in space. According to international treaties, the territory of a state stops at 80 km of altitude above the sea level. Anything above and in space is considered as an international territory. The question that remains is: who is legitimate to govern those international territories? A United Nations agency, such as WARSEC, would be the most legitimate to regulate space affairs.

After all, it embodies all the UN members through its executive committee and subordination to the Fourth Committee of the General Assembly. In my view, WARSEC indeed preserves the sovereignty of each state on Earth, including the United States of America, by preventing space from becoming a zone of lawlessness."

The Republican lady went on: "Having an international agency setting space regulations may threaten the interest of American companies."

Fuck Vahlroos, Ralf thought, he must have spent some millions in lobbying, the bastard.

Ralf pondered a while and said diplomatically: "What is good for American companies is not necessarily good for the United States of America. However, having laws known to all and applying equally to all is good for all corporations, including American companies."

The chairwoman continued her questioning: "Mr. Åhman, my religious colleagues, and I respect their beliefs, question the need to spend resources in interstellar exploration or colonization."

This was an easy answer for Ralf: "First of all, I believe that exploration can be achieved at a reasonable cost. Second of all, WARSEC will have their own income taken as a fee on commercial space activities. This will therefore greatly reduce the financial burden for its member states, including the United States of America."

The chairwoman took some notes and commented: "Giving WARSEC its own resources is highly questionable, however I expect it to be a marginal part of your income, so I shall not insist on it. More generally, what is the purpose of interstellar exploration? What is there to win?"

That was typical American. They always needed to win something. Ralf decided to be open:

"Honestly, I don't know if there is anything to win. What I do know is that mankind has a lot to lose by not attempting it."

"What do you mean?" another senator on the hearing committee asked.

Ralf looked at him and said: "We will soon have 11 billion people living on a planet that has exhausted most of its resources. It is now believed that the Earth can sustainably support maximum 6 billion individuals with our current living standard. Many scientists believe that the climate has been so irreversibly changed over the last century that 95% of the species are doomed to go extinct within one hundred to one thousand years. Therefore, I think that WARSEC is relevant."

"Why? Do you think you can save the Earth?" a third senator asked.

"Quite frankly, Mr. Senator, I don't give a damn about the Earth. The Earth has been there for four and a half billion years, and it will still be there for another four billion years before it gets swallowed by the Sun. We know for sure that mankind will not be there in four billion years. But we now even fear that mankind will not even make it the next three hundred years. The goal is not to save the Earth, but to try and preserve humanity."

"Do you really believe humanity is presently at risk, Mr. Åhman?" the chairwoman asked Ralf.

"Yes, I do. Currently, mankind is not only demographically, economically, and socially challenged, but also environmentally, geologically, and geophysically challenged. Yes, Madam Senator, we are presently at risk."

"This is bullshit!"

It was the senator to the far right of the hearing committee who had erupted. He was an old, white-haired gentleman slouched in his chair. He wore a black suit, white shirt, and a red tie: he was a Republican. The senator went on:

"God created the Earth. God created mankind, and God cherishes mankind. If there is any risk for the survival of mankind on Earth, God will do something for us. In the meantime, we should instead focus on being good Christians, rather than sinners. We should encourage birth, rather than abortion, enforce law and order rather than tolerate the intolerable."

Most of the democrat senators were now laughing in the hearing room, and Ralf was uncertain what attitude to adopt: "Madam Chairwoman of the committee, do I have to comment on this?"

"No, you needn't, Mr. Åhman," the chairwoman replied.

"Outrageous, Madam Chairman!" the religious senator exploded. "*In God we trust*! That's the motto of our country! You are insulting the founding fathers of our nation!"

"And you are insulting the credibility of this very committee," the chairwoman replied firmly to the senator. "Mr. Åhman. Please talk about space cooperation. What is your view on it?"

"145 years ago, the space race was started as part of the competition between the west and the east under the Cold War. Yet, as early as 1957, the United States of Eisenhower, a Republican president by the way, and the Soviet Union of Khrushchev felt that outer space affairs had to be discussed within the framework of the United Nations. That's how the office of which I am currently the director was created. Since then, major powers and smaller countries have always efficiently cooperated in terms of space exploration, regardless of the geopolitical differences on Earth. UN space cooperation is, in my opinion, the most successful UN cooperation since World War 2."

"UN cooperation? What is it worth?"

It was the religious senator again: "One billion dead worldwide under the Qatari flu. 87 Million Americans lost their lives in that pandemic. Don't you think that the USA would have done better by staying out of the UN and the World Health Agency? Has the UN succeeded in eradicating poverty or diseases, or even avoiding wars?"

The other members of the hearing committee looked at Ralf

intently, waiting for his answer. Ralf took a deep breath and said very slowly:

"Mr. Senator, the United Nations is only the sum of its part. The goal of the United Nations has never been, repeat never been, to bring heaven on Earth. The only goal of the United Nations is to save humanity from hell."

"Has it worked so far?"

"Soon there will be 11 billion people on Earth, more or less at peace with each other. Yes, it has worked so far."

Ralf hadn't liked the hearing at all. Being fired at by so-called 'realists', who doubted the purpose of international organizations, was not his cup of tea. The only good moment had been when he had the opportunity to use a line inspired by a statement made by Dag Hammarskjöld at Berkeley University, back in 1954.

However, Washington was also an opportunity for him to eat lunch with Glover Johnson. Ralf was even allowed inside the Pentagon for that occasion, which was a first for him.

Glover had some good news. The US president had managed to have her 33rd amendment ratified by all 51 states. As a result, she assessed that her chances of being re-elected for another term were pretty high, as socially excluded people would automatically become enrolled voters and hopefully vote for her. President Fang was, therefore, willing to follow a longer-term strategy as far as the US collaboration with the UN was concerned. As such, she had accepted the request from the Hira Dorjee-Sherpa to let Glover Johnson quit the Pentagon and start working full time for the UN.

The following Thursday, Ralf took the high-speed train to New York City and the UN headquarters. On the 38th Floor, the UN secretary general was waiting for him in her spacious office.

Once again, her earGlasses were charging. Hira Dorjee-Sherpa invited Ralf to sit down on the sofas, where he gave her a quick update on progress. Not only had he hired Glover Johnson, who would start in Vienna as soon as February, but he had also hired Anatoli Govorov and Alice Fù, two of the lead scientists behind warp technology, as well as two doctors who had worked on the optimization of the warp field: A certain Mikko Andersson and a Valeriya Limonov, both from Luleå University. Ralf joked that he had a team good enough to start designing interstellar exploration spaceships.

"Is it our role to build spaceships?" the UN secretary general wondered.

"It will have to be clarified with the respective national space agencies," Ralf admitted. "However, we are responsible for the sharing of space technology, be it the EM-drive developed by the Americans, or the Alcubierre metric, alias warp drive, developed by the Sino-Russians. So, it makes sense to look into the possible design. Moreover, we will administrate the resources of the Moon, which could turn out to be a perfect spot to build spaceships efficiently."

Hira Dorjee-Sherpa smiled and said: "You should you have become a CEO, rather than an international public servant. You seem skilled."

Ralf felt slightly embarrassed: "Except that I am more interested in the return of investment for mankind as a whole than for a handful of shareholders."

The secretary general closed her eyes, and finally said: "When WARSEC officially takes over UNOOSA, we will need a director. It's a more senior position than being just the director of UNOOSA. WARSEC will become much more than a coordination bureau."

Ralf wondered if he was to be moved to another department. Either he would remain as an advisor to the new appointed WARSEC director, or perhaps he would get a position as a political advisor in New York instead. He was fine with any of these alternatives, as long as he did not have to be the new WARSEC director himself.

But Hira went on:

"To make it work, it will require someone with both leadership and management skills, but also with a keen sense for diplomacy. I have already proposed your name to the Fourth Committee."

Ralf was taken aback. "Me? But Hira, I haven't even applied for the job. I could stay for a year, but sincerely, I am more interested in working as a political advisor in New York… I'm a diplomat, from the beginning, not a manager."

Hira Dorjee-Sherpa smiled. "Ralf, I know you are a diplomat. You were the UN mediator in Cyprus enabling the reunification of the island. When was it?"

"6-7 years ago. 2088 to 2089."

"Time flies by… But, after that, you applied for the Vienna office, didn't you?"

"I did, because my ex-girlfriend wanted me to stay in Europe. We are separated now. And if I could choose between Vienna and New York, I would prefer New York."

"First of all, no one knows where the new head office of WARSEC will be. We know for sure that the Austrians would like to kick some UN organizations out of Vienna. They accuse us of jacking up the housing costs for Viennese people. Second of all, every country trusts you. You cannot just leave now. Can I count on you?"

Did he really have a choice, when the SG was asking so insistently? Anyway, it was only for five years, and the first five years at WARSEC should be manageable.

As he left Hira's office on the 38th floor of the UN building, he noted that a member of the secretariat was reading *The Chained Palmiped*. The headline was: '*Republicans in favor of WAR…SEC*'.

17: UNOOSA BECOMES WARSEC (MAR 2095)

On that Tuesday morning of early March 2095, Ralf was late to the office. For some reasons, he had not woken up when the alarm went off. He jogged the few hundred meters from the *Kaisermühlen* subway station to the Vienna office and found himself quite satisfied with his present shape. He was only panting slightly when he came through the gates of the Vienna International Centre.

At the reception desk, a young man notified him that Tatjana Aydemir, the production director of the European Space Agency had just arrived. Since she was to attend the meeting chaired by Glover Johnson, perhaps Ralf could take her up there.

Ralf led her to the elevator. Tatjana was a short, dark-haired lady with blue eyes. She wore jeans and a polo with the ESA insignia on. That was a good sign, Ralf thought. Her clothes were saying: "*I am so good at what I do that I don't have to impress anybody by wearing a fancy suit.*"

Glover had booked the Alpha Centauri conference room. Ralf and the ESA director were last to arrive.

As they entered the room, Ralf introduced Tatjana Aydemir to the rest of the attendants. Glover shook her hand and introduced the rest of the team.

Around the conference table were Dr. Alice Fù and Dr. Anatoli Govorov, who had flown the *Alcubierre* during the first warp-test. Also there were the two Doctors who had contributed to the optimization of the warp field: Dr. Valeriya Limonov, a short but stout Russian lady in her mid-twenties with brown hair, and Dr. Mikko Andersson, a brown-haired Swede with Asian-shaped grey eyes, giving away his Sami origins, also in his mid-twenties.

All wore polo shirts with the UNOOSA insignia. Ralf and Glover were the only attendants wearing suits and ties.

Ralf started the meeting:

"As you know, the ratification of the Vienna treaties is going well. China, Russia, the USA, the West Asian Union and the South Asian Union have all ratified the treaties, including their respective member states. Basically, when the European Union has ratified them, WARSEC will become effective and take over from UNOOSA. This should happen before June."

He went on: "Now, WARSEC will have not only to lead the first wave of interstellar exploration but also to manage the outer space resources exploited by mankind. The closest celestial body to exploit is the Moon. In order to embark on interstellar journeys, we need spaceships with warp capabilities. Yet we will have a limited budget. I would like you, therefore, to study the possibility of designing a warp spaceship that could be manufactured on the Moon using mostly the resources available there."

Anatoli looked puzzled: "Is the *Alcubierre* not good enough?"

Glover Johnson decided to answer the question: "The *Alcubierre* does not have a big enough cargo bay, and hydrogen propulsion for conventional maneuvers is not optimal."

The ex-US Navy admiral started a slide presentation, using the touchpad on the table, and went on: "What we want is safety and efficiency. First, we need to set warp communication devices. If a spaceship travels at warp 10 to Alpha Centauri, the closest star to the Sun, it will still take 160 days for the crew to get there. But if something goes wrong over there, it will take four years and a half for us to receive an SOS message. This is not acceptable."

"That's a good point," Ralf said. "What do you suggest?"

Glover looked at the UNOOSA director. "When the Chinese Space Agency and Roscomos first tested the warp drive, they did it with a so-named 'warpedo.'"

"Yes," Alice jumped in. "First in the Black Sea, and then in orbit, before the decision was made to build the *Alcubierre*. But the warpedo was lost."

"Well," Glover said. "We need Warpedo devices that don't get lost and can warp at least 50 times the speed of light to carry messages. That way, it would take only 31 days for a message to reach Earth from Alpha Centauri. This is more acceptable."

"The warpedo we built would only go at warp five," Anatoli said.

"Warp 50 is possible," Valeriya assured. "The thinner the better, when it comes to warping. Two meters in diameter, and with the proper green matter oscillation, and it should be feasible."

"Yes," Mikko confirmed. "We just have to skip conventional propulsion: no hydrogen and oxygen tanks, then it is fine. An EM-drive would be good enough for the docking maneuver."

The Electromagnetic-Drive developed by the Americans used electromagnetic waves to propel itself in space, thus only requiring electric power generated by the compact fusion reactors. No room was wasted for oxygen and hydrogen tanks.

"Are we getting the EM-drive technology from NASA?" Mikko added.

Ralf smiled: "Yes, that's the purpose of the Vienna treaties."

Having covered the first topic, they moved to the next one: Designing warp ships for interstellar exploration. Glover tapped on the touch screen to show the next slide, and explained:

"We need warp ships that are cheap to manufacture and,

ideally, can be built on the Moon, rather than in Earth orbit. These spaceships will need to have decent cargo space, for at least 4 communication warpedoes, two SX-White Parrots or one AF5 Dachshund S, not to mention a great many navigation and observation satellites. There should be room for up to a hundred passengers."

"Well you want something big, Glover," Alice said.

AF5 Dachshund S were smaller aerospace shuttles, developed by Airbus Space and currently used by the ESA. They were able to transport maximum six passenger and crew into orbit and were almost 30 m (98 ft) long.

Alice made a quick calculation: "Even if you disassemble the wings, a Dachshund is still 30 by 4 by 4 meters. That's 480 cubic meters [ca 17,000 cubic ft]. And what about White Parrots? They are shorter, but bulkier, and can't be disassembled."

SX-White Parrots were space-only double decker vehicles developed in emergency by NASA to help with the construction of the orbital station. They were 15 m (49 ft) long, 5 m (16.5 ft) wide and 4 m (13 ft) tall. They were brought in to orbit using space elevators and were now mostly used to shuttle astronauts between the orbital station and the two space elevators. They could have up to twenty passengers onboard.

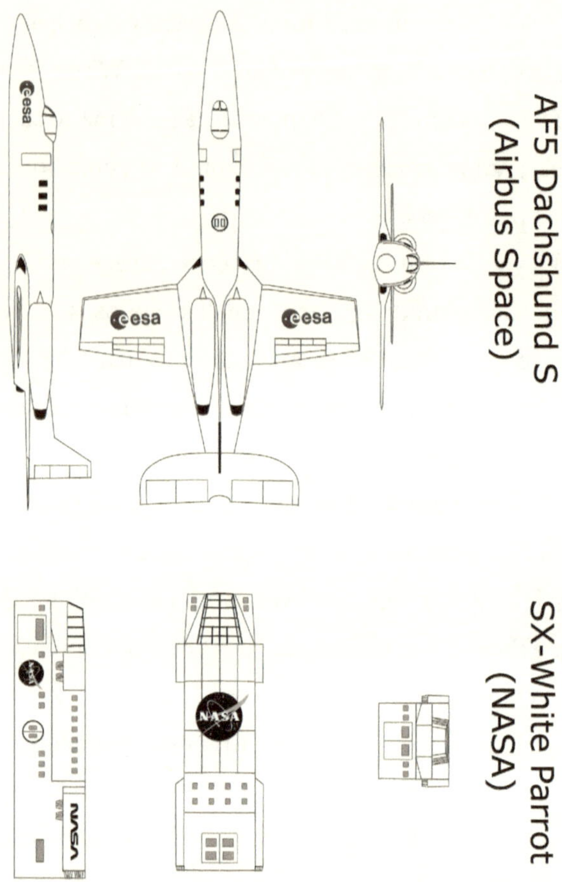

Figure 7: drawing of the AF5 Dachshund S (Airbus Space) and the SX White Parrot (NASA), which will be required to fit in the cargo bay of the Forward-class ship to be designed. The AF5 Dachshund S has the insignia of the European Space Agency (ESA).

"This will be a challenge," Glover admitted. "However, I would like you to all work with Tatjana here from the ESA and think not only about the design to meet the requirements, but also how it could be built on the Moon, using mostly materials that can be extracted there."

The four scientific doctors all looked at Tatjana.

She thought a while and said: "That should be manageable. After all, all the national space agencies are currently working on expanding the recent lunar base. It's all about partnering with them. What should this class of warp ship be called?"

"I was thinking of calling it the 'Forward'-class," Glover replied. "Like the polar ship in *Captain Hatteras*, the book by Jules Verne. Interstellar explorers will be a lot like polar explorers, confined several years in their vessels, with no way of communicating in real time to the rest of human civilization."

There were some whispers in the room, but Ralf brought their attention back by pointing at the projection canvas screen: "I would like to come back to the intention of trying to make it possible to manufacture the Forward-class ships on the Moon. It is not only in order to avail ourselves of free materials. The other reason is that the regulations from the International Labor Organization do not apply on the Moon. Manufacturing there could be done by as many robots as possible, without WARSEC having to pay any tax on robot labor."

Since a treaty in 2048, robot labor on Earth had been strictly regulated. Companies using too high a ratio of robot labor had to pay a tax, whose minimal rate had been decided by the International Labor Organization.

"All the private space corporations will be jealous," Tatjana noted.

"True," Ralf admitted. "However, we plan on involving them as well. Currently, I am in negotiations with national Space agencies and private corporations, like Boeing, Comac and V-Space, to set up a joint venture on the Moon. The goal of this WARSEC Ventures will be to manufacture aerospace shuttles cheaply and sell them or lease them to airline companies. We want to encourage space travel and space sightseeing."

Valeriya looked surprised: "You mean that any reasonably wealthy tourist will be able to go to the Moon in five years?"

Ralf nodded: "Hopefully, to the orbital station in four years, to the Moon in seven, and Mars in ten. And that's mostly for our own sake."

The four doctors and Tatjana cast wondering glances at one another and Ralf decided to expand a bit more: "At best, the contribution of all the member states to WARSEC budget will amount to a half of an ESA budget."

"And an ESA budget is peanuts," Tatjana added. "It is a quarter of the NASA budget."

"Of course, our goal won't be to replace the space agencies, which spend a lot on research," Ralf admitted. "Our *raison d'être* will be much more practical. But still the public funded budget will not take us on an interstellar mission. We must, therefore, be more creative in finding sources of income; selling aerospace shuttles to airline companies and encouraging private space activities, for example. We can, after all, levy a tax on commercial space activities, so successful space corporations are good for us."

Anatoli looked impressed. "It sounds like a real business idea. I like this."

The little task force from UNOOSA thus set out in their efforts to design a new class of exploration ships that could be cheaply produced. Ralf was in the meantime in contact with the New York UN office about the development of new recruiting procedures for when WARSEC would be launched.

There was also the question of the migration of their information service, and Ralf was more and more feeling he had become the director of a real agency rather than of a diplomatic bureau.

In the middle of March, Ralf had an appointment with a Marketing Bureau in downtown Vienna. He was introduced to a little room and sat down with two young ladies, both wearing thick-framed glasses.

"Good afternoon, Ralf," said one of the ladies. "Are you excited to see our proposition for the logo and flag of WARSEC?"

"Excited is perhaps not the word," Ralf replied, "But let's say I'm curious."

"Ingrid, please show Ralf."

The youngest of the ladies brought forth a set of A3 sheets of paper. He was totally surprised.

"You are kidding?" Ralf exclaimed. "You cannot copy the flag of the United Federation of Planets!"

"The United Federation of Planets?" said Ingrid sheepishly. "I don't know what that is. I didn't plagiarize anything."

"The United Federation of Planets, like in *Star Trek*," Ralf explained. "You do know *Star Trek*, don't you?"

"I've heard of it, but I have never seen an episode."

"Well, this is the same flag."

Ingrid, however, had a different opinion: "I do not think so. Look, in the background, you have the UN blue, with on top of it white laurels surrounding a circle divided in two. Here you have the planets of the solar system, and there the Milky Way."

"Please google Flag of the United Federation of Planets, and you will see," said Ralf, irritated.

The older of the two ladies opened her tablet and googled it.

"It's not exactly the same," she said. "Their blue is much darker and is definitely not the UN blue. Besides, they don't have the planets of the solar system, and they don't have the earth as on the regular UN flag."

Ralf was comparing the two flags, the proposed flag of WARSEC on the sheet of paper, and the *Star Trek* flag of the United Federation of Planets.

He eventually said: "You are right, they are different flags. However, I do not want to run the risk of infringing any copyright. Besides, your version is too overloaded. Too many stars and celestial bodies. It will not look well if we print it on shoulder patches. Please do a new version. Keep the UN globe, the sun and only a few planets of the solar system. Decrease the number of stars to a minimum."

Later that evening, Ralf received by email five new propositions from the marketing agency. He had a quick conference call with Glover, who had already gone home for the day. The agreed to pick the agency's fourth proposition as their first choice. They would submit it to the UN Fourth Committee.

Figure 8: the WARSEC flag proposition chosen by Ralf Åhman and Glover Johnson, in white on a UN-blue background.

On Thursday 24 March in the evening, the UN secretary general Hira Dorjee-Sherpa called Ralf Åhman. With the ratification by the European Union and South Africa, the Vienna treaties had become effective. Ralf was expected before the Fourth Committee in New York the next Monday. First, they would validate Hira's choice of appointing Ralf as the new WARSEC director. Then, they would have to agree on the location of the new headquarters of the agency.

18: VODKA DIPLOMACY (MAR 2095)

It was early afternoon when Ralf Åhman arrived in New York on Sunday 27 March, and he went directly to the hotel. After taking a power nap to overcome his jetlag he met with Sanne for dinner in the Radisson's restaurant.

Sanne complimented him on his shape. He had now lost 20 kilos (44 lbs) in twenty-one weeks and had stopped his diet. He had donated his over-sized suits to the Red Cross. It was a mental incentive not to grow fat ever again.

Sanne started to like New York. Even though the city felt a bit too dark for her liking, due to the shadows cast by the tall skyscrapers, she had been impressed by the huge dyke systems and the giant sluices that the New Yorker had built to protect the city from the rising sea level, which had already increased by five meters since the beginning of the century.

Besides, New Yorkers were the right kind of people for her initiation to large societies. They were welcoming, tolerant and socializing, while respecting one's needs to be cold and distant at the same time. It was a perfect compromise for her and she now felt more at ease in larger groups of people.

At Colombia University, she had been forced to give presentations to other students. The first time had been terrible and she had almost peed herself, but through adequate coaching, she could now make eye contact with members of the audience as a way of gaining reassurance. In summary, she was progressively, centimeter by centimeter, becoming a normal being.

Ralf mentioned that he would be formally appointed as the director of the new WARSEC.

"What about the new WARSEC headquarters?" Sanne asked as they were served some panna cotta for dessert. "Any clue where it will be?"

"Sincerely, Sanne, not the foggiest idea," Ralf answered. "Quite messy at the moment. Nobody seems to agree. We will go through it in the coming sessions of the Fourth committee. It will probably make me feel like being in a lunatic asylum."

Sanne took a piece of panna cotta with her spoon, hesitated one moment and said: "Do you remember Thierry Diakité? The PhD student from Kigali who designed the Martian robots to build the rocket?"

"Yes, have you been in contact with him?" Ralf replied, his mouth full.

"Yes, through some social network. He currently works

at V-Space, in Burkina. Apparently, he does not like working there. If you need a good robotics engineer, you may want to contact him. He is also friends with Tintin Mutombo, the co-author of Anatoli's article on the unified gravity theory."

"Good that you mention them," Ralf said as he grabbed for his glass of water. "I need to start some talks with V-space about future cooperation. I will see if I can arrange a meeting in Bobo-Dioulasso. It could also be an opportunity to meet Thierry and Tintin."

"Could I join you for the trip? I may be able to pay for the journey with the money I've got left."

Ralf drank water from his glass and put it back. "Don't you have classes?"

"I have the defense of my Bachelor thesis next Wednesday. And then this is the spring break, and I will be available."

"Your Bachelor thesis was about space economy? I will try to come to your defense."

The next morning, Ralf was formally appointed director of WARSEC. It happened in the large aula that served as the Fourth Committee's room. It took one minute after Hira Dorjee-Sherpa had officially asked the question. With electronic voting, everything went so fast.

On a PowerPoint projected on a large canvas screen, he showed the proposition for WARSEC flag to the Fourth Committee. Two minutes later, the Committee had approved the new flag.

"I have also been in contact with several philanthropic organizations," Ralf said. "Among them, the Gates and Carnegie foundations. You see the list on that slide. They are willing to donate a significant sum of money to WARSEC for the construction of the headquarters. That's perhaps only 10% of a NASA budget, but enough to get us a long way. Do you agree with WARSEC receiving these private donations to build the headquarters?"

There was some chit-chat but, five minutes later, the vote went through. Ralf's morale was quite boosted. In fifteen minutes, three of the four main discussion topics had been resolved.

"Now," Ralf said, "the last remaining topic is the choice of the location of the new WARSEC headquarters. The only request from us is to have it as close as possible to an airport. We have the funding to build it. Austria has already made a formal request *not to* have WARSEC in Vienna. They claim they already have enough oversized international organizations in their city. The first proposition we got was from the South Asian Union."

The new representative of the South Asian Union (SAU), who had taken over after Hira, after the latter had been nominated secretary general, was suggesting having the head office in Kashmir. Kashmir was the symbol of the peace between India and Pakistan, the two main member states of the SAU. They now had shared sovereignty. The whole province was technically a half autonomous condominium belonging to both Indian and Pakistan. Every second week, the Indian governor would let his Pakistani counterpart take over and vice versa. A journalist of *The Washington Post* had coined the term of 'quantum geopolitics' to describe these arrangements where a territory was simultaneously in two different States. Likewise, Taiwan was both independent and attached to China. European geopolitical students had enormous trouble understanding this idea. Asian students seemed to have less trouble.

After the SAU representative had done his exposé, the other representatives fully acknowledged the peace signal it would give to the world to have the new headquarters in Kashmir. However, they seemed to question the very idea of building a new head office in a zone so vulnerable to earthquakes.

"My dear representative of the SAU," the Chinese representative said, "I fully understand the symbol of Kashmir for the South Asian Union. However, as a Chinese person, I would like to remind you that the Indian subcontinent is, geologically and tectonically speaking, *taking* us from behind. This is not your fault, and I don't blame you, but the result is an irritatingly high number of earthquakes."

There were some laughs, after which the Chinese offered a location close to Shanghai.

"Silly," the Indian representative replied. "Shanghai is too expensive; the agreed donations would not even suffice for a couple of chairs. Besides, this location is vulnerable to Tsunamis and typhoons."

Instead, the American and Canadian representatives proposed a location at the Americano-Canadian border, between Seattle and Vancouver.

"Outrageous," the Chinese representative replied. "You want to set the WARSEC headquarters basically on the headquarters of Boeing. You want to favor an American company."

"Please," Ralf tried. "Currently, WARSEC means to involve all private aerospace corporations. We are having talks to start a joint venture, and there is no question of discriminating any players."

This did not help. When the Europeans suggested Toulouse, in France, to be the new headquarters, they were accused of wanting to favor Airbus.

"We want to propose Macapa," the Brazilian delegate said. "It's very close to the joint NASA ESA space elevator in European Guyana. It is located by the water. Real estate does not cost much there. It will be the cheapest and best proposal you will ever get."

Ralf tended to agree. But both the Chinese and South Asian delegates burst into anger.

"Do you know how far it is from China?"

"And from the South Asian Union?"

"We, China and the South Asian Union, will stand for most of the cost. We cannot accept that it is located so far from us,"

The Chinese delegate summarized.

"Not to mention the risk of tropical storms," the US delegate said.

"What about the gold panners making inroads into European Guyana?" The French delegate said. "As long as Brazil does not improve the situation, you should not get any benefit from the UN."

Ralf decided it was high time for a lunch break. When the committee gathered again in the afternoon, no progress was made on that front. The UN member states would simply not agree on the location of the new WARSEC headquarters.

That evening, Ralf decided to take shelter in the little UNOOSA office on the thirty-fifth floor, the one that had *Star Trek* and *Star Wars* posters together with pictures of famous statesmen and diplomats.

The office was messy, a sign that the interns using it were brilliant minds. Brilliant minds are seldom tidy. He sat down on the couch and closed his eyes. The day had been exhausting.

"There you are. Look what I got. A bottle of *Koskenkorva.* You know how hard it is to find one in the States?"

It was Esko Punainen, the representative of the European Union. This time he was talking English rather than Finnish. The tall, overweight Finnish diplomat closed the door behind him.

Ralf looked at him and sighed. "You are really not afraid of getting fired, Esko."

"I'm already fired. My position here ends in July, and President Bonavita, our dear European president, has appointed me EU ambassador in Kirghizstan."

With a hand gesture, Ralf invited Esko to sit on the couch beside him. "What are you complaining about? There is more snow there than in Finland. You like cross-country skiing. You will enjoy it."

Esko sat down and put the vodka bottle on the side table. He looked at the new WARSEC director. "You don't follow geopolitics anymore, do you, Ralf? You only keep your head in the stars, nowadays. You, who arranged the reunification of Cyprus. They were close to giving you a Nobel Peace Prize."

Ralf looked down at Esko's shoes. His were more polished and shining than his own. He sighed and said: "They had to give it to the Greek and Turkish leaders of the Island. Not to the UN middleman."

Suddenly, Esko laughed. "I've heard other rumors according to which you shouted somewhere 'The Norwegian bitches!', and that indisposed the Norwegian parliament."

"Bullshit," Ralf retorted. "My ex-partner is Norwegian. Why would I insult a Norwegian?"

"I won't insist. Anyhow, there are tensions in Kirghizstan between Kirghiz and Uzbeks. A new transition government is trying to ease them, but it could go nasty anytime."

Ralf glanced at the vodka bottle on the side table. "That's

why you have the bottle of *Koskenkorva*?"

Esko smiled. "When things don't go your way, my advice is always: 'drink'!"

Ralf could not help laughing. "Esko, you are so Finnish."

"*Kiitos,* so are you," the Finnish diplomat replied ('Thanks').

Ralf grabbed the bottle from the side table, unscrewed the cork and took a slug directly from it. "God, that's good," he said. "*Koskenkorva* is definitively the best vodka in the world."

"I enjoy seeing you in this mess, Ralf," said Esko grabbing the bottle from Ralf's hand. "A bunch of 235 angry representatives unable to agree on something so trivial."

"Not so trivial," Ralf corrected. "Everybody wants their share."

Esko took a big glug from the vodka bottle and said: "Do you know what we should suggest? A shithole in Finland; that would be funny."

Ralf laughed. "What would you pick? Jyväskylä? That's where I was born."

Esko shook his head. "That wouldn't be credible. It is a true shit hole. We need a shit hole, but not that shitty a shit hole."

"Helsinki?" Ralf suggested.

"No, it's too conventional. Too easy to access. Too neutral, too peaceful. Too many peace conferences have taken place in Helsinki. We would need a city more challenging."

"Turku?"

"Turku is not bad." Esko admitted. "But I would recommend

Vaasa."

"Vaasa!" Ralf Exclaimed. "But there is nothing there!"

"Precisely. It's cheap to build," Esko continued. "It has already been five years since the tunnel between Vaasa and Umeå opened. Yet the development of northern Sweden and Finland is not taking off as quickly as expected. There are probably some municipalities and county councils that would grant generous subsidies for the UN to build there."

"You are right," Ralf admitted. "And Finland is easy to access from Russia, China, and Japan, the most important countries to convince…"

"The only nations that would not benefit from it, geographically speaking, are in South America and Oceania."

"Yes, but they are used to being far from everything, so it's not a big deal," Ralf said.

"Moreover, there are no earthquakes or tropical storms in Finland," Esko added.

They were now both laughing and breathing vodka like regular drunk Finns. Suddenly, Ralf became serious. "Esko, sincerely, it could work. It could be a good proposal. You should try it."

"You mean I should stop drinking, and draft a proposal?" Esko asked.

"You can draft it tomorrow morning. Just don't drink too much, so that you don't have a black-out. You may forget all we've just said."

"Don't worry, my brain works better with some alcohol in it."

"No wonder the EU president is sending you to Kirghizstan," Ralf said.

The next morning, the Vaasa proposition was initially welcomed with laughter. However, in the afternoon, more and more representatives seemed to show a genuine interest in it.

The choice for Vaasa as the new Head office of WARSEC was finally approved by the Fourth Committee the following day in the early afternoon. As soon as the vote was over, Ralf rushed out of the room, left the UN building, and took a taxi to Columbia University.

He took some time finding the room where Sanne had her defense but he arrived only two minutes late. The content of her bachelor's thesis impressed him, and he was already thinking how it could be put into practice for the hypothetic colonization of a planet in a remote system.

At the end of the defense, Ralf congratulated Sanne. If she wanted to work for WARSEC after her master's in Cambridge, he would arrange it. She was genuinely interested.

Ralf also mentioned he had booked a meeting with V-Space in Burkina Faso on Wednesday 20 April, just before the Easter weekend. He had to go to Vienna before that, but they could coordinate to arrive in Ouagadougou at about the same time. However, it was important that Sanne should get vaccinated against malaria and yellow fever as soon as possible.

19: COMPETITION VERSUS COOPERATION (APRIL 2095)

When she first got off the plane at Ouagadougou, Sanne thought that she would choke to death. She had a short moment of panic: where was her spacesuit? Why was the oxygen turned off? Was she back on the red planet? The earth on the ground was indeed red.

She nearly collapsed, but a passenger held her up and said:

"Welcome to Ouga in April. It's only 49 degrees. Celsius, not Fahrenheit." (49° C = 120° F)

After some time, Sanne managed to breathe normally, but she realized she was drenched in sweat after only one minute outside the aircraft. Was it possible?

Inside the terminal, she found a bar which was air-conditioned and in which the temperature was only 31 degrees (88° F). She sat there and ordered water bottle after water bottle.

It was Tuesday 19 April. She had taken a direct flight from

New York. Since V-Space had expanded their activities in Burkina Faso, airline traffic between the two cities had greatly improved.

Ralf arrived on the mid-afternoon flight from Paris. He wore a straw hat and a very light shirt, and trousers. His face was also covered with sweat.

"Burkinabe say that Burkina in April is hotter than hell," he commented. "This is certainly true. Let's go to the train station. I've heard there is a good AC in the high-speed train to Bobo-Dioulasso."

The temperature was indeed much cooler in the high-speed train. Sanne enjoyed the scenery through the window. The red earth contrasted with the dark green of the trees. At the end of the afternoon, the night fell suddenly, and it was pitch black when they arrived in Burkina Faso's second largest city.

In Bobo-Dioulasso, they checked in at the Astronaut, the new hotel built in town. Because of power shortage, the AC, however, was not working. They were told it was because V-Space premises outside the city were being given priority for power supply. As a result, it was an inferno in the rooms. Ralf decided to spend the evening in the swimming pool. He was a very good swimmer. As he was swimming back and forth, he realized that Sanne was just standing in the pool.

"Not interested in swimming?" Ralf asked.

"I can't swim," Sanne said, a little ashamed. "Not many

swimming pools on Mars"

Ralf realized he had made her feel awkward, but Sanne was mostly worried about the heat:

"It's really hell, here. How can anybody sleep in these rooms?"

Ralf advised her to sleep on her balcony, putting her duvet on the floor and wrapping herself in a mosquito net. He informed her he would go to the V-Space premises early the next morning. He should be back early in the afternoon. They would meet Tintin and Thierry in the evening.

Ralf slept particularly badly that night. It was damn hot. And when at last the air temperature had cooled enough, he was awoken by the call of the nearest Muezzin for the morning prayer ("*Allah wa akbar*"). A moment later, some loudspeakers were broadcasting the "Jesus-loves-you" kind of songs, after which, the Catholic churches started ringing their bells.

Though he was exhausted, Ralf didn't even try to go back to sleep. He got up, took a shower, applied a lot of deodorant, then put on his cream trousers and a light white T-shirt. In his briefcase, he packed a second shirt and a cream suit jacket. After a short taxi ride, he was at the premises of V-space. He headed for the lobby and used the bathroom to change into his suit. He did not put on his tie, as Vahlroos did not like ties. A moment later, he was sitting on the sofas by the reception, working with his laptop. The AC in the V-Space building was really enjoyable.

At 9:30, he finally went to the reception and introduced himself. He was given a visitor badge and led to a large conference room where they offered him different kinds of coffee. He accepted a double expresso.

"Good morning, Ralf," Michael Vahlroos said cheerfully coming into the room. He was wearing a navy-blue suit and light grey shirt, but no tie. "You don't mind me calling you Ralf? You may call me Mike."

Swedes had been on a first name basis with each other for a century and a half. So, no, he didn't mind. He was introduced to Sophie Couillard, a tall, athletic blond woman who was the general manager of V-Space. She was wearing a light blue skirt-suit.

At the conference table, Ralf was invited to sit opposite them. Michael commenced the meeting by congratulating Ralf for his new position as the director of WARSEC.

Ralf politely thanked him and announced his intentions straight away: "I will be straightforward. I'm here to discuss hypothetic future cooperation between WARSEC and V-Space."

"We are listening, Ralf," Michael said.

"You have received my proposal concerning WARSEC Ventures," Ralf went on. "Our first objective is to encourage private space travel within the solar system."

Michael seemed not to be surprised, and acquiesced: "Of

course. You do not have enough public funded resources to even consider launching an interstellar exploration. I have done the math. But you can levy a tax on any profit-driven activity in space. In order to launch your first interstellar expedition, you must first ensure you have enough thriving space corporations around the Earth."

Ralf was relieved to see that they had understood his intention. He went on: "We are planning to expand the orbital station, to let hotels and other businesses benefit from it. To that end, we need to make space travel affordable. We need to mass produce aerospace shuttles."

Sophie looked perplexed: "Do you want us to increase the production of the Albaspace?"

"Not exactly," Ralf replied. "We would like to start a joint venture with other aerospace companies. Airbus and Boeing have already expressed their interest. The goal would be to mass-produce cheap aerospace shuttles on the Moon using the materials available there."

"And the fact that robot labor is not taxed up there," Michael added.

"This, also," Ralf admitted.

"You are planning to do some kind of social dumping to mass-produce aerospace shuttles that will compete with my Albaspace," Michael pointed out. "Aren't you afraid of this leaking to *The Chained Palmiped*?"

"Your Albaspace will remain the best in the class for a while.

Currently, we are planning to resuscitate two cancelled projects. The failed A980 from Airbus, now nicknamed Space Bear, and the cancelled Boeing 637, which we will call Space Hound."

"They were both cancelled after the success of the Albaspace," Sophie noted.

Ralf took a deep breath. He had to be more diplomatic. "The goal is not to compete with you in your top-notch segment. But we must make it more affordable for people to get to space. You can be part of WARSEC Ventures, help with the manufacturing, and take parts of the profit home."

"What about the manufacturing of warp ships?" Michael asked.

"We also plan to do this with WARSEC Ventures," Ralf replied. "We are currently designing a new class of exploration ships that could be cheaply assembled on the Moon. You will also be part of that."

"Why would I want to share all of our expertise with you?" Michael wondered.

"Because we would all benefit from it," Ralf tried. "Mankind would benefit from it."

To Ralf's surprise, Michael rose to his feet and eyed him scornfully: "You say you want cooperation. In fact, all you offer is competition to my business. Some cheap aerospace shuttles to compete with my Albaspace. Some cheap warp ships to compete with my V-liner. You are pretending to be a business-minded player, while you are in fact both playing and making the rules. Do you have no decency?"

"I am treating all private corporations alike," Ralf defended himself. "I believe I do not make any discrimination."

"The way I relate to people is easy," Michael said. "Either you are a business partner or a competitor. I believe you are a competitor. Do not expect my help for your business venture. And make no mistake, I will beat you."

Ralf took a deep breath and remained courteous. "Fine. At least I tried to convince you. What a pity, however, that you are the only aerospace corporation not wanting to join. Boeing, Airbus, Comac, Bombardier: they will all be part of the venture."

Michael had a self-satisfied smirk on his face: "Not all our competitors are as smart as we are. Otherwise we would not be market leaders in the aerospace shuttle segment."

Ralf decided to move to his next topic: "What about the extension of the orbital station? We need a business partner. You would also benefit from that. It will also boost the sales of your Albaspace."

Michael sat back and said: "For this, we may have an agreement. I am planning to found Vahlroos Travel for increased sightseeing in space. Vahlroos Travel will have an interest investing in the orbital station."

"Happy to see that we have a few agreements despite everything," Ralf said.

"Please do not take it the wrong way," Michael replied,

"But I still believe you are only trying to artificially create a regulatory hell which can only compromise the very divine nature of destiny."

Ralf was not sure he had understood.

Michael indicated his general manager and said: "Sophie here will also show you the manufacturing line of the Albaspace. Perhaps, WARSEC may want to acquire one or two. Both the US and EU presidents have chosen it as their personal plane. Should the UN secretary general decide to acquire a private jet, the Albaspace is definitely the best choice."

During the tour, Ralf was secretly impressed by the manufacturing lines of the Albaspace, but he tried to conceal it.

"Sophie," Ralf asked the general manager, while they were in the sections where the curved wings of the aerospace shuttles were assembled to the fuselage. "Why can't Michael even contemplate the idea of cooperating with WARSEC Ventures? It would increase his profit anyway… Is it ideological?"

"He has grown up all his life being told that big government equals evil. You are like big government. You are almost communist for him…"

"And for you?"

"I'm Canadian… I'm a bit more tolerant of public initiatives."

Ralf had his eyes fixed on the Albaspace standing behind Sophie Couillard. From the front, the canard wings looked like a moustache and the cockpit windows like slightly closed eyes.

The plane really looked like an evil cat.

"Don't you think the Albaspace looks like a grumpy cat, from the front?" Ralf said, changing the subject.

"I had never thought about it," Sophie said.

Albaspace (V-Space)

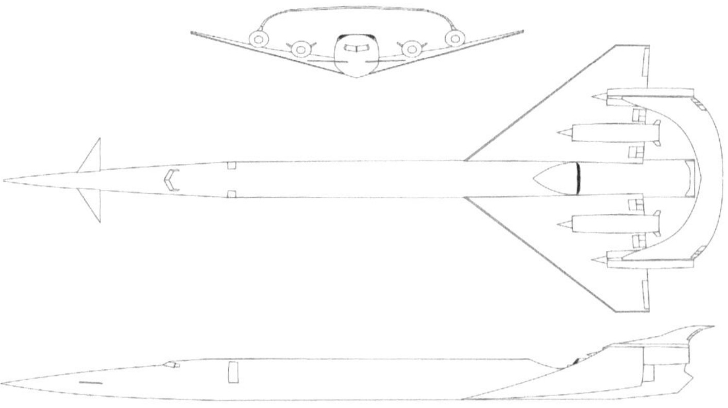

Figure 9: The Albaspace developed by V-Space has no windows, but the cabin is equipped with a multitude of screens. It is equipped with four CUBIC-R engines on the wings and one scramjet, at the rear of the fuselage. The US president has picked it as her Air Force One, and the EU president as her EU Flight One.

An hour later, Ralf was back at the hotel. He saw that Sanne was in the swimming pool. She had set her old Martian laptop by the side of the pool and was learning how to swim by doing exercises as shown in demonstration videos.

Ralf went to his room, stripped his clothes off and sat down in just his underpants with his computer on the balcony of his room, under the sunshade.

At the beginning of the afternoon, he got a phone call from the hotel reception: Sanne was feeling quite sick. Ralf went to her room to check on her. She had thrown up a few times already and had a bad headache.

"Well, that's sunstroke," Ralf said. "Next time, it would be good to wear a cap, even if you are in the water. Damn it, you are quite red. You forgot the sun cream."

"I thought the sun would only be strong around midday," Sanne answered sheepishly.

"The sun is always strong, here. I also see that the mosquitoes have not missed your face either. The best is just for you to rest before we go out tonight."

Later that evening, at around eight o'clock, Ralf and Sanne took a taxi to the Sankara. At the bar, they asked for Tintin and Thierry, and they were led to a table in the back-yard. Ralf recognized the tall Tintin immediately from the pictures Anatoli had shown him. He introduced himself and Sanne. They decided to drop the titles and not call themselves 'Dr.'"

Sanne told Thierry how she was grateful to him for developing the Martian robots that enabled her to be brought to Earth, to which Thierry modestly mentioned that it was in fact Tintin who had done most of the work: Thierry's robots had only taken her into the Martian orbit, while Tintin had been one of the designers of the *Alcubierre* which had brought her all the way to Earth.

They ordered cold *Sobebra* beers and some salads. It was so hot that it was impossible to be tempted by any other kind of food.

When Sanne asked Tintin and Thierry how they enjoyed working for V-Space, they both looked at each other and burst out laughing.

"We hate it," Tintin said finally when he had recovered himself.

"They have good finance, good people, but they want to pursue a stupid project," Thierry added.

Ralf wanted to hear more. Tintin explained:

"They want to build a warp-drive equipped spaceship with atmosphere entry capability, but they want it to be too ambitious, technically infeasible, and for the wrong market."

"Why is that?" Ralf wondered.

Thierry took a few sips of his beer and said: "They want to have a spaceship big enough to pursue extraterrestrial mining activities, which we don't think will be an interesting market before at least twenty years, or even thirty years' time."

"I agree with you," Ralf said. "But why is their spaceship technically infeasible?"

Thierry took forth his smartphone and showed the two demonstration videos of the so-called majority and minority projects. Both rocket scientists emphasized the high risk of a vertical entry into the atmosphere for the V-Liner. Meanwhile, the smaller V-Craft was unable to embark on an extraterrestrial mining expedition, but light enough to take off and land like an airplane. While a vertical entry in the atmosphere would be very risky, a low angle entry would be fully manageable. However, their V-Craft would be so small that it could only be used to transport passengers in near-orbit or even to Mars, hence it had been kept as a 'minority project' only.

"How long before their V-liner is ready?" Ralf asked. He was curious about Michael Vahlroos's possible next moves.

"At least five years," Thierry answered. "But even if it makes it into orbit, it will crash on the first landing attempt."

"With ten compact fusion reactors onboard?" Sanne asked.

"Yes, but they are developing a new kind of reactor to be certified by the FAA," Thierry said. "Crashproof, or so they say."

Ralf considered the two rocket scientists for a short moment. They were quite brilliant. He turned to the theoretical physicist:

"If you could decide, and apart from your alternative V-Craft, what project would you pursue, Tintin?"

"Build faster spaceships," Tintin answered without hesitation. "Currently, we can build a spaceship going at warp

10. Ten times the speed of light still means five months to go to Alpha Centauri, the closest star from our sun. By using more energy and making the ship thinner, we could reach warp 50 or perhaps even 70. But there would be no room left for a crew. However, I believe the Alcubierre metric can be redesigned to enable a tenfold efficient warping. That's the project I would rather pursue."

"You mean, it would be possible to have a spaceship reaching its destination at warp 100?" Sanne wondered.

"I'm convinced," Tintin answered "If the warp field could be maintained slightly elliptical rather than perfectly cylindrical, and if it could oscillate the right way, it would be possible to warp ten times faster but requiring only twice as much energy. Though, in practice, it would be hard to build."

Sanne did a quick mental calculation. "That would mean only nine days to Alpha Centauri. That would be something."

Thierry changed the subject: "How was your meeting with Vahlroos? Is V-Space going to cooperate with WARSEC?"

"Sadly, no," Ralf replied. "At least not for our ventures on the Moon. But he showed interest in being a stakeholder in the development of the orbital station. But overall, he does not seem to like us."

"It's not surprising," Thierry commented. "He has always got what he wanted since his father died. The Vienna treaties are certainly the first things ever not to go his way. You are challenging his very conception of the world."

"Not everything has always gone his way," Ralf corrected. "You should not forget that his son was kidnapped and murdered."

"Yes, and yet, he has a very clean conscience," Thierry objected. "Though it was him who refused all negotiation with the kidnappers and instead put a bounty on their head. How couldn't he anticipate their reactions?"

"Kidnappers? I had read they had only caught one," Sanne said.

"The one that will be executed next summer?" Tintin wondered. "I'm not a detective, but I doubt his culpability."

"They just arrested him because he is black," Thierry added. "I'm pretty sure he is innocent. Have you seen all the demonstrations to have him released?"

"I'm afraid he may not be the first or the last innocent person to be executed…" Ralf said in a low voice.

As they were still waiting for their salads to be brought forth, Ralf switched the subject to hiring opportunities at WARSEC.

Currently there was a hiring freeze. Since UNOOSA had become WARSEC, all the hiring procedures were to be processed by the UN recruitment agency. They were setting up a Young Professionals program for graduates under 28 and both Tintin and Thierry were welcome to apply in July. It was a competitive exam and the written test would be in October and the oral tests in December.

Both Tintin and Thierry promised to apply.

20: DAMAGE CONTROL (JUNE 2095)

In his villa in Casablanca, Deng Hoang was restless. Cursed be the Chinese condoms! He should not have used any. That was folly. They should have waited for him to get a new supply of German condoms. There were not many options left to mitigate risks in Morocco.

It had a happened in the middle of April. The Chinese condom they had used had just failed. Getting an emergency contraceptive pill in Morocco was impossible. He had booked a flight to Europe to buy some and come back. They thought it had worked, but obviously not. In the middle of May, Aisha started to have some morning sickness. A pregnancy test confirmed that the worst had happened.

Deng was furious with himself. He should have known better. Aisha's parents had begged him to arrange an abortion. They had told him it was much better than infanticide. This was how they usually solved it in Morocco. Abortion was strictly forbidden in Morocco, but it seemed somehow acceptable to kill unwanted babies after they were born.

The Moroccan government would, of course, deny the very existence of that issue: for what mattered was that there was no proof these babies had been killed because they were unwanted. They could just have died of a natural cause. No autopsies were done. It was only the pro-choice militants who were claiming that the high death rate of babies under a month old was due to the fact that abortion was forbidden. The government dismissed all these claims as nonsense, and as such there was no need to legalize abortion, which was morally wrong anyway. Deng sometimes wished China would invade Morocco and teach these people how to use their brains.

He had to organize an abortion for Aisha. Otherwise she would not be able to finish high school and apply to the police school. But it had to be done in secret: Abortion was illegal and she could face four years of imprisonment, even if she had her abortion abroad.

The border between Algeria and Morocco was closed for reasons he failed to understand. Spain was the closest European country, but Spain was also the only European country where abortions were still illegal. Cursed be these Catholic fanatics!

It took a few days for Deng to find a solution. His logistics manager was a European citizen from Ireland, where the right to an abortion was one of the most extensive in the EU. Deng smiled at that. It had not always been like that in Ireland.

However, when rights were denied too badly and for too long, it would often bring about a brutal change that would have them fully granted.

He had arranged an employment contract for Aisha so that she could travel with the supply chain manager to the Irish affiliate of Wong-Hò. Once in Ireland, she would easily be able to have an abortion. She would be away only the last week of June. Aisha would only tell her teachers at the *Lycée Fatima Mernissi* that she was to take a short onboarding program in Ireland before starting an internship at Wong-Hò, back in Casablanca. They would let her go.

At school, after class, Aisha notified her mathematics teacher she would do a short internship in Ireland.

"I see, you are gonna have an abortion," the teacher said.

"No," Aisha lied. "It's just an internship."

"How did you get it, that internship? I'm not stupid, I teach mathematics. I'm not blind either. But don't worry. Your secret is safe with me."

"I'm not having an abortion," Aisha said insistently. "I'm starting a six-month part-time internship at Wong-Hò. There is a one-week onboarding program in Ireland, that's all."

"It's OK, Aisha. Islam does not forbid abortion. In fact, I would even say that Islam authorizes abortion. You see, all the rules in the Coran related to intercourse have a single purpose: that no child should have to live without knowing its father. If you push the reasoning, it would mean that abortion is legal if there is a risk the child may never know its father. This is mathematics."

Aisha noted suddenly that someone was eavesdropping and asked the teacher to shut up. She failed to see who it was.

Deng tried to reassure her. There was no need to be paranoid. It would go well. Aisha tried to relax by punching and kicking the punchball on his terrace all the harder. She was also practicing knife throwing on a target hanging on his outer wall. She looked like she was in a mood to kill.

Deng remembered Aisha had told him she had been expelled once from her junior high school: she had kicked in the head of the son of a politician who had been stealing her shoes and bullying her friend. Now that Aisha was pregnant, she was displaying more aggression than ever.

Aisha finally left on Saturday 26 June, to Deng's relief. Since it was the first time she would get on a plane, she was quite excited despite the circumstances. That was good, Deng thought. An abortion was not a big deal after all.

On Tuesday 28 June, Deng was having lunch when he received a message from his logistics manager. The abortion had gone well. Aisha did not seem to have been the least morally affected and had compared it to 'having a malign tumor removed'.

Deng felt relieved. Aisha would now come back at the end of the week, and everything would go back to normal.

Except that it did not.

Later that afternoon, Deng received a call from Aisha's mother. Someone had reported her daughter to the police. She was now wanted for having an illegal abortion abroad. That was expressly forbidden by Moroccan law.

Aisha was now facing four years of imprisonment, and most of all would not be allowed to study at university, or, of course, to join the Moroccan police. Her whole life was now ruined.

Deng was once again angry with himself. He had to find a solution. The only way was to help Aisha emigrate abroad. He could perhaps move to China and take her there?

On Thursday, the logistics manager called Deng again: Aisha had vanished.

Deng's first reaction was anger. Why had she run away?

Then, he became worried. She would have to be careful. Europeans could hardly be trusted. A sordid story had just made the headlines. An inspector of the French police had just set free a girl from India who had been detained as a sex slave by a French humanitarian worker in the Paris suburbs. That worker had gone to India, last September, to give assistance in the aftermath of the earthquake that had hit the Bihar province. He had found the teenage girl, whose mom had been accused of witchcraft and burned by an angry mob. He had taken her back to Paris and locked her in his apartment, where he had sexually abused her at will.

Europe was a dangerous place indeed. On the other hand,

Aisha was an intelligent and strong young woman who could fight. But could she really make it, on her own, on a foreign continent? She was only seventeen.

21: THE UNITED KINGDOM OF SOUTH BRITAIN (JULY 2095)

Samir Benyamina hated the trip already. He had left the parental flat in Beaudottes for the commuter train station early in the morning with a duffel bag and a smaller backpack. That had been the best part of the journey. He had not said goodbye to his father, and his father had just ignored his departure. At last, he would live away from Fat Ali. It was gratifying. But the rest of the journey had been less pleasant so far. As it was rush hour, he had to stand all the way in the commuter train from Sevran-Beaudottes to Paris Gare-du-Nord.

At the train station, he had to make his way through a thick flow of rushed Parisian passengers to the departure terminal of the train shuttle to the UK. He finally found his coach (number 6) and his seat (number 66). So far, he was the only one in his *carré* of four opposite seats. It would probably not last long.

It was July 1st, 2095, and the vast majority of young

Europeans of his age was starting their European Service on that day. It seemed that almost all the passengers stepping into the coach were eighteen-year-old *slavants. Slavant* was a contraction of *slave* and *servant* and it was the nickname of the participants in the European Civil Service. The EU officials did not like that denomination, but everybody used it anyway.

In the *carré* on the other side of the aisle was a single young man wearing glasses. He had dark hair, brown eyes, light-framed glasses, and looked a bit lost. Eventually, all the passengers sat down, the doors shut, and the train started. The young man with glasses came over to Samir's *carré*.

"Hi. Name is Jordi. Jordi Puigdemont, from Catalonia. Mind if I sit with you? I am bored over there."

Samir did not mind. He introduced himself as 'Samir from France' and asked Jordi where he was going.

"UK," Jordi replied. "Going to Cambridge. Civil Service. Will be detached to the social services."

Unlike Samir, Jordi spoke English with a perfect East Coast American accent. That was because he was Catalan, Samir thought sarcastically. Catalonia had fought hard to become independent from Spain. It had allegedly been to promote the Catalan language, but in reality, what had mattered most had been to distance themselves from the Spanish language.

In the broader European context, Catalan had quickly turned out to be an unpracticable official language. Though it would have been logical for Catalonia to make Spanish their second official language, the Catalan authorities had refused. They had preferred to give that status to the English language. The Catalan constitution was written in both Catalan and English. The advantage was that all Catalans spoke perfect English and Samir was a bit jealous. Unfortunately for him, he had grown up in France, where movies in English had been dubbed into French until he had turned fifteen. Though he spoke better English than the French presidents of the first quarter of the century, Samir still had a marked accent.

"So where are you going?" Jordi asked.

"I'm also going to Cambridge. I will be detached to the healthcare service."

"What a coincidence," Jordi said.

"It's not," said someone standing beside them. It was a tall and athletic young man with slicked back blond hair.

"Pardon me?" Jordi said.

"It's not a coincidence," the blond man reiterated. "They have algorithms for sitting arrangements. They ensure people serving in the same geographic location get to know each other on the train trip. It's the very least they can do, given the taxes we pay for it."

The blond man pointed at Jordi. "By the way, you are sitting in my seat."

"Your seat?" Jordi said.

"I have seat 67. You are in it. Please step aside. I want my seat."

"Sure, I will take seat 68," Jordi said. "By the way, I am Jordi Puigdemont, from Catalonia. Nice meeting you."

"I am Johan Staël von Trollstein, from Germany."

Samir started to laugh.

"Is my name funny?" Johan Staël asked.

"Not at all," Samir replied. "My name is Samir ibn Ali ibn Aziz, from the hidden oasis kingdom in the Sahara."

"You wish," Johan replied. "I can smell you come from a shit hole in the Parisian suburbs. At least, I have the courtesy to sit next to you."

There was a sudden chill in the *carré*. Jordi moved back to his *carré*, put his earphones on and listened to some music. Johan Staël was watching some movies on his tablet. Samir, who had neither a smartphone nor a tablet, was looking through the window.

"I love this guy," Johan Staël said aloud, looking at his tablet and imitating someone from TV as he announced: "*I'm Wolf Welsh. I have served in the EU Marine Parachute Regiment, I have climbed to the top of Everest, I have swum across the melted glacial Arctic ocean, I have skied across the South Polar ice cap. I'm going to show you what it takes to survive in the most hostile environments.*"

Samir looked at Johan Staël as if he were an idiot.

The train stopped in Lille, northern France. More passengers were boarding, most of them *slavants*, from the northeastern part of Europe, also heading for the UK.

A flat-faced blond man squeezed himself into Samir and Johan's *carré*:

"Hi, guys. I'm Carsten, Carsten Nielsen from *Danmark*."

The fourth person in their *carré* was a very tall but rather thin brown-haired woman with blue eyes. She was trying to squeeze a disassembled bike into the overhead luggage compartment.

"It's never gonna fit in here," Samir told the young woman. "Let me help you. We can have it by the door of the coach."

"I don't want it to be stolen," The tall woman said.

"No worries. If I see a thief, I will punch him in the face. Let me guess, you are also heading to Cambridge?"

The tall woman acquiesced and a moment later, they all sat in the *carré*, and the lady introduced herself:

"I'm Sanne, Sanne van der Maas, from the Netherlands."

"I've heard your name before," Johan Staël said. "I remember, when I was a kid watching *The Martian show*, there was a girl called Sanne van der Mars, or van der Maas. The girl who never laughed and was always so serious."

Sanne reddened.

"Yes," Johan Staël went on. "This could be you. You were rescued from March last October, weren't you? But why are you doing your civil service? You shouldn't have to."

"I volunteered," Sanne replied.

"You what?" Johan Staël exclaimed with wide open eyes.

"You had the opportunity to save two years of your life, and you volunteered?"

After six months spent at Columbia University, Sanne was confident enough to retort to people like Johan Staël: "Of course. First of all, it's a perfect opportunity for me to meet people. Then, in my case, I will be doing only one year, and not two. Last but not least, I want to do my duty to society."

"Duty to society?" Johan Staël wondered. "We are already paying too much tax, to finance wasted benefits on people like that Samir over there. Should we furthermore spend two years of our lives to what, help poor kids be better at mathematics? Poor people do not deserve our help."

"And why not?" Sanne wondered.

"They put themselves in that situation. We are helping them well enough by just being rich. Trickle-down economy."

Sanne felt as if she was back in a debate at Columbia University, except that she had a bachelor's degree in economics and Johan Staël had just finished high-school. She felt confident arguing with him. "Johan, the purpose of the economy is to serve society, not the other way around. Now, if you had read *Feedback from the Earth*, by Sheldon Cooper, you would know that the very survival of mankind is presently at risk. The good news is we can handle these risks, provided the whole of society works as a team. Society can work as a team, only if it feels like a team. The European Service is what makes team EU."

Johan slowly clapped in his hands.

"I'm impressed," he said. "I would never have guessed that the only Martian to make it to Earth would be a communist, but it makes sense: *red* planet."

"I'm not a communist," Sanne objected.

"Very close," Johan Staël said, smiling. "You should be happy to know to you belong to the 19%."

"What 19%?" Sanne wondered.

"The 19% of people on Earth who care about the future of mankind," Johan Staël replied. "Sadly, you are nothing but a dreaming minority. You will just be unhappy for the rest of your life. The other 81% are reasonable people who care for themselves, instead. Samir, do you care about the future of mankind?"

"Never given a thought about it," Samir admitted

"Precisely."

Samir hated Johan already, but he was starting to like Sanne. An announcement over the train's intercom told them they would soon cross the tunnel under the Channel. Samir could not speak for the others, but as far as he was concerned, it would be his first time in the UK.

"Will you take your driving lessons in the first year?" Carsten asked as the train was entering the tunnel under the Channel.

"And why not?" Samir wondered.

The flat-faced Dane looked at Samir. "You know, currently they drive on the left. But next year, they will switch to right-hand traffic. My dad told me."

"Are they switching?" Samir asked.

"Yes," Johan Staël confirmed. "It has just been voted on by the UK Parliament… Five years after the South-Britons said no in a referendum. But it was only logical. Ireland and Scotland have been driving on the right for more than thirty years, now. Southern African countries switched to right hand-driving twenty years ago, and South Asia fifteen years ago because of commercial pressure from China. Currently, cars designed for left-hand driving are solely produced in Japan and Australia."

"Yes," Carsten went on. "But it may be confusing to learn how to drive on the left, and then start driving on the right when you get your license."

"Then we should learn it now," Samir replied without hesitation.

"Why?" Sanne wondered.

"Well, everybody will think like you," Samir explained. "If everybody waits one year, there will be too many slavants wanting to take driving lessons at the same time next year. Not everyone may get a slot. If we apply now, we will surely get some slots."

"Your brain is perhaps not as slow as I had feared," Johan Staël said condescendingly to Samir.

The train finally arrived at Waterloo station, in London. They had to find their way to King's Cross station to catch the train to Cambridge. Johan Staël led the way, and Samir helped Sanne carry her bike. Jordi was with them.

In Waterloo station, they contemplated the white flag with the two red crosses of England and Wales respectively. The flag of the *United Kingdom of South Britain*.

"Seventy years ago, the flag used to be different," Johan Staël said. "There was some blue in it. Scotland and Northern Ireland were still parts of the kingdom."

In the subway, they had to force their way through the crowd, which was not easy while carrying Sanne's bike. After a change in Leicester Square, they made it to King's Cross, where they managed to board the next train for Cambridge.

It was a nice Friday afternoon. The clouds had now completely vanished, and it was sunny. Many passengers were drinking beers on the train, and it was said that fare inspectors were not working on June 30th and July 1st in order not to clash with drunk slavants.

Carsten brought forth cans of Carlsberg beer, but both Samir and Sanne declined for very different reasons. Sanne was planning to bike from the train station to the Civil Service dormitory, while Samir claimed that beer made one fat.

Once in Cambridge, Sanne removed the bike from its cover and assembled it. Samir wondered where she had bought that flashy green mountain bike.

"How many locks do you have, for your bike?" he asked Sanne.

"Just one," she replied.

"If I were you, I would have three," Samir said. "One for the front wheel, one for the back wheel, and one for the frame. Otherwise your bike will get stolen pretty fast. Trust me, I used to steal bikes."

"Thanks for the tip," she said, strapping her duffel bag onto her luggage carrier.

"See you at the dorm!" she added while pedaling away.

About 800 young Europeans were doing their civil service in Cambridge. Every year, between June and July, four hundred new slavants replaced the four hundred who had just served their two years.

The dormitory for the European Service people was located between Hauxton Road and the M11 Highway, about five kilometers from the train station. Slavants had to put up with some noisy roads!

On that sunny afternoon, there was at least ten dozen slavants walking from the station to the service dormitory, and Samir and Carsten decided to just follow the flow, while Jordi had been looking for a bus and Johan had taken a taxi.

Car drivers were honking as the slavants were dangerously drifting onto the road and Samir felt he was really not used to left-hand driving.

It was twenty past four when Samir and Carsten arrived at the dormitory, made of eight dozen old truck containers of all possible colors. They were greeted by Sanne. She had requisitioned two old bikes.

"You can have them if you want," Sanne said. "They were abandoned by their former owner, according to the dormitory caretaker. If you can break the lock and fix the flat tires, you can use them."

Samir was good at breaking locks and Sanne had all the equipment to fix flat tires. Twenty minutes later, both Carsten and Samir had their own bikes.

The dormitory complex was arranged in twenty-four two-story barracks, made of four truck containers each. On each floor, a kitchen and bathroom unit had been grafted to the adjacent containers. Windows had been pierced into them, and each container had five rooms furnished with bunk beds. The ten slavants living in the same container shared the same bathrooms, and the twenty slavants living on the same floor shared the same kitchen.

Sanne had obtained a room in Barrack 12, where Jordi was also staying. Carsten and Samir were directed to barrack 5. Carsten got his room in container 5-A on the first floor and happened to be sharing his room with Johan Staël von Trollstein. Samir got his in container 5-C on the second floor. He was sharing his room with Magnus Li, a slim Swede of Chinese descent wearing thick-framed glasses.

Because he was last, Samir had to take the top bed. He didn't mind. He was used to sharing a room with three brothers. This was, after all, an improvement. On his bed was his welcome package: thirty condoms.

"The caretaker is holding an information meeting at 17:00 in front of Barrack 1," Magnus said. "We should go, we are already late."

In front of Barrack 1, about four hundred slavants had gathered. There was a little stage in front of the barrack, and a middle-aged man with long brown hair tied behind his head was standing on it with a microphone.

"Good evening all, my name is Mark Lowcock, and I am the caretaker of this dorm. This can either be your hell for two years or… perhaps, heaven. It is up to you."

"Let's talk about hell first. Most of you fuckers are only teenagers who have never done a chore at home, never swiped a floor, and done nothing but be cuddled by your parents. This is fine. Nobody chooses their parents. Whatever your childhood was, now it is time for a change. If you are not able to keep this place tidy, I'm gonna give you hell. If after two warnings your corridor is not tidy enough, you get a fine. An expensive fine. It's two months of your slavant's miserable salary. So, don't fuck with me, and I won't fuck with you."

Samir was certain he had not been one of these so-called 'spoilt fuckers', but Johan Staël looked very sore.

"Talking about fucking," the caretaker went on. "This can

be your heaven. Your salary is miserably low. A third of the minimum wage. Of course, housing is free, part of the food is free, and we pay for your driving lessons. Most importantly, condoms are free. Use them. Not to build water bombs but to engage in active intercourse. This is one of the purposes of the civil service: fuck, don't fight."

Most of the slavants were laughing.

"However, should there be any kind of male supremacist behaviors here, the strange sensation you will be feeling in the seat of your pants will be me kicking your ass."

Most of the males stopped laughing, while some young ladies were still giggling.

"The purpose of the European Service is integration. To have all of you, from different backgrounds and countries, live and work and clean and fuck together. Integration is about bullying each other equally. That's not what the fancy brass in Brussels say, but it is what I say and I am the boss here."

Mark Lowcock paused and looked at his audience to gauge their reaction. He then resumed his speech.

"As you have heard from my accent, I am Irish. Here we are in the UK. You will be working with Brits. Some of them are still using the Imperial system, using feet instead of meters, using fucking stones and bloody pounds instead of kilograms. It is your sacred duty to bully them into using the metric system, is that understood?"

Half of the slavants cheered.

The caretaker looked around and asked: "Is there anybody from Paris, in France, here?"

Samir tried to remain as invisible as possible. Unfortunately, Sanne pointed at him.

"Parisians are assholes," Mark Lowcock went on. "It is the sacred duty of all of you to bully this young Parisian into stopping believing Paris is the center of the world."

There was some more cheering after which Samir said in a loud voice: "No worries: I already hate Paris. No need to bully me".

There was some laughter.

"Good start, young man," the caretaker went on. "Please bully each other, *kindly*, into becoming true Europeans. This is the only purpose of the two years you are going to spend here. Of course, you will assist with taking care of senile people, helping deficient kids at school and assisting poor homeless devils, but the main purpose is for you to become European."

A few applauded, including Sanne.

"Thank you for listening. Now go and fuck each other. And be nice to the second years. They are your seniors."

The crowd slowly dismissed and wandered around aimlessly.

"If this guy is Irish, then I love Ireland already," Samir said to Magnus.

"He was kind of a jerk, wasn't he?" Magnus objected.

"Hey, I saw that there was quite a bit of food left in our kitchen," Samir said. "I can cook something. Guys, what about dinner in barrack 5 at seven o'clock?"

"No thank you," Johan Staël said. "I'm going to a pub in town. It's Friday night. Only losers with no money stay in the dorms on a Friday night."

"*Vilken skitstövel!*" Magnus said in Swedish, referring to Johan Staël ('What an asshole!').

"*Det ved jeg.*" Carsten replied. "*Jeg sad ved siden af ham i toget. Og vi deler samme rummet!*" ('I know. I sat beside him in the train. And we share the same room!')

"What the fuck was that language?" Samir said disgustedly. "It sounds like straight out of a sci-fi movie."

"Fuck you," Carsten retorted. "That was Danish. It's no sci-fi."

"I'd love to come for dinner," Sanne said. "I'm biking now to the city to buy some extra lockers for my bike. Anything else we need?"

"I'm coming with you to buy some alcohol," Carsten said.

Later that evening, Samir was cooking a mushroom risotto and also some *crèmes brûlées* in the second floor kitchen of his barrack, and the odors were luring slavants out of their rooms: Marta and Giuseppe were two slavants from Italy living in nearby corridor 5-B.

In corridor 5-C, Myriam was from Wallonia, Gabriela from Poland, and Ingrid from Germany. They were first-year slavants. Camilla from Spain, and Ivo from Germany, were both second-year slavants.

At seven thirty, Carsten and Sanne also turned up with some alcohol and a bike locker.

Samir ask them to help themselves to the risotto. The slavants were packed in the small kitchen, some sitting on the couch, other on the available chairs.

"I have some cans of Carlsberg," Carsten said.

"Yuk. Carlsberg is certainly the most disgusting beer in the world," Ingrid said, "You should have got German beer."

"Or Walloon beer," Myriam said. "No offence, but Danes can't brew."

"Fuck you."

"Fuck me?" Myriam replied to Carsten. "I've not said no, but I've not said yes either. Please behave." She put a fork of risotto in her mouth and licked it in a sensual manner.

"The risotto is really good," Giuseppe said. "You could almost be Italian, Samir."

"Hm, a male who can cook, and cook well, moreover." Camila said, opening a can of Carlsberg. "Samir, you are going to get laid a lot."

"That's why we get thirty condoms a month," Samir answered.

"We ladies get only ten condoms a month," Sanne said.

"Why do you get condoms at all?" Magnus wondered, focused on eating his risotto without spilling as he was sitting uncomfortably on the sofa's armrest.

Ingrid looked at him with a malicious smile: "Because one out of four times, men forget to bring their condoms with them when they go out. You should know it. Swedish males are particularly known for never having any condoms on them. I know what I am talking about."

"Ten plus thirty equals forty," Carsten counted "Do they really expect us to have sex that much?"

"Why? Can't you?" Myriam said, winking her eye at him.

"Not everybody is Kennedy," he commented.

On the wall of the kitchen, there was an ad poster, featuring a black-and-white picture of former US president, John Fitzgerald Kennedy together with actress Marilyn Monroe. It read "*Ich bin ein Berliner. Aber bei mir hab' ich immer ein'n Pariser.*" ('I am a Berliner, but I have always a 'Parisian' on me.). *Pariser* was the brand of the condoms that were distributed to the slavants.

"There are 38 member states in the European Union," Carsten said. "I'm hoping to have sex with a least a girl from each of these states… plus the Vatican. I'm gonna also have sex with a woman from the Vatican!"

"Who will that be? The Pope's mother?" Samir asked.

"Anyway, that's the spirit," Carsten retorted. "If a minister of health decided we should have condoms as part of our salary, let's use them!"

"Sex without borders!" Myriam shouted.

"Let's be true integrationists!" Carsten replied.

When they were done with the dinner, it did not take long before Carsten was leading Myriam to his room downstairs, explaining that Johan Staël was out at a pub. A moment later, it was Magnus who took Marta into his and Samir's room. Ingrid made some advances on Samir, but he declined, saying he had to clean the kitchen. The truth was that she was too fat for his taste.

As he started the dishes, he realized that only Ingrid and Sanne were left and he could hear that most of the other slavants were having fun in the rooms or in the bathrooms. He would have to buy earplugs.

Sanne and Ingrid offered to help him to clean up the kitchen. He declined, but they insisted on helping him. He switched on the corridor's TV, so that they didn't have to talk. It was Channel 8, from the Bolloré group.

"Bollox news," Sanne whispered.

"And so what?" Ingrid replied. "I think they have much more reliable information than the European Public Channels."

"Look, they are talking about the plans to expand the orbital station," Sanne said. "When I am done with my studies in economics, I will apply to WARSEC."

As the two young women stood and watched, Samir kept tidying the kitchen. He had absolutely no interest in space travel. That was for the rich anyway, not for him. When he was done, the kitchen was probably the cleanest of all those in the dorms.

22: THE EUROPEAN CIVIL SERVICE (JULY 2095)

For Samir and Carsten, the European Civil Service started on Saturday 2 July. They had both been assigned to the same department at the elderly folks' home, located near Addenbrooke's hospital. They were in charge of residents suffering from dementia.

On that first day, there was no supervisor. Todor Bogdanov, a second-year slavant who was stronger than a wrestler, was showing them around.

"This place is a mess," he said. "There are cutting down on everything. There are barely enough plastic gloves to last the month, so we have to be *parsimonist*. Don't waste."

"Otherwise, we have to go to Addenbrooke's hospital and steal some," said Magalie Petit, also a second-year slavant. "Dr. Green, the visiting geriatrician, hates the savings. He's a weirdo, but he helps to steal equipment from other departments."

"Carsten, you come with me," Todor said. "Samir, you can go with Magalie. That way you can speak French."

"*Viens*, Samir." She said ('Come'). "The alert display showed that Mr. Hill's diaper needs changing. I will show you how to do that."

Samir wondered what kind of health institution would have diapers equipped with electronic detectors while there were not enough plastic gloves for the personnel. The world was crazy.

"*Attention,*" Magalie said. "*Il peut* être *assez violent quand on lui change la couche, ce pauvre type. Il est assez relou.*"('Careful, that poor devil can be rather violent when we change his diaper. He is a pain in the ass.')

Samir's first experience with assisting a mentally deficient patient turned into a nightmare. The two of them were barely enough to handle the operation, and Mr. Hill punched Samir in the face. Samir hit him back.

"*Du calme, Samir,*" Magalie said ('Calm down, Samir'). "We are not allowed to hit the patients, or the relatives complain. It's not his fault if he punches you."

They had to catch his hands and tie him to change his diaper. It was brown and slimy and smelly, and Samir almost felt he would throw up.

"Come on, Samir," Magalie said. "Be a man. There are worse things than that."

Samir hated his first day at the elderly folks' home. He hated the second day. He hated the third day as well. In fact, he hated the whole first week, and so did Carsten, but they were both getting better at what they did.

Thursday evening, Carsten was waving a bottle of alcohol, standing in front of Barrack 5.

"*Gammel Dansk,*" he said. "Usually, we drink it for breakfast, but if I don't drink now, I will dream about poop all night. You want some?"

"Yes please," Samir replied.

Carsten poured some alcohol into a plastic mug and handed it over to Samir.

Samir took a sip; the *Gammel dansk* was disgusting, but then he felt the warmth of the alcohol fill his stomach and radiate to his brain. He felt lighter and smiled. "Wahoo! "I want some more. Let's forget the poop for tonight."

They were joined by Magnus Li, the Swede sharing Samir's room. "I also want some," he said. The slim Asian-Swede looked exhausted. "I need to forget what I saw… There are some families… you would not even believe that they can exist…"

"Is it so bad assisting social workers?" Carsten wondered as he deployed three long chairs in front of the barrack and sat in one.

Magnus took the bottle from Samir, took a few sips, and sat down on one of the long chairs.

"I grew up in Borås, in Hässleholmen, a shit hole. People there get shot all the time for drug smuggling. But at least my mother had a job, and I always managed to stay out of trouble… If you compare Cambridge South, it's a mess."

"How messy?" wondered Samir who was now sitting in the remaining long chair.

"I had to assist a social worker and the police to take two children out of the father's custody. He is a drunk asshole, and he was beating them badly. The mother… she was sent to the hospital… never seen anybody in such bad shape."

Magnus's eyes turned red and wet, and he took another sip of the *Gammel dansk.*

Samir gazed in front of him. "I grew up in an asshole family," he said. "The social workers never did anything for us. Every time they came, my father would show himself as a proud cock, and they would buy everything they saw. In the end, my sister took care of the problem."

"How?" Carsten wondered.

"She beat my father up. Now, he daren't be mean to us," Samir replied. "Unlike what they said at school when it comes to bullying, violence solves a lot of issues."

Sanne came and met them.

"English kids are a horror!" she complained as she glanced around for an available long chair. There were none to be seen.

"I think kids are a horror everywhere, not only in England," Samir smiled.

"How is the municipality's summer camp?" Carsten wondered.

"The horror," Sanne answered. "These kids, they are nine, and they know more about sex than I do."

"I can remedy that," Carsten proposed.

"Fuck you, Carsten," Sanne retorted.

"Anytime," he replied. "Still have not had any intercourse with a Dutch lady, even less with a Martian."

"Well, you will be dating your left-hand tonight, Carsten. Good night."

Sanne left.

"Carsten," Samir said. "Sometimes, you behave like a kind of a male supremacist. Believe me, it's becoming old fashioned. Update your firmware. You are not in a Danish farm anymore."

"That's the problem," Magnus added. "He cannot do it to his father's pigs anymore. Carsten: Ladies are not like farm animals. They demand respect."

It started raining, and they went inside the barrack.

The following Friday, it was still pouring with rain, as Carsten and Samir biked to the elderly folks' home. Once again, the work was exhausting. Samir was punched again by Mr. Hill when changing his diaper and beaten by another senile lady while assisting her in the shower. *Only a few hours left before the weekend*, he thought.

He decided to take a break, went downstairs to the main entrance, and stayed a while under the porch, breathing in the wet air and watching the pouring rain. He remembered he had some cannabis left. He had not given all of it back to Inspector Chautel. It was highly appropriate to smoke a joint. Friday was cannabis day in all decent places. He had enough cannabis left for two more joints. This would be his last joint but one. He rolled it carefully and lit it.

"God, you have a cigarette? Do you have one for me? It's impossible to buy cigarettes in Europe since the whole goddamned continent has become cigarette free."

Samir turned around. It was a bald man with square glasses and wearing a white tunic, on which there was a name tag reading '*Dr. Doug Green, Geriatrics*'.

"It's not a cigarette," Samir replied. "It's a *joint*."

"You are too young for this shit," The doctor replied. "It may destroy your brain. Never smoke a joint before you turn twenty-seven, is that understood?"

The Doctor took the joint from Samir's hand and took a puff.

"What's your name, laddie?"

"Samir."

The Doctor inhaled a large quantity of cannabis, exhaled through his nose and said: "Listen up Samir, you know what's the problem with old people?"

"They can't take care of themselves?"

The doctor took another puff before answering: "Almost. The true problem is that there are too many of them. The more of them die, the more of them come."

"That's the definition of an ageing population."

"In 2071, twenty-four years ago, the Qatari flu killed a lot of them. That was really nice. But now they are back. Yes, quite a few died ten years ago, in that heat wave. But it was not enough."

Samir looked at the Doctor, flabbergasted: "Doctor, are you all right?"

The Doctor took another puff. "I'm perfectly fine, Samir. So is your joint. Did you know that the Aztec forbade people to live longer than fifty-two years in their society?"

"No, I didn't know that."

"Fifty-two years was the duration of their holy calendar cycle. As a result, when Aztecs turned 52, they were given a choice. Either they would go into exile and try to survive on their own in the jungle, or they would accept to be sacrificed for the sun, which most of them preferred. After all, if at 52 you had not already been killed in battle, you were a real loser!"

"Really?"

"True story. Thank you for the joint, Samir, I have to get back to work. By the way, if you have some cannabis for sale, I'm interested."

Samir went back into the building and made it to the third floor, where his department was. On the stairs, he came across Carsten.

"Damn it. I feel I am in a lunatic asylum," Samir said.

"Of course you are," Carsten replied. "We work in the

dementia department, remember?"

"I just wonder who is the craziest here. Sorry, sir, excuse us."

A middle-aged man of athletic shape was trying to get past them with his slightly overweight son. He was talking to his lad.

"You see, boy. That's why you have to work out more and strive to be in good shape, like Daddy. If you don't, you will never be accepted for the military service, and you may end changing your grandparents' diapers like these two losers."

"*Enculé d'Anglais de sale bourge! Tu la vas fermer ta gueule?*" Samir shouted at the man showing him his middle finger ('Dirty English bourgeois fucker! Are you gonna shut up?').

The athletic man showed him two fingers instead and said calmly to his son: "The brown frog has lost his temper, it seems. Typical."

"Come on, Samir," Carsten said, "let's get back to work. By the way, I have just met a student nurse; Emily. She will start in our department around mid-July. At last, a good-looking English girl. She is mine, so don't touch."

"You are really obsessed! Why don't you have a try at Mrs. Blake, instead?"

"I don't do rape," Carsten replied.

"But if you did, they would probably be the best rapes in the world! Bloody Dane!"

"Do you hear yourself?" Carsten asked amused. "You swear like a bloody Englishman! By the way, could you bring lunch to Mr. Fraser? He is nice, and definitely not senile. I wonder why he is here. But he talks too much, and I can't stand his talking."

A moment later, Samir was in Mr. Fraser's room carrying a tray with his lunch.

"Mr. Fraser," Samir shouted. "This is Samir, the orderly. I am here with your lunch."

"Please, Samir, don't shout. I can hear you perfectly. You may put the lunch here on the table."

Samir obeyed. Gareth Fraser was sitting on a chair beside his bed, reading a tablet. He was wearing jeans and a polo shirt.

"Sir, you don't seem to suffer from dementia," Samir dared. "Why are you here, and not in a normal retirement home?"

Mr. Fraser looked Samir in the eye. "I like to be in a senile department. At least, I am not disappointed by the intellectual capacity of my fellow residents. Believe me, a regular retirement home is barely more intellectually challenging."

Mr. Fraser burst into hearty laughter, restrained himself, and added: "More seriously, as you see, I have very limited mobility and I wanted to stay in Cambridge, so this was the best compromise."

"You were born in 1998, sir. You have just turned 97 years old?"

"Correct. Please don't call me sir. Just call me Gareth."

"Ok, sir… Gareth…"

The old man smiled at Samir.

"How do you like your Civil Service in Cambridge? You've

not landed in the easiest department."

"To be honest, I don't like the job," Samir replied bluntly. "But I like being out of my father's apartment, I like to know I will be able to get my driving license without having to pay through the nose for it. So, overall, being a slavant is not too bad."

"I'm impressed," the old man said.

"What by?"

"Young adults usually don't have balanced opinions. What were your A-levels in high school?"

"Cooking. I went to a professional high school. I am not eligible to go to university."

Gareth pondered over this and said: "You know, there is a community college in Cambridge. You should consider applying for it, at some point. I think you are more intelligent than you believe you are."

"Yeah? A police inspector also told me that."

"You certainly had a tough childhood," Gareth said. "But now, the Civil Service is about setting the clocks right. You are being given opportunities, don't miss out on them."

"What opportunities?"

"I would recommend you a book, but it is a very long book. It is called a *European Dilemma*. You would understand what I mean."

"I have no time for reading. Now, if you will excuse me, I have to tend to other residents."

In the late afternoon, the rain had completely stopped and the evening even turned sunny when Carsten and Samir were biking back to the dorms. They were greeted by Sanne who suggested that they should eat outside.

Samir cooked Asian food with prawn fritters, goat cheese and mozzarella fritters. It was quite unhealthy, but it was Friday. They all gathered on the outdoor tables in front of Barrack 5.

As Samir seemed lost in his thoughts, Sanne asked him: "What are you thinking about, Samir?"

"I was thinking about how many weirdos there are at the home," Samir replied. "Dr. Green, the geriatrician. He wants to kill old people. And then, there is this Gareth Fraser, who talks and talks."

"Gareth Fraser?" Sanne asked. "About ninety-seven years old? The lead author of the *European Dilemma*?"

"The *European Dilemma*? Why is everybody talking about it? Samir wondered.

"It's a comprehensive sociological study that was done in the 2030s," Sanne replied. "This is the book behind the European Civil Service."

"So, he is the reason we are here," said Carsten as he swallowed a mozzarella fritter.

"Oh, I would like to meet him," Sanne said.

"You're more than welcome to come by our department," Samir replied. "But I warn you, this guy talks too much."

Later that evening, most of the company decided to head for downtown Cambridge, to see if there were some student parties they could crash. Samir was not in the mood and decided to stay at the outdoor table and smoke a joint. This time, his last joint.

He reflected on the purpose of the European Service. Perhaps it served an integrationist goal, after all. His older sister Soraya was now studying engineering in Sweden. Could that have happened if she had stayed at home, at Fat Ali's?

"Hi, do you still have some food left?" a voice asked.

The night had now fallen, but Samir could make out a young, athletic lady, slightly shorter than he was. She was wearing black leggings, a green T-shirt and a dark blue veil.

"Sure. Got lots of fritters: shrimps, goat cheese, mozzarella, crabs. Take your pick. There is also some wine."

"I don't drink much, but I could have a glass of wine," the girl said as she sat down by the table, across from Samir.

"Are you a slavant? Which barrack?" Samir asked. "I don't remember seeing you before"

"No, unfortunately not. I'm not a European citizen. I'm from Morocco. My name is Aisha."

"Samir."

"You are French?" Aisha wondered. *"Si tu veux, on peut parler français?"* ('If you want, we can speak French.')

Samir declined: "Sorry, girl. I've been smoking, and my

brain is messed up. Can't switch to French right now. What are you doing here?"

Aisha looked embarrassed and finally said: "I have traveled from Ireland, and I have noted that the best way to get free food was to squat in the dorms of the European servants."

"*Slavants,* not servants," Samir corrected. "Why have you traveled from Ireland? You look like you're just fifteen."

"I'm seventeen." She took a shrimp fritter and swallowed it.

"Still! What are you doing here on your own, if I may ask?"

"Came to Ireland for an abortion. Not a big deal. It's like having a tumor removed. But it's considered a crime in Morocco. Somebody reported me. If I go back to Morocco, I face four years in jail. Moreover, I am no longer allowed to go to university."

"Really? That sounds crazy."

Aisha ate some more before she added: "I really would like to finish high school. I wanted to be a police officer."

Because of the joint, Samir was too messed up to feel really sorry for anybody. He said bluntly: "As long as you are an undocumented person in Europe, it's not gonna happen."

"What can I do?" Aisha asked.

"Honestly, you are pretty fucked. From where I sit, I see you have only two options. Either you go back to Morocco and sit in jail, or you continue your life as an undocumented person in Europe with no prospect of integration other than pretending to fall in love with a European, live with him for five years, and then perhaps marry him and get some documents. You would lose at least four years in any case. I would choose jail in Morocco."

Aisha cast him an evil eye: "You are an asshole."

Samir did not reply. He was either too tired or too messed up. He was contemplating Aisha eating the mozzarella fritter.

"You may have a third option," Samir finally said.

"What?"

"You wanted to become a police officer: Do you like to fight and sweat?"

"Yes"

"You look rather athletic. You could apply for the European Foreign Legion. As far as I know, women are allowed, and you may be under eighteen, provided you have authorization from your parents."

"Can we check?"

"I don't have a smartphone, but my roommate has a laptop in the room. Het lets me use it and he is in town. We could borrow his internet. Just help me to clear the table and bring the stuff up to the kitchen."

Samir insisted on first doing the dishes and cleaning up the kitchen, after which they went to his and Magnus's room to check the website of the European Foreign Legion.

"You see," Samir said as they looked at Magnus's laptop. "Women have been admitted to the Legion since 2044. It was still the French Foreign Legion, back then. You can apply at seventeen, provided you have the authorization from one of your parents."

"Can I check the physical requirement?" she asked.

She browsed through it.

"It should be OK," she said. "May I send an email to my parents?"

Samir watched Aisha write the email on the computer. She looked rather cute, despite the veil that was hiding her hair.

"To be honest," Samir said "It's not that easy. I tried to join the Legion four weeks ago. I did not want to do my Civil Service. I was dismissed after two days. I did not pass the physical tests."

Aisha clicked on *Send* and looked up at Samir. She stood up as the computer was shutting down.

"Take off your shirt," Aisha commanded. As Samir hesitated, she added: "I want to see if you are physically stronger than I am. I doubt it."

Samir opened his shirt while he saw Aisha removed her veil, disclosing shoulder-long black hair. She took off her T-shirt and leggings and stood there in panties and sports bra. Samir had never seen a woman with as many muscles as Aisha.

"You don't have much fat, but I don't see many muscles either," she said, kneeling down and dragging off his pants and underpants simultaneously. Samir started breathing nervously as he felt her breathing on his private parts. He had an erection.

She stood up again and looked at him in the eyes.

"If you want better stamina, you'd better quit smoking and

try exercise instead," she said undoing her bra.

With her hands on his shoulders, she forced him onto his knees.

"I see you have German condoms. Good. They are better than the Chinese ones. But if you want me to ride you, you'd better lick me first. Drag my panties down."

23: ENGLISH SUMMER
(JULY – AUGUST 2095)

The second week of July went way too fast for Samir. Aisha crashed in his and Magnus's room, waiting for the letter from her father. Magnus did not mind Aisha sleeping with Samir in the top bed.

Aisha had no trouble blending in with the other slavants. One evening, they played soccer, and she scored five goals, while Magnus, in the opposite team, scored an own goal.

Samir was fascinated by Aisha. Not only was she dominating and attractive, but she was also more intelligent than he was and, as strange as it sounded, more religious than him. Samir had described himself as a 'bad Muslim', so bad that he was more of an atheist, and could not understand why Aisha would put so much faith in religion. Aisha would reply that it was a question of interpretation. She would gladly debate it together with Sanne, Carsten, Ingrid and Samir.

Islam was, in her view, the most joyful religion in the

world, and full of hope. Christianity, on the other hand, was rather a pathetic religion, not that she wanted to be perceived as offensive to Christian believers if any of them were, but sincerely, Jesus was nothing more than a virgin loser, who let himself get killed without resisting. How could a religion make a model of him?

On the other hand, the Prophet Mohammad was a much more interesting character. In the first half of His life, He had had a unique wife, Khadija, who was older, had been His boss and had proposed to Him. After her death, the Prophet changed his lifestyle completely and started to have several wives, not that He really wanted them, but just that He could not really say no to all the girls who were lining up to marry him. Though, on two occasions, He had been dumped at the altar. But still, at last, a happy Prophet! In His prime, he could sexually satisfy all His nine wives on the same day! Which, by the way, was the evidence for Islamic feminists that oral sex was authorized within Islam. Nine wives on the same day! There was no other explanation. In Aisha's view, Islam had been in the beginning a very progressive religion. However, the influence of the male supremacist Medinans had altered its interpretation.

And no, she was not wearing a veil as a sign of submission, but only as a sign of self-respect. She only wore a veil when in the presence of unknown people and on the street, never in another context. No, there was no contradiction for a Muslim female believer to be bossy. The Prophet's first wife had been very bossy herself. Yes, a good Muslim could drink alcohol provided they did not get drunk. No, a good Muslim could not eat pork, unless there was nothing else to eat, but the modern interpretation was mostly because pork could make one fat.

And yes, it was OK for Muslim women to have sex outside the bounds of marriage. The only rule was that no child had to be born without knowing her or his father. Condoms and other means of contraception had solved that issue. DNA tests as well, for that matter.

Aisha received the letter from her father on Friday 15 July 2095 and on the following Sunday, she and Samir went to London by train.

The recruiting center of the Foreign Legion was located at the periphery of London in a newly built industry area, on Deadstick Street. As they were standing in front of the barracks, Aisha spent some time contemplating the flag of the European Union.

"You are still sure?" Samir asked. "It's a five-year contract."

"It's the best option I have," she replied. "I will be granted European citizenship in three years. I will have food and lodging, and it's pretty safe. We have checked: the legion has not been deployed on any external war-like operations over the last two decades."

"They were deployed in some peacekeeping in Greenland," Samir recalled.

"Yes," Aisha admitted. "I read about it. But it was pretty soft. No casualties."

"The EU president is a hawk, though," Samir said.

"Come on, Samir. Warp travel is now possible. Everything is pointing toward world peace. I think the Legion is pretty safe at the moment."

"Do you like the European Flag?"

It was a Sergeant passing by, wearing a legionnaire's képi, who had spoken. He added:

"It has not always been that flag. It used to be twelve yellow stars forming a circle on a blue background. It used to be a pussy flag that had something to do with harmony or some Catholic bullshit."

"How is that flag better?" Samir asked. "It's also twelve stars on a blue background."

"Yes, but they are arranged as in the atomic structure of a diamond. The diamond represents strength and unity. You cannot break a diamond."

"You are a legionnaire? I would like to join," Aisha said.

"You? How old are you?"

"I am seventeen, I have my passport. But I also have an authorization letter signed by my father."

"Do you see the bar there in front of the building? Show me you can do at least four pull-ups."

Aisha went there, took off her veil and put it in her bag and started doing pull-ups. She did one pull up, two, three, four, five, six, seven, eight, nine.

"OK, OK, I got it, stop it," the legionnaire said impatiently. "Follow me."

Samir did not even the time to kiss Aisha goodbye. The legionnaire took her to the barracks' front door and opened it. He and Aisha disappeared behind the door.

Back in Cambridge, Samir felt a sudden void. His brief relationship with Aisha had been terminated. If she got in and, according to Sanne, Aisha had a good chance of landing on the right side of the statistics, then she would not be able to communicate with anybody outside the Legion for the next six months. By then, she would have forgotten about him.

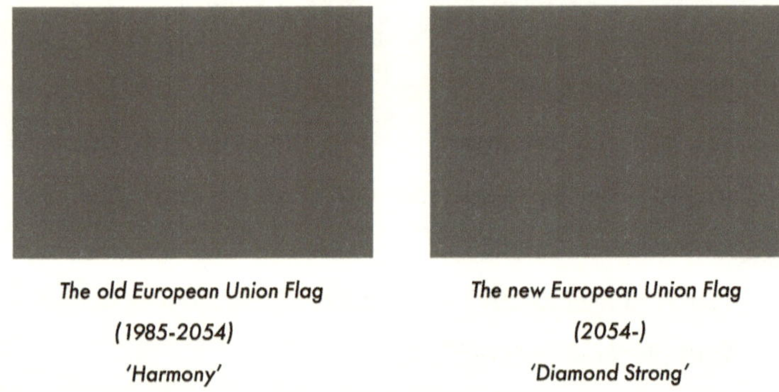

The old European Union Flag
(1985-2054)
'Harmony'

The new European Union Flag
(2054-)
'Diamond Strong'

Figure 10: the old European Flag, and the new EU flag, with the dark -blue background and the 12 yellow stars arranged in the atomic structure of a diamond, supposed to symbolize strength, rather than harmony.

The more she worked at the summer camp, the more Sanne hated young kids. She was looking forward to September when she would be working as a math tutor to junior high-school pupils instead. Meanwhile, it was hell.

A kid had filled a condom with water and thrown it at her head. She had grabbed him and slapped him in the face. A supervisor had told her she was not allowed to. She had got a warning.

Her sexual life was not satisfactory either. Cute and interesting guys were all too short for her. It seemed that tall men were mainly jerks. Or at least here, in Cambridge.

Besides, Johan Staël would constantly tease her for being a *Red Martian with a 'Red' like in communist."* What a dickhead!

After having been on Mars, at the Vienna Conference and at Columbia University, it seemed that reality was hitting her in the face. But was it not one of the purposes of the European Civil Service? To make naïve young Europeans like herself understand that life sucked? If it was the purpose, it was certainly succeeding.

She found, however, comfort in knowing that *the* Gareth Fraser behind *The European Dilemma* was staying in Samir's and Carsten's department. She decided to take the time, on Saturday, to go and visit him.

She just knocked at the door and introduced herself. She mentioned she had read *A European Dilemma* at the recommendation of one of his former students. Gareth Fraser invited her to sit on a chair opposite him.

"Which student?"

"Ralf Åhman, the new director of WARSEC."

"Ralf Åhman? Does he still remember me? He has not visited me in ten years. Fifteen years ago, I was still the dean of the institution of political sciences, here, in Cambridge. At 82, I was a dinosaur, so they ousted me."

"Sorry to hear that," Sanne replied.

"So, you are the only survivor of the Martian colony? Always thought it was a stupid project," the old man grumbled. "How do you like your first weeks of Civil Service?"

Sanne smiled. "I hate it. At least the summer camp babysitting part. Kids are mean. But I understand the purpose of it."

"The European Service," Gareth said slowly, "is the most important thing that has ever happened in Europe since the fall of the Roman Empire. It is the victory of Integrationism over congregationism, of cooperation over competition, of daylight over darkness. It is the recognition that the human factor outweighs the marketization of labor, money, and natural resources."

"I know," Sanne said.

Gareth's eyes lit up, as if talking about the civil service gave him new energy. "Of course, it is imperfect. People complain about the cost of having it. Trust me, the cost of *not* having it is greater. You see, I was twenty-one when the UK became independent from the EU, as they called it. A horrible time. It marked the end of the United Kingdom of Great Britain and Northern Ireland, but only a few of us understood it. Scotland declared their independence a couple of years later, and it took barely more than a decade for Northern Ireland to merge with the Republic of Ireland. It was only in 2063 that the UK joined the EU again. By then it was already a federation. All of this would not have happened if we had had the European Civil service back then. Europe would have suffered less."

Samir and Carsten were right, Sanne thought. Gareth Fraser talked a lot. Back at the dorm, Sanne realized that her antique Martian computer was dying. She went to Samir's and Magnus's corridor. Magnus was boiling water in the kitchen. She turned to him:

"My computer is dead. Can you help me get a new one? I looked at the prices; it's crazy expensive."

"On Earth, you don't own your computer, unless you are super rich," Magnus said as he was retrieving a tea bag out of his private cupboard. "You lease your computer. The VAT on the acquisition of goods is ten time higher than on the leasing of goods."

"That's called *parsimonism*."

It was Johan Staël. He was coming out of Ingrid's room.

"This was the answer to *consumerism*," he went on. "Consumerism was goods-centered. People used to buy their computers, use them, and throw them away after two years."

"I know that," Sanne replied.

"Then you should know that *parsimonism* is service-centered." Johan Staël said. "You pay every month for the use of a computer, not to own it. In a consumerist society, computer manufacturers have an incentive to make fragile computers which break down after two years. In a parsimonist society, manufacturers want their computers to last as long as possible. They lease them to you, and they change some components when needed."

"That's how mankind has managed to give a decent standard living to almost eleven billion people while making do with limited resources," Magnus added. "I can show you how to lease a computer."

"The best part with *parsimonism*," Johan Staël added with a quirky smile, "is that economic inequalities have increased. The middle class does not own their cars, their washing machines or computers anymore. The patrimony of the superrich has increased, while that of the others have decreased: I like."

Sanne looked at him. "I've heard that some would like to introduce a universal tax on capital, to tackle just this issue."

"Well, send me an email when it happens," Johan Staël said and he left the corridor. When Magnus had his cup of tea ready, he led Sanne to his room, where they found Samir in shorts and T-shirt.

"Hi guys, I have to bike at full speed to the annex. I work

night shift this weekend, and I am late already."

Samir was panting and sweating when he arrived at the home. It was damn hot. In Mr. Fraser's room, there was a young Doctor, who looked Pakistani. Gareth introduced him as Dr. Windsor, a psychiatrist from the nearby Addenbrooke's Hospital.

The Doctor of South-Asian descent shook Samir's hand: "You can just call me Eamon. I'm a Democrat."

He was interrupted by Dr. Green, who asked Samir to join him outside Gareth's room. In the corridor, the bald geriatrist exposed the situation: "Be ready, laddie, it's gonna be a tough night. We are gonna lose patients. Inevitable. It's too hot, and five patients are in a terrible state."

The doctor then said for himself: "Hopefully, they will die in the early morning. Else, we won't sleep much."

"Doug, if you want to consult a shrink, I can recommend someone."

It was Dr. Windsor. He had come out of Fraser's room.

Dr. Green looked at him with a theatrically irritated look: "Why don't you go back to the psychiatrist emergency room and scan for serial killers, instead, Eamon? We are all mentally fine here."

"I doubt that, Doug. Good luck for tonight," said Dr. Windsor as he headed for the stairs.

When Dr. Windsor had left, Dr. Green said to Samir:

"When you think about it, this guy is the Crown Prince. He

may be our next King."

"Yeah, and I'm gonna be the next Napoleon," Samir replied.

He was saved from Dr. Green by Emily Chapman, the new student nurse. The athletic red-haired and blue-eyed nurse needed extra arms to carry Mr. Flinkur from his wheelchair to his bed. Samir followed her to the room.

As usual, the two robots designed to help carry heavy patients were both out-of-order, and the department was waiting for a technician. Samir tried to help, but even two people to lift the 230 kg (507 lb) old man were not enough.

"Damn it, Samir, you need to work out," Emily said. "I can pick up 110 kg [242 lbs] in a deadlift. You are a man, you should be able to manage at least 160 kg [352 lbs]. I guess you can barely manage half that."

"Fuck you."

"I know you'd love to. If you work out more, you may have a chance. Until then, not even in your dreams. You're still higher on my potential list than this irritating Dane, though."

"Show me how to work out, then," Samir tried.

"If you want. There is a gym at the hospital nearby, for the staff. But if you prefer more challenging sports, we could go and climb. There is a climbing gym in downtown Cambridge.

"Climbing? I'd love to try." It was Carsten who just came by. He added: "If you two go climbing, I want to be there."

Samir and Emily did not mind, as long Carsten helped them carry Mr. Flinkur.

Later that evening, Emily called the families of the five patients at risk of not surviving the night. Most were on holiday, far from Cambridge; two were stuck at some important barbecue parties. None would come.

"Bunch of assholes," she said.

Samir remembered when his mother was treated for breast cancer, a year and a half earlier. She had been on the wrong side of the statistics, as Sanne would have said. Immunotherapy had not worked on her. It worked on a third of the patients at best. Samir's mother belonged to the wrong two thirds. She had gone through chemotherapy, making her weaker and weaker. Despite this, their father had kept on treating her like a bag of shit. One evening, after receiving treatment, his mother had been unable to cook. Fat Ali had decided to take the children to the nearby McDonald's. When they had come back, they had found their mother lying in her own vomit. The following day, she had been transferred to a palliative department.

Palliative departments were where patients were allowed to starve to death. They were packed with painkillers but given no glucose in their IV. As they could barely eat, they would just die. There had been nothing glorious in what he had seen. Fat Ali believed in God, the Prophet, Heaven and other religious nonsense, but he would not show up for his wife's last moments on Earth. He was an asshole. Samir was an atheist, but he had been the only one of the family there when his mother had exhaled for the last time.

"Samir? Are you sleeping?" It was Emily. She added: "Mr. Flinkur has just passed away. We need help to bring him to the morgue."

Mr. Flinkur was only the first to die that night. In the early, morning, he was followed by Mr. Hill and Mrs. Blake.

"Only three dead?" Dr. Green said the next morning. "I was exaggeratingly pessimistic."

When Samir biked back to the dorms, he enjoyed the morning breeze, the blue sky, and shining sun. Life should be embraced while one could still do it.

The following Monday evening, Carsten and Samir went to the climbing gym, located in front of Parker's Piece, in downtown Cambridge. Emily was already there. Samir was impressed by the climbing wall structures and all their colored grips. It looked really thrilling. There were some impossible overhanging sections, and he wondered if he would be able to climb that one day.

"Oh my God," Carsten said entering the hall, "I now understand why there are no good-looking English women on the streets. They are all hiding in the climbing gym! This is heaven."

"And here goes the obsessed Dane!" Emily commented.

Emily had brought some extra harnesses, and the two young men rented some climbing shoes. Emily belayed them with a top rope. Samir, who was really thin, turned out to be quite good at climbing, but the flat-faced Dane, who was taller and slightly more potbellied, had difficulties.

Seeing that no girls were impressed by his performance, Carsten decided to leave for a student party at the nearby Geological Institution. Samir and Emily kept climbing until the gym closed at 10 o'clock in the evening. It had been a successful session for Samir, and he had even obtained his green card, meaning he was now allowed to belay other climbers' top ropes.

Emily thought that they should go out and celebrate and she took him to a pub, which was located a fifteen-minute bike ride from the gym.

Samir thanked Emily for taking him climbing. It was a fun sport and he had to work out more, anyway, in order to be more appealing to girls, to which Emily fully agreed, laughing.

Emily Chapman thought that Samir was lucky to do European Service. She had not done it. Healthcare students didn't have to do any kind of European Service, as they did a lot of internships as part of their studies and it was already considered as public service. Now, she regretted it. She was still living with her father nearby.

Suddenly, Emily realized that it was one in the morning already.

"We should go," she said. "But you've drunk too much. You should not bike home."

"What shall I do? Walk home?"

"No, you could crash in my room, in my father's flat. He doesn't mind."

Later in the night, as Samir was asleep spooning Emily, he was awoken by a phone signal. It was Emily's smartphone. She answered.

"No, Johnny, not tonight… It's four o'clock… I'm with somebody else… I can see you on Monday or Tuesday… OK… Bye."

"Who was it? Your boyfriend?" Samir asked.

"I have no boyfriend. He is just a fuck-buddy. And so are you. For the time being. But I'll gladly see you again on Friday and Saturday nights."

Of course, the incident made Carsten appear hilarious. Sanne liked the concept. If Samir was just a fuckbuddy, at least he had guaranteed sex on appointed days, unlike the serial one-night-stander Carsten was.

For a student in economics like Sanne, it all made sense. In a liberal economy, a monopoly was forbidden. A company was not allowed to have an exclusive right to sell a service without any fair competition. It was only logical that the principle should apply to sex life as well. Nobody should have the right to claim exclusive access to their sexual partner. It was anti-liberal.

Besides, the fuckbuddy approach was sounder, when it came to building up lasting relationships. In a traditional boyfriend-girlfriend relationship, parties were faithful to each other at the beginning, but would most of the time progressively cheat one another until they broke up. However, in a fuckbuddy relationship, parties were knowingly unfaithful to each other at the beginning and then would progressively decide to commit to each other after a reasonable reflection time. Or not.

Sanne convinced Samir that being Emily's fuckbuddy was a very good deal. She also wanted to meet Emily, in order to be coached into the fuckbuddy market, and Samir brought her to the climbing hall. At first, Emily believed that Sanne was one of Samir's fuckbuddies, but she became quite friendly when she understood she was not.

During the second half of August, Sanne obtained both her green card and red card at the climbing gym. She was now even allowed to lead climb, like Samir and Emily. She did not like it, though. That was scary.

As a lead climber, she would clip the rope in quickdraws (QD) while climbing upward, to secure herself. She would always fall above the last clipped QD, and it would always take some time before the rope stopped her. She hated it. Both Emily and Samir admitted they were also scared. That did not stop them from liking climbing in general.

In a way, Sanne thought climbing had similarities with being in space, or on Mars. It was scary, committed and, in a way dangerous, if one screwed up. But as long as one was following safety procedures and was comfortable with them, one could well find it enjoyable.

There, at the climbing gym, there were also a lot of tall, handsome climbers with no strings attached. One of them was an elite climber, heavily tattooed, and often to be seen wandering around topless in the gym. She somehow managed to nail him. They even became each other's Tuesday and Thursday fuckbuddies. It was not as good as being each other's Saturday fuckbuddy, but still.

The only problem with that dude was that, when he was not talking about climbing, he was only talking about finger pull-ups and muscle-ups. He had no interest in space and was barely impressed to know that Sanne was a Martian: she had not even been on Mount Elysium, the highest mountain of the solar system. What was there to be proud of about being a Martian?

The future of mankind? He did not give a crap about it. He was definitely not part of the 19%. The only thing that mattered to him was climbing, and Sanne was not remotely interested in having a sentimental relationship with him. The sex was awesome, though, and when you were nineteen, that was what mattered.

Every time she slept with him, he snored, and she could barely sleep, so she would think about space. When she had been on Mars, she'd wanted to come to Earth. Now she was on Earth, she wanted to go back to space.

The orbital station was to be extended, they were planning to manufacture spaceships on the Moon, and the first small steps toward interstellar exploration and space colonization were slowly but surely taken forward. She had not heard any news from Ralf. She had better contact him.

She had to keep a good relationship with him. She wanted to work for WARSEC after her studies.

24: LETHAL MISTAKE (AUGUST 2095)

Some days, Sophie Couillard hated her job. This was such a day. All of this was Michael's fault. His sentiment of election and entitlement would often make him a difficult person to work for, but sometimes it just made it impossible. This was such a time.

She was at last back in her office and shut the door. She needed to be alone for a while. The setting sun was lighting up her westerly oriented office in orange. It was located on the seventh floor of the main V-Space building, adjacent to the airport of Bobo-Dioulasso, Burkina Faso.

She went to her desk, picked up a pair of sunglasses, put them on, and stood in front of the large bay window. August in Burkina was the rainy season and the heat was bearable. She opened the window bay and went out on the balcony.

She was assailed by the noise of a passenger jet landing on the runway. It was only a Boeing operated by Burkinair. She looked to the north. There were the large V-Space hangars serving as assembly lines for the Albaspace. In front of them, six sleek Albaspaces, painted in the colors of Quantas, Qatar Airways, and Lufthansa were waiting to be flown to their new airline companies.

This was why she was there. This was why she was at V-Space. She had been the project manager of the Albaspace and it had been a hell of a success. She would continue to succeed whatever unnecessary trouble Michael Vahlroos had in store for her.

When the engines of the passenger jet shutdown, she could hear a clamor. It was the Muezzin calling to the Evening's prayer, as the sun was disappearing behind the Horizon. The air was filled with a deep *"Allah wa akhbar"* singing. When he was done, some loudspeakers informed the inhabitants of Bobo-Dioulasso that Jesus loved them. Finally, the bells of the nearby Catholic Church rang so as to convince those who still doubted that 'God was great' or that 'Jesus loved them'.

As for Sophie, she was rather loved by mosquitoes, it seemed. She smashed a few on her arms and went back in into her office, closing the balcony door behind her. She sat down behind her desk, laid her sunglasses in front of her keyboard, and looked at the screen.

"Always enthusiastic, not always right, but never in doubt."

So was entitled a blog entry that had been written by an American Lawyer in Florida. It was about Michael Vahlroos.

Eleven months earlier, Michael Vahlroos's son had been kidnapped. Instead of following the FBI's recommendation to negotiate a ransom, he had offered twice the demanded amount to whoever bounty hunter would bring him the kidnapper. It had seemed to work. Bounty hunters had brought back the suspect kidnapper alive, but found his son dead.

The suspect, a black man, had been convicted of kidnapping and second-degree murder, which, in Florida, meant being sentenced to death.

The blog entry had been written by the inmate's lawyer, to denounce what had happened. She had conducted her own investigation and found out that her client had been innocent. He had just been a random black man at the wrong place at the wrong time.

The real culprits had been those who had called themselves 'bounty hunters'. Surprised by the unexpected move by Vahlroos, who had been more interested in doing justice to the culprits than saving his son, they had just killed the kid, kidnapped the first uneducated black man they met, and sold him to Vahlroos for twice the price.

Unfortunately, the lawyer's investigation had taken time, too much time, all the more since Michael Vahlroos had had his friend, the governor of Florida, arrange the execution as fast as possible, since, as Michael allegedly told the lawyer, he wanted justice so that he could 'move on': he did not want to 'mourn for years before the execution took place.'

The execution had finally taken place.

Execution in Texas and Florida, the two remaining states with the death penalty, were no funny things. They were conducted with so-named 'Texan guillotines'.

Still, according to the lawyer, Michael had allegedly referred to them as "ingenious French design with American technology and know-how."

Throughout the 21st Century, carrying out executions in the United States had become more complicated. Pharma companies were refusing to sell lethal injections on moral grounds, and electric chairs, hanging, and firing squads had been judged as too traumatizing to be permitted.

A Silicon Valley firm had therefore invented the laser guillotine, which would behead the convict with a light ray. However, this had also been ruled out as two traumatizing since it burned the convict for an unacceptable time before they passed away.

Texas had therefore devised their 'Texan guillotine', equipped with both a blade, like in a traditional French Guillotine, and lasers. As the blade beheaded the convict, lasers would be triggered simultaneously in order to instantly cauterize the opened arteries. The result was a less bloody execution than that of a French guillotine.

According to the manufacturer, which the lawyer was quoting in her blog entry, the purpose of the Texan guillotine was to render execution 'pleasant for the victims' families'.

Sophie had reading the lawyer's blog entry five times. She was furious with Michael. His deadly mistake had not only been an unfortunate error for the innocently executed inmate, but it was putting in jeopardy the whole reputation of V-Space.

Her African colleagues had taken all this very badly. All the more since Michael did not seem to show any remorse. They accused him of being racist, which was certainly an exaggeration: Michael was only Michael.

The Trade Unions had even started a wild-strike earlier in the morning. They were refusing to manufacture any more Albaspaces as long as Michael Vahlroos was the CEO of Vahlroos Corporation.

The Unions' reaction had been very understandable but was, however, not acceptable. The behavior of a CEO in his private life had to be kept strictly separate from his business.

A negotiation marathon had followed in an attempt to avert the strike. To Sophie's surprise, Thierry Diakité and Tintin Mutombo had offered to act as mediators. They had been successful and the strike had been prevented at an acceptable cost: workers would be given three extra days of paid holidays.

Now things were moving. Vahlroos Travel had been founded. The extension of the orbital station had been resumed. Space business was expected to be booming, provided V-Space's reputation was not to be ruined by Michael's personality.

She cast a glance through the window behind her. It was now pitch dark outside. About time to go home. She was about to shut down her computer when the face of a blond man with blue eyes and a Swedish nose popped up on her screen.

It was an incoming video call from Michael Vahlroos. It was only lunch time in New York City. She sighed and accepted the call.

"How are things going in Burkina?" the CEO asked.

Sophie took a deep breath and smiled at the webcam. "Things are fine, here. There was no rain today. How can I help you?"

"Just wanted to be sure. There are a lot of assholes in New York. They are all against the death penalty. They are just pussies."

"An innocent has been executed," Sophie pointed out. She hoped Michael would just hang up and leave her in peace. He did not.

"Yes, I know. Everybody makes mistakes. That's not a reason to oppose death penalty. I prayed for that innocent and I am sure the Lord will open his doors to him."

"Sure, Michael." Perhaps if she agreed with him, he would leave her alone.

"That's the real problem, in this world. People are pussies nowadays. They can't take brave and courageous decisions anymore. People who are against death penalties are hypocrites anyway."

"Agreed, Mike."

"Just look at the Europeans. They don't have the death penalty, but they still kill suspects anyway, and without giving them a chance to a fair trial. That's worse."

"Certainly."

"They have all these so-called 'accidents,'" Michael said doing a quote hand gesture on the screen. "Remember in the 2030s?"

"No."

"There was that Norwegian male supremacist who had killed a lot of leftist youngsters. The Norwegians released him after serving twenty years or so in prison, and he was immediately killed in a 'hunting accident,'" he added, doing a quote hand gesture again.

Michael starting laughing on the screen.

"Hunting accident!" he repeated. "The 'hunter' was an eighty-year-old Swedish admiral, former Special Forces. He allegedly missed an elk within two hundred yards and hit the guy almost a mile away! And it was not even the hunting season!'"

Michael laughed again. "Do you believe that, Sof'? Norwegians really take us for idiots. Why don't they reintroduce the death penalty? That would save them a lot of trouble!"

Sophie was looking at Michael laughing through the webcam top of the screen of her screen. She was in no mood to laugh.

When Michael had finally stopped laughing, he said: "It was

nice talking to you, Sof'. Gotta go. Good evening." And he hung up.

Sophie sat a long moment at her desk, gazing aimlessly at her screen. They were losing focus. V-Space's goal was not to get involved in politics, but to go to space. The media were now all over the place, commenting on Michael's personality. This was understandable, but meant the world was losing focus.

As far as the conquest of space was concerned, things were about to change tremendously, and this was what the media should be writing about. She wanted to write an opinion piece. Vahlroos Corporation had some connections with *The Wall Street Journal*.

She opened her word-processor and started typing.

25: WARSEC VENTURES (AUGUST 2095)

August in Vienna was hell. The heat wave had hit central Europe head-on and, of course, there was not enough power supply for everyone to have access to air conditioning. That third week of August, Ralf had had the custody of his kids. It was not helping. Dag was five years old while Eleonore was only three, and they were getting on his nerves.

"*Pappa*," his son asked in Norwegian. "*kan vi gå og svømme? det er for varmt.*" ('Papa, can we go swimming? It's too hot')

"*Inte nu. Jag måste jobba,*" Ralf replied in Swedish. ('Not now, I have to work.')

They were in Ralf's office, in the Vienna International Center. The kids were drawing on some pieces of paper on the side board by the small sofa corner. He was sitting at his desk, trying to focus.

Ralf had, at first, wanted to work from home. It was easier with the kids. But it was too hot. Instead, he took them to his office, where he had hoped the air conditioning would cool them down. However, the AC stopped working slightly after lunch. It was typical. The windows could be opened, but the heat was radiating in the office directly through the badly isolated concrete walls. Stupid engineers from the 1970s, he thought.

Sweat dripped down from his foreheads over his trousers. Damn it. There was nobody in the office anyway. He took off his shirt and pants and let them dry over a chair.

"*Pappa,*" his daughter Eleonore asked. "*hvorfor går du med undertøy?*" ('Papa, why are you only in underwear?')

"And why would the director of an international agency not be allowed to go in underpants in his own office?" he replied in English.

"Come on, kids," you must drink. "Why don't you watch a movie on the tablet? You have to practice English. Norwegian is fine, but useless."

Ralf took his tablet, tapped a few times on the screen and handed over it to the children.

"You can watch this movie," he said. "It's called *Ratatouille.*"

"Pappa, what does this text read?" asked Dag, who could not read yet.

"It reads," Ralf replied, "*The story of this movie is set in 2006. Back then, the world population was about 6.9 billion. In 2095, the world population is about 10.4 billion.*"

"Why does the world population grow so fast?" Dag asked.

"That's a very good question," Ralf replied. "We can talk about it later, now watch the movie."

Ralf went back to his desk. He looked at his cactuses he had brought to the office for the summer. Even they looked dry. He poured the rest of his mineral water on them.

He still had to send a report to the secretary general. He reviewed the attachments and started drafting his emails. When he was done, he proof-read the email.

Object: WARSEC Proposals to be ratified by 4ʰC on 2095-08-25

Dear Mme Secretary General,

On Thursday 25 August, the fourth committee will decide to ratify our current proposals on the orbital station, the new HQ in Vaasa, and WARSEC Ventures.

<u>Executive summary:</u>

- *Orbital station:*
  - » *Project to extend the station from 2 rings to 4 rings: 1 ring for WARSEC, 1 ring for current national space agencies and two rings for private corporations. Expected completion date: 2098-01-31 (provided ratification next week)*
  - » *Private companies to finance 80% of the extension cost, WARSEC 20%*
  - » *WARSEC to gradually become one of the leading administrators of the station, with the NASA, ESA, JAXA CNSA and Roscomos.*

- » *Orbit control to be operated by the consortium of space agencies until 2098-12-31. WARSEC will then have to take over.*
- » *Representatives of US, EU, SAU and China known to support the proposal.*

- • *Vaasa HQ:*
  - » *Municipality has agreed to donate the ground beside the airport. Impact studies done, and no opposition to the construction of the HQ.*
  - » *See enclosed proposal from Finnish architecture agency. Includes astronaut training center, but also permanent room for the 4th Committee, for it to be closer to the WARSEC operations.*
  - » *Construction cost will be largely covered by donations received previously. Expected completion date: 2097-01-31 (provided ratification next week)*
  - » *Representatives of US, EU, SAU, Russia, and China known to support the proposal.*

- • *WARSEC Ventures:*
  - » *Leading space corporations have all accepted to join WARSEC Ventures (with the notable exception of V-space).*
  - » *Ambition to start manufacturing cheap aerospace shuttles on the Moon by 2097-02-28 (provided ratification next week)*
  - » *Objectives: a) increase WARSEC income, b) decrease the cost of space travel.*
  - » *WARSEC Ventures necessary to finance and further develop new interstellar exploration spaceships. Class Forward currently under design.*
  - » *Representatives of EU, SAU, Russia, and China known to support the proposal.*

<u>*Expectations on the first interstellar journey:*</u>

I have also been made aware that some of my staff are under pressure from national representatives to set-up a first interstellar exploration journey now. I believe it is our role to decrease everybody's expectations:

- *The Alcubierre is not fit for any interstellar exploration journey, as it can barely transport any scientific equipment and there is no point in risking the lives of a crew just to make an interstellar journey and say ''mankind went there'.*
- *The new ships of the Forward-class will be much safer and more adapted. However, it is not reasonable to believe the first exemplar will be ready before the end of 2098. I, therefore, find it very unlikely that we will be able to carry our first interstellar journey before 2100-01-01, as everybody would like us to.*

I will be in New York for the ratification votes on 2095-08-25

Best regards,

Ralf Åhman
General Director
World's Agency for the Regulation of Space Exploitation and Colonization
United Nations Office at Vienna
Vienna International Centre,
Wagramerstrasse 5,
A-1220 Vienna
Austria – European Union

Ralf decided he was happy with the mail and sent it. He looked at Dag and Eleonore. They were still absorbed with the movie, on the tablet.

When they were done, he would take them to the swimming pool, though it would probably be packed with people. It was about time to teach Dag how to swim anyway, and Eleonore had to get better at breaststroke.

He still had the time to complete a few things before they were done with the movie. But when he looked, he realized, he had nothing left to do. Working at WARSEC was not at all as time-consuming and stressful as working as a political advisor at the UN. He liked it.

Besides, WARSEC was getting almost no attention from the media. This was the best of it, he thought, as he sat in his underpants in his office.

He was silently attempting to build the most powerful UN agency ever seen, but the world was not quite realizing it.

The world still seemed to be sleepwalking into what would become an interstellar era.

Published Books in the WARSEC Series

Book 1: Regulation
Book 2: Oscillation
Book 3: Exhibition
Book 4: Exploration

Available now for paperback and Kindle on Amazon!

ABOUT THE AUTHOR

Ash Gawain is an EU citizen living in Northern Europe. When not working, writing, nor drinking, Ash is being kept in adequate physical shape by an ex-Swedish military, in order not to die of heart failure before the WARSEC series is complete.

About the WARSEC series:

When I went to the cinema and watched Christopher Nolan's INTERSTELLAR, in January 2015, I first thought I had got into the wrong theatre room. The film opened like a kind of documentary about farmers. After overcoming the first moment of surprise, I admitted the concept was brilliant, though I was willing to challenge everything else about the film.

At that time, I was studying political science, while spending a lot of my time with earth and ice scientists. This, added to a good dose of Finnish Vodka, led to the WARSEC interstellar series.

More on: **www.ashgawain.com**

ACKNOWLEDGEMENTS

The first four books of the WARSEC Interstellar Series could not have reached their final stage without the help of Deborah Murrell, whose thorough edits and comments in the margin have been critical. Any error or mistake is my sole responsibility. I am also forever grateful for Lisa Robbins's valuable feedback and advice, and most of all for her patience with a non-native English-speaker.

Of course, the book could never have been without a book cover. I would like to thank Mark Thomas, not only for his wonderful cover design but also the beautiful paperback edition.

Finally, I would like to thank my family and friends for their support and encouragement, especially Eliah, for reading so many of drafts, and Lumi for forcing me to spend less time in front of my screen and more time exercising.

www.ingramcontent.com/pod-product-compliance
Lightning Source LLC
LaVergne TN
LVHW042351190726
843493LV00005B/971